The Case of the Red Phantom

A Cruise Ship Cozy Mystery

Cheri Baker

Published by Adventurous Ink, Seattle

This is a work of fiction. Names, characters, places, and incidents either are the product of the author's imagination or are used fictitiously. Any resemblance to actual persons, living or dead, events, or locales is entirely coincidental.

First edition. April 7, 2021.

978-1-952200-12-0

Book design by Patrick Baker
Cover art by Cheri Baker

DC3859493D

Chapter One

ELLIE STEPPED OUT ONTO THE lido deck and stretched her shoulders back. The long flight from Orlando to San Diego had left her feeling stiff and sore, but now that she was back on board the *Adventurous Spirit*, the memory of a too-tight seat and packets of stale pretzels seemed unimportant. Sunlight cast a blanket of heat over her bare arms and shoulders. Over at the Seashell Bar, Manny frowned in concentration as he buffed the polished wooden counter. Behind him, colorful liquor bottles faced forward like rows of stalwart soldiers, ready for the engagement ahead. Her heart lifted at the sight of him. "Hey, stranger!" she called out. "Did you miss me?"

Manny slung his white bar towel over one shoulder and looked up. "Ellie! Welcome back. How was your vacation?" He came around the bar and enveloped her in a big, soft hug. Manny smelled like clean white cotton and lemon oil, and when he let her go, crow's feet crinkled at the corners of his deep brown eyes. His black hair stood straight up like Astroturf, and it was as flat on top as a newly mowed lawn. Above the bar, strung between two posts, a trail of triangular flags fluttered in the breeze.

"My vacation was lovely. Granted, it would have been nice if you'd waited for me in Miami. Give me a cruise ship over an airplane any day! No one offered me cake, the seating was atrocious, and no one burst into song. Not even once!"

The wind picked up, ruffling the pages of the drink menus standing upright on the tables nearby. Strands of silver hair pulled loose from Ellie's ponytail and blew into her eyes. She reached up and tightened the elastic. The temperature was in the high eighties, not too different than it had been in Florida, but the sea smelled saltier here. Cool wisps of air shot across the lido deck and flicked at the bare skin beneath her capri pants.

Manny raised an eyebrow. "Oh. Should we have put the *Spirit* up on rollers and pushed her right up to your house in Florida? It's a shame that we inconvenienced you."

Ellie beamed at him, feeling her happiness spreading outward like the illumination from a lighthouse. She'd missed Manny's good-natured teasing. "Very funny. Oh, and before I forget, Junior says hello. He's enrolled in college for the fall. And my youngest, Cole, has a new girlfriend! She's a professor of biology and so very smart. I took hundreds of pictures."

"You took pictures of her smartness?"

"Yes. I cracked her head open and snapped photos of her pink and wriggly brain. Just for you, Manny. Because I knew you'd ask."

"Brains don't wriggle," he shot back. "Have you seen the captain yet? Word is he's been moping around like a lovesick teenager ever since you left." He picked up a glass and polished it, inspecting it in the light before setting it back down with the others. "Not that I have any direct knowledge, you understand."

Ben had greeted Ellie at the dock as soon as she'd arrived. In fact, he'd picked her up mid-hug and swung her around like she weighed nothing! The poor man would probably be sore tomorrow, she thought, her mouth quirking up on one side. "Yes, I saw him."

Sudden pain in her hip made her eyes water! She exhaled slowly. No matter how hard she tried to stay stable, she kept shifting her weight, and whenever she did, it hurt! She tightened her grip on the nubbly blue handle of her cane and exhaled slowly, pressing the rubber stabilizer firmly against the wooden deck. Her agony subsided, shifting from sharp to dull, but slowly. Two more exhales later it had subsided to an angry ache, hot prickles over a tender spot the size of a tangerine.

The tinny beeps of distant trucks floated on the air. She turned toward the noise, hiding her grimace from Manny. Down below, on the concrete dock, crews were loading pallets into the cargo hold. Further down the lido deck, near the starboard railing, a crew woman straightened lounge chairs into perfect parallel lines while a young man followed behind her. He wiped each chair and set a thick plum-colored beach towel on each seat.

Beyond the outer rail, the Pacific Ocean was a churning expanse of dark blue, hunter green, and the deepest grays. These were new waters – rougher ones, perhaps – and the white-capped waves went out as far as her eyes could see. The view was different than the serene blue waters of the Caribbean, but it was no less beautiful.

God is good. Ellie thought, focusing on the horizon, where the waves met the sky. *He made this world, and he made everyone I love. Hallelujah.*

If Manny had noticed the return of her cane, he didn't say anything. He was a sweetheart that way. Ellie's last visit to the family physician had been disappointing, to say the least, but she wasn't in the mood to discuss it. Not on such a beautiful day when there was so much to do! She shot Manny a conspiratorial smile. "Well, tell me! Did anything interesting happen while I was away? What did I miss?" She gritted her teeth and hoisted herself up onto a bar stool. Her cane disappeared between her legs, out of sight, if not out of mind.

Manny spoke in a stage whisper. "Oh, you'll like this! Victor and Wynona went on a *date*."

"They didn't!"

Victor Vasquez, the ship's hotel director, had a good heart and a keen mind. But he also happened to be one of the stuffiest men she'd ever met. Victor kept time on a gold pocket watch, raised a stink when rules weren't followed to the letter, and he wore a vest with shiny buttons, like an old-timey train conductor. The man probably ironed his underpants, with starch! In contrast, the ship's theater manager was loud, extroverted, and always losing things. Wynona had a big voice and even bigger hair. She wasn't much of a disciplinarian, preferring to boss her performers around with high-energy shouts and eager claps of her hands, like a cheerleader.

Ellie tried to imagine them together and failed. "I guess opposites do attract?"

"Rumor has it there will be a second date." Manny opened the ice bin beneath the bar, poking at it several times with his metal scoop. On Ellie's first cruise, he'd accidentally served a cocktail with a finger in it. His apprehensive expression as he poked the ice was almost funny. The poor man would never look at an ice bin the same way again! Not that she blamed him.

He shut the bin with a satisfied grunt. "Maybe you and Ben can advise them. From what I understand, Victor isn't thrilled about having the crew stare at them while they walk around the ship together."

"I can empathize. It's hard to enjoy a romantic dinner with everyone spying on your dates."

"Well, the crew doesn't get much time for recreation. I can't remember the last time I sat down to watch an entire episode of TV. But when our coworkers pair up, it's like: *Days of our Lives: Cruise Ship Edition*." Manny spread out his hands in the air like he was highlighting a theater marquee.

Ellie laughed. He wasn't wrong! And wasn't she just as curious about Victor and Wynona as others had been about her and the captain? "Speaking of TV, I assume you've heard about our new guests? My daughter-in-law Marcie is so jealous. She adores Raquel and Vick."

Everyone knew about the Sweetie Pie Baking Competition. The once-modest television show had spawned multiple seasons, a rotating cast of celebrity judges, and a bestselling line of cookbooks. But this was the first time they'd filmed aboard a cruise ship. In just a few hours, the current batch of culinary hopefuls were coming aboard the *Spirit* to film the final two episodes of the upcoming season.

"I can't say I've watched it," Manny said. "But the film crew was waiting at port when we pulled in at three in the morning. They don't let grass grow under their feet; I'll give them that. Speaking of which, you should check in with Violet. Roberta canceled karaoke for the entire sailing and Violet's feelings are hurt."

Violet Wolfe, the ship's cruise director, was Ellie's dearest friend aboard the *Spirit*, and Violet's trademark show, Karaoke Crush, was always a hit with their guests. That made Roberta's decision surprising. Roberta Crowley might own a good chunk of the cruise line, but she tended not to meddle in day-to-day affairs without a good reason. "What happened? I thought the baking competition was being held in the big theater? And a cruise without karaoke is like..."

"It's like a day without sunshine! It's like Christmas without a tree! It's like a birthday party with no cake! At least, that's what Violet told me when she was drowning her sorrows in a martini. I take it Roberta hasn't told you about our last-minute booking? We're hosting a paranormal convention called Secrets of the Dead. The headliner is the world-famous medium, Chryss Tiano. He talks to ghosts. Or they talk to him. I'm not entirely sure how that works."

"And ghosts are afraid of karaoke?"

"Apparently he needs the Moonlight Lounge for his séances."

Ellie huffed out her breath. "Well, that sounds *awful*."

"It's just one sailing. Violet will have her lounge back in a week."

"Oh, I'm not upset about *that*. I'm upset about this so-called convention. A medium? And séances? Why would we host something so tacky?"

Manny looked surprised. "Why would you say that? You pray to your departed loved ones, do you not?"

"It's not the same, and you know it. Don't get me wrong, I enjoy a good ghost story as much as the next person. But that's different than pretending that you can talk to the dead. Mediums are hucksters and charlatans! They fool gullible people for profit. And we're going to help them do it? Yuck."

Manny fixed her with the same look he used with junior staff when they'd been caught slacking. "Well, I'm sure you will be respectful of our guests, no matter their personal beliefs. Correct?"

That stung! "When have I *not* been courteous? You know I don't let my personal feelings interfere with my duties." One of Manny's napkin dispensers was cockeyed. She twisted it into position.

"Indeed." Manny raised an eyebrow. "So, when you meet our VIPs, please tell them we've created two special cocktails for the sailing. There's a delicious apple pie martini for the foodies, and a spectral sangria for the ghost hunters."

"A spectral sangria?"

"Tell them it's full of..." Manny leaned across the bar and beckoned her forward to whisper into her ear. "Spirits."

She laughed. "Very cute. I'll tell them. I told Roberta I'd be our liaison to the Sugar Network. But hopefully she assigned someone else to handle the circus." When she caught Manny's sharp look, she quickly added, "But I'll be fine either way."

"Uh huh."

"I will!"

A cool wind blew across the lido deck hard enough to make goose pimples rise on Ellie's arms. Something whooshed behind her. She turned to see the sliding glass doors closing. Behind the panes of glass, the vestibule was empty.

ELLIE TOOK THE ELEVATOR DOWN several levels and headed toward Roberta's suite at the front of the ship. It felt good to be back! She admired the long, blue-carpeted hallways, the art on the walls, and the way every nook, restaurant, and shop had a distinct look and feel, while still fitting into a harmonious whole. The ship smelled fresh and clean, like freshly vacuumed carpet and crisp linens. Sunlight streamed in through the windows. Ellie waved at the manager of the jewelry store and received a smile in return. A young housekeeper fist-bumped her as they crossed paths in the hallway. Ellie paused at the railing when she reached the upper level of the atrium. The shiny black piano rested quietly below; the rectangular bench was empty. A crewman with a dark brown ponytail mopped the dance floor with long strokes. There was tea downstairs at the cafe, and she wanted some, but it would need to wait.

The new seasonal itinerary would take the *Spirit* back and forth along the Mexican Riviera. According to her new guidebook, the word *riviera* meant coastline in

Italian, and Mexico's western coast was dotted with charming cities and towns, all set against the wind-roughened waters of the Pacific Ocean.

A familiar voice grabbed at her from a distance. Ellie turned toward the sound and saw the black double-doors of the Moonlight Lounge, shut tight. The lounge wouldn't open for hours. But Violet's frustrated voice was loud enough to project through the closed doors and into the hallway.

Ellie hurried inside. The Moonlight Lounge was dim and cool. The round booths to the left and right of the central aisle gleamed softly like they'd been freshly polished, but the room stank like someone had set a floral arrangement on fire.

Two figures stood in the aisle, Violet and a stranger. Next to Violet, beneath her, almost, was a petite woman in dark slacks and a moss-green sweater. She had blunt-cut black hair that went to her chin and a round, pleasant face with olive skin. Beyond the women, on the low stage, two leather chairs waited like a tableau in a high school stage play. A frosted glass orb sat on a round table between the chairs, and a long, black power cord ran out of the orb and spiraled across the stage in search of an outlet.

Ellie rolled her eyes. Who needed ghosts and magic when you had a 100-Watt light bulb? But with Manny's stern rejoinder still fresh in her mind, she kept her observation to herself. Some people believed Elvis was alive and living on Mars. Was that sane? No. Was it her job to correct them? Not when they were guests of the cruise line. Their misguided beliefs weren't any of her business.

Beliefs? her mind responded acidly. *Delusions are more like it!*

Two bored-looking workers waited on the right side of the stage. They were looking up at the ceiling, at the bar at the back of the room, and at one another. They seemed to be going out of their way not to look at the women in the aisle.

"I don't mean to be difficult," the short woman was saying, "but our contract clearly states that we have the right to redecorate this room as we see fit." She pointed at the clipboard in her hand. "It's in section twelve, subsection A. I negotiated this clause personally with Roberta Crowley."

Violet looked pained. "Yes. I know. But we're talking redecorating, not remodeling. And we can't allow—" Her expression brightened when she saw Ellie approaching. "Oh! Here's our event coordinator, right on time. May I introduce Ellie Tappet? Ellie, this is Cora Wise, personal assistant to Chryss Tiano, the celebrity medium."

Ellie held out a hand. "Pleased to meet you. I'm sorry for not being here to greet you when you arrived. I just got in myself."

Cora's handshake was brief and warm. She didn't seem at all put off by her debate with Violet. "I'm looking forward to working with you."

Ellie bit her tongue. She'd sort the details out with Roberta. First things first. "You want to make changes to the lounge?"

"Yes. As I was explaining to your colleague, I need those purple curtains taken down. They're nice, to be sure," she shot Violet a sidelong glance, "but purple is a very *assertive* color and Chryss Tiano will be channeling delicate energies this evening. They need to come down."

Over the woman's shoulder, Violet was trying to communicate something telepathically. Her green eyes flicked imploringly between Cora and the curtains surrounding the stage. Probably she was screaming: *Don't let these freaks destroy my lounge*. Ellie smiled at Cora. "I'm sure we can get this sorted out. Can I see your contract, please?"

"Certainly." Cora reached into her pants pocket, pulled out a small yellow sticky flag, and affixed it to the contract next to the relevant section. Then she handed over the clipboard, turning it to face Ellie. "I believe you'll see everything is in order."

Ellie scanned the document. It did indeed say that the crew of Chryss Tiano's Fantastical Events LLC could redecorate as they liked. She felt a jolt of surprise when her eyes grazed section fourteen of the contract. Roberta had promised Cora *24/7 access* to an event coordinator from the cruise line. Ellie's fingers tightened on the clipboard. 24/7 access? When was she supposed to sleep?

She ran her finger down to a bit of fine print on the back page. "It says here that you must return our rooms to their original condition. If not, you'll lose your deposits, which were..." she flipped to the correct page, "substantial. Can you guarantee you'll put everything back?"

"You have my word."

Ellie shot Violet an apologetic look. "Then go right ahead." She handed the clipboard back.

Cora nodded, then she strode over to the workers. She snapped her fingers and one of them ran to the far wall to retrieve a ladder. She stood attentively while they began taking the curtains down. She called out, "Careful! Don't crease them."

Violet leaned toward Ellie and whispered, "This blows chunks. Roberta *canceled* karaoke. Do you know the last time we had a cruise without karaoke? No. You don't, because it's never happened. Ever. It's...." she shivered, "It's unlucky is what it is."

Ellie hid her smile. People who worked at sea were superstitious in all sorts of ways, but this was the first time she'd heard about the protective value of the evening karaoke show. Still, she knew how important it was to Violet. "I'm sorry to hear that, hon. Maybe we can squeeze you in somewhere else?" Violet didn't reply, so she pointed at the frosted glass orb on the table. "Is Chryss Tiano supposed to talk to ghosts with that thing?"

Cora, who was a good twenty feet away, turned back, her expression bland. "Don't be ridiculous. The orb is merely stage lighting. Chryss Tiano's power center lies within him. He's not reliant on external totems to access the spirit realm."

"Good for him," Violet called back. "That's gotta come in handy when you left your totem in the car, and you need to get the ghost of your great-great-grandma on speed dial."

One of the workers, the one holding the ladder, barked a strangled laugh. But he quickly turned it into a cough when Cora turned her laser-beam eyes in his direction.

"Excuse us," Ellie called out. She gently maneuvered Violet toward the back door.

"I'm sorry," Violet said, once they were out in the hall. "It's just that I spent a week coming up with food-themed songs for cupcake karaoke and at the last-minute Roberta hands my lounge over to those people."

"Well, with two different groups on board, I imagine we're pinched for space. But—"

The lounge doors swung open and Cora came out. The woman moved fast! She was already flipping to a new page on her clipboard. "Ellie? Before you leave, I have another matter to discuss with you. Section four of our contract states that—"

Ellie held up a hand to forestall her. "Cora, I'll take your word for it. You don't need to show me the contract every time. What do you need?"

"Oh! Well, Chryss Tiano needs a stateroom that faces the sunrise. He begins his day with an intensive Yogic ritual that requires direct access to morning sunlight. It's essential for his energetic flow."

Did Cora believe what her boss was spouting? She did seem faintly embarrassed. Perhaps she felt bad about taking down Violet's curtains? "Cora, I'll do all that I can to make your boss's stay comfortable. But I don't hold with all this mystical energy talk, and in all honesty, I don't want to." Ellie smiled to show there was no offense intended. "Just tell me what you need in plain English, and I'll hop to it."

Cora's mouth quirked up on one side, and a dimple appeared in her cheek. She was younger than she'd appeared at first glance. Late twenties, perhaps? Young or not, she had the self-assurance of someone who was used to getting what she wanted. Cora looked left and right, to make sure no one else was listening. "Look, Chryss wants to be on the other side of the ship. Open water makes him nervous, and he'd like to be able to see land, even at a distance. He'll sleep better that way." She winced. "I know it sounds silly, but—"

"It's not silly at all. I'll see what I can do. Is there anything else?"

Cora's black leather purse was slung under her arm. She unzipped it and pulled out a large cellophane bag of foil-wrapped chocolates. "He'd like one of these on his pillow every night. We put the request in his contract, but this was a last-minute booking and I doubt your housekeeping team had a chance to shop for Ayurvedic chocolate. Can you get these to his housekeeping crew? Don't tell Chryss you got them from me. He'll like you better if he thinks you bent over backward to accommodate him."

Ellie took the chocolates. "Thanks for thinking ahead. That was very thoughtful."

Again, Cora looked surprised. Was she so unused to being treated politely? She glanced at Violet. "Ms. Wolfe? I took reference photos of your lounge. We'll put it back just as it was, I promise. And I completely understand your hesitance. When you're a performer, your stage is an extension of your talent. You don't want anyone messing up your flow." She zipped her purse back up and shot them a businesslike smile. "Please, excuse me. My checklist is ten pages long and I'm already behind."

"She's not so bad," Violet said, once Cora was back inside.

"No. She isn't," Ellie smiled at Violet. "I'm off to see Roberta. Do you want to come?"

"No. I'm going to look for a new spot for karaoke. I don't care if I need to perform inside a bathroom stall. There *will* be Cupcake Karaoke on this sailing. I swear it." She raised her fist in the air. "I swear it on my favorite black dress!" Violet was halfway down the hall when she turned back, a sheepish smile on her face. "Oh, and welcome back. I want to hear all about your trip. Soon."

Ellie blew her friend a kiss. "I missed you too. Go on. I'll find you later."

Chapter Two

STUART ANSWERED ROBERTA'S DOOR AFTER the first knock. The old man's eyes twinkled as he stood stiffly in his tuxedo, holding the door open with his spine ramrod straight. Stuart, formal as he was, managed to express a great deal with his eyes. Ellie felt a sudden urge to hug him. But she hesitated. Was it improper to hug your boss's butler-slash-lover? Pauline Phillips hadn't covered this situation in her weekly advice column in the Gainesville Sun. And since she'd passed away, there was no asking her now.

Maybe I'll ask Chryss Tiano to ring her up for me.

Stuart pivoted like a toy soldier as she stepped inside. The small pink rose on his lapel matched the massive floral arrangements to the left and right of the entryway. He turned his head at a forty-five-degree angle toward the room and announced, "Eleanor Tappet has arrived," in tones crisp and round enough to please the Queen herself.

Stuart was laying it on thick! There must be company over.

Roberta's suite smelled like black coffee and freshly baked chocolate chip cookies. Her parlor sofa was upholstered in velvet. Plump silk cushions rested in the corners. A handsome leather wingback chair rested next to a lamp in an opulent reading nook, and a brass telescope stood proudly near the floor-to-ceiling windows. Near the dining room table, a tall glass cabinet held curiosities collected during a lifetime of travel.

A man sat across from Roberta. He was in his early fifties, but his open, friendly expression and messy thatch of sandy brown hair gave him a boyish charm that was undeniable. He wore a dark blue blazer over his wool slacks. He looked ready for a business meeting, not vacation.

Roberta stood, gathering her long skirt in one hand. She'd pulled her white hair back in a loose bun, and soft little tendrils escaped near her ears. She wore diamond-accented hair combs. Her necklace pendant was a dangling pair of red rubies, hanging from golden stems like ripe cherries.

"Greg, meet Ellie Tappet," Roberta's voice was as rough as an old crow's, but there was plenty of warmth in it. Her cheeks were flushed with pleasure, as if she'd been chatting with an old friend. "Ellie's a minority owner of *Adventurous Cruises*, and she's volunteered to be your liaison for the sailing. Ellie, this is Greg Norris, executive vice president at The Sugar Network."

Ellie hurriedly transferred her cane to her left hand and offered her right hand to shake. Greg's hand hung awkwardly in the air while she shifted her position. "We're honored to be hosting the Sweetie Pie Baking Competition," Ellie said. "In fact, my daughter-in-law is one of your biggest fans."

Greg glanced down at the cane. His gaze rested momentarily on her new "sensible" walking shoes, and his sunny smile faltered for a second, like a screen glitching.

"And we're thrilled to be aboard the *Adventurous Spirit*," he replied, making eye contact. "We've held our competition in five different countries, inside the Empire State Building, and one time, at the base of an active volcano. But this is our first time filming at sea, and I can already tell this will be an epic season of television."

They sat, Greg and Ellie on the sofa, Roberta across from them in her velvet chair, her head held high like a duchess. Stuart was already heading toward the kitchen, his patent leather shoes squeaking with every step.

"I understand you're filming two episodes during the sailing?" Ellie asked.

Greg picked up a small glass of sherry from the coffee table. "Yes. Your ship will host the semi-final and the final showdown." He glanced at Roberta. "She's signed the non-disclosure agreement, right?"

"Of course," Roberta lied smoothly.

Greg sipped his sherry and grimaced as if the taste pained him. "I'm glad to have your assistance, Ellie, but there will be little for you to do. This is our seventh season, and my crew is a well-oiled machine. The riggers are already setting up the baking platform in the theater. We've made arrangements for ingredients, portable ovens, costume changes; the whole nine yards. In fact," he glanced at his watch, "my director Linda did all the onboarding videos yesterday, down near the docks. We call that the 'Nervous Nellies' segment." He leaned back against the fawn-colored cushions with a self-satisfied smile. "Our audience loves it when our contestants are full of terror and self-doubt. A typical baking contest can't hold the attention of nine million viewers every week. If it could, your average county fair would be pulling in millions of dollars in corporate sponsorships. It's our job to showcase the personal journey of each baker, showing where they came from, what they want, and what their triumphs and struggles are. It's all about storytelling, and that's what makes our contest the best in the business."

Ellie listened with interest. It wasn't too surprising to hear that some of the on-screen drama was manufactured by the production company. Still, it was strange to hear Greg put it so plainly. But she understood his meaning. Assigning ratings to cakes and pies wouldn't be half so interesting if you couldn't connect with the people behind those baby blue aprons. "Well, it sounds like you have things handled," Ellie said. "But I'll be around if you need anything at all. You can call me," She shot Roberta a bemused look, "day or night."

Stuart returned with a hot cup of Earl Grey tea and set it carefully on the coffee table next to Ellie's knee. She shot him a grateful smile and picked up the cup and saucer. The porcelain was delicate, and the beautiful roses around the rim of the saucer were accented with hints of white gold. Roberta had brought out her fanciest china for Greg Norris. Ellie sipped her tea and turned to Roberta. "I understand we have a convention on board?"

Roberta waved her hand like she was shooing away a troublesome gnat. "Just a small one. Ellie, keep them contained. I don't want the paranormal enthusiasts interfering with the baking competition. We're happy to have the convention, but they're not our top priority. The Sugar Network is."

Ellie was about to ask how she was expected to keep hundreds of people "contained" when Greg broke in. "Oh, there's no need to worry about that, Berta. We want to capture the vibrancy of the sailing — all that hustle and bustle! Your other guests are welcome to move freely about, except on a closed set. And I want your theater full when we film the final showdown. Let's extend an invitation to everyone, first come, first serve. Maybe we can hand out free drink coupons to spread the word. Can you get those printed up for us?"

"Certainly." Roberta's half-closed eyes reminded Ellie of a cat being stroked. Behind that smug smile of hers she was no doubt adding all those drink coupons to The Sugar Network's bill.

"Greg, what can you tell us about the contestants?" Ellie asked.

"Oh, we've got an exceptional batch of bakers this season. We have our very first husband-and-wife competitors, Teddy and Ariana McIntyre. Teddy is passionate about healthy eating — he's a personal trainer in Chicago, you know — and his wife Ariana makes the most scrumptious wedding cakes you've ever tasted. Then we have Mindie Burton, our Aussie contestant. She's completely self-taught, and she runs a small chain of French patisseries in Sydney. Mindie is starting up a school for aspiring pastry chefs, and the show is tremendous exposure for her. She's got a real shot at taking the Golden Cupcake home, and that would be fabulous for our overseas viewership, by the way. Harvey Fleming is from Leeds, and he's the sweetest grandfather you'll ever meet. He worked for the National Rail service in England for over thirty years. But his scones..." Greg kissed his fingertips. "They're to *die* for."

"And the fifth finalist?" Ellie asked, when Greg didn't continue.

Greg's mouth took on a pinched appearance. "Ah. That would be Kitty Gilbert. An exceptionally beautiful young woman. She's as dumb as a weathered wooden post and irritating to the nth degree. But she's popular with our viewers. And our judges, apparently."

Ellie and Roberta exchanged a look.

"Forgive me," Greg said. "It's been a long day, and I'm speaking out of turn." He scratched his ear. "It's funny. They tell you that when you become a VP for the network, you'll get more sway over programming decisions, but cable television is a cutthroat business. You end up doing favors left and right to keep your shows afloat. I shouldn't let it bother me, but I do."

Greg leaned forward. "Kitty is our CEO's niece, you see. Nora likes it when we keep one of the less talented bakers around through the semi-finals. And hey, I get it! If a weak baker manages to hang on, our viewers at home feel like they too could be a star. It's good optics. I can respect that. But I believe it diminishes the value of our brand. The Sweetie Pie Baking Competition is about finding the *best* bakers in the world. Or at least it should be. And can you guess which baker has survived round after round, despite a lack of talent?"

"Kitty Gilbert?" Roberta asked, her tone sympathetic.

He nodded. "Exactly. Anyway, I'll stop my grousing. You two aren't interested in my management problems. Besides, I've run six seasons without a single scandal. And I'm not about to ruin my streak because Nora's niece's brownies taste like expired box mix."

Ellie smiled at him. “Don’t worry about it. We all need to vent, now and again. Why don’t you walk us through the next couple days? Let’s make sure you have everything you need.”

⚓⚓⚓

ABOUT AN HOUR LATER, ROBERTA walked Greg to the door, chattering happily the entire way. But as soon as the door clicked shut, she turned back, scowling. “That man is going to be a pain in my rump.”

Ellie set her teacup down in her lap. “Why do you say that? He seemed perfectly nice to me.”

Roberta scoffed lightly. “You *would* think so. That’s why I asked you to be his handler. You’ve got an ability to tolerate all sorts of irritating people. As for me, I lost that knack years ago. I lost it, and I have no desire to dig it back up again.”

Ellie smirked. “I’ll interpret that as a compliment.”

“Didn’t you notice his little game? He kept griping about his boss, and then he kept apologizing. Every time, you’d smile and insist that we’d keep his gossipy little secrets. And then he gossiped all the harder!”

Roberta was right. “Maybe he’s having a bad day?”

“Your naiveté never ceases to amaze me, my friend. No, Greg Norris knows *exactly* what he’s doing. I’ll give him credit for that. He doesn’t like Nora Blay. He wants to be CEO of the network, so he’s making sure everyone knows about the nepotism with Nora’s niece. *Someone* will leak it to the press, eventually, and either it will be juicy gossip, which is great for his ratings, or it will be a scandal, and Nora will take the hit, leaving him free to slide into her spot." Roberta sat carefully, adjusting a tasseled cushion to her liking before leaning back. "In fact, I bet Greg's been stroking Nora's ego the whole time, saying how *talented* her niece Kitty is, fueling the fire. I know these scheming types very well. And they always cause trouble, one way or another."

"I'll keep an eye on him then."

"Do that. But don't get in his way if you can avoid it. I'm prepared to tolerate a fair amount of nonsense from Greg in the interest of getting more business from The Sugar Network."

"Did they pay us all that well?"

"No. Corporate events are usually more trouble than they're worth." Roberta's smile took on a dreamy cast. "But imagine the *Adventurous Spirit* on every television across the globe! We have five ships right now. How would you like to have fifteen? That's within reach if we play our cards right."

"I like that we're small," Ellie said, thinking out loud. "But I see your point. If we were bigger, we could do more for the crew, maybe look into a profit-sharing program. So I'll do my best to keep Greg happy." She fixed Roberta with an impatient look. "But we need to talk about Secrets of the Dead. Are you aware that you gave them

24/7 access to me? When do you expect me to sleep? I'm not as young as I once was, and even then, I needed six or seven hours a night!"

"Oh, they won't be calling you in the middle of the night. But feel free to deputize Violet. Half of her events are postponed until the next sailing; and Violet, God love her, is exactly like a cat. She's gorgeous and smart and a pleasure to have around. But when she gets bored, she starts shredding the furniture and knocking things over."

Ellie laughed out loud at the comparison, and a naughty smile burst through Roberta's grouchy expression.

"How was New York?" Ellie asked. "I went on vacation before you got back, so I never had a chance to ask."

Roberta sighed happily. "New York is New York! The faces change, but the city sparkles, the food is incomparable, the performances are world-class, and anything you could ever want is at your fingertips. For me, New York lives right here." She put her hand over her heart and adjusted her long shimmering skirt so it hung neatly over her slender legs. When she looked up, the pale blue eyes that peeped out from her wrinkled face were vibrant and full of joy. Some people were young no matter how old they were, and Roberta Crowley was one of them.

Ellie glanced down at her ugly white shoes. Her doctor had recommended them, along with the cane. They were huge and white, puffy enough to serve as floaties should she fall overboard. She needed stability, her doctor had said. But they were *old lady shoes*, and she hated them so much she wanted to light them on fire. Sitting next to always-fashionable Roberta, it was hard not to feel dowdy and out of place.

Roberta reached out with one slipper-clad toe and pointed at the cane resting next to Ellie. "What happened?"

"It's nothing."

"You flinched when Greg looked at your cane. Are you embarrassed?"

Trust Roberta to get right to the heart of things. "No, I'm not *embarrassed.* And I didn't flinch! I have osteoarthritis. It's a degenerative condition."

"And you're starting to degenerate?" Roberta peered at her, looking her up and down from shoes to hair and back again. "You seem relatively intact to me."

"No! Well, not exactly. And I wasn't upset with Greg. I'm just annoyed that I need a cane again. I had some problems last year, before I came aboard, but they went away. And I was doing great! My pain was almost gone, and I was exercising, and I hadn't had any problems in months and months. But now..."

"Your condition has worsened."

She nodded. "My hip hurts. All the time. And my doctor says it might not get better, so I should get used to this." She nudged the thick silver cane with one foot and sighed. "I'll be fine."

"But you're disappointed," Roberta pursued.

"I'm not *thrilled.* I mean, Ben's younger than me. And I don't think he signed up for a girlfriend with a cane."

Roberta tilted her head. "May I give you some advice?"

Ellie's gut tightened. Roberta wasn't the type to ask before giving advice. At least not usually. "Go ahead."

"You need to own it."

"I need to own what, exactly?"

"Everything. You need to own absolutely everything about yourself. Stop apologizing. Stop cringing! A cane is only shameful if you *feel* shame, Ellie. And I can guarantee, your feelings aren't coming from Ben, or Greg, or anyone else." She pointed at her right hip. "Look at me. I had this hip replaced fifteen years ago." She pointed at her lower teeth, pulling her lip downward to show them off. "Half of these are implants. My original set rotted right out of my head and now I'm half cyborg. After all that flossing! What a colossal waste of time *that* was."

She lifted her long skirt and pointed at her slender shin. Thin blue lines ran beneath her pale skin like delicate threads. A faded scar went up to her knee. "This bone snapped right in half during a river cruise. I was playing roulette with a gang of Russians — dreadfully entertaining, Russians are — and after I spun the wheel, I hit the carpet. Osteoporosis, the surgeon said. I've got more rods in me than a nuclear reactor. But do I seem ashamed of my body?"

"No."

"No, I don't. And do you know why? Because it's nothing to me! What matters to me is my life and how I live it." Roberta held her head even higher. "Most people have never lived half so well as I have! Most people haven't even *tried* to reach their full potential. Your life is your canvas. So, Ellie Tappet, I don't want to see you wincing like you've been struck when someone glances at your cane, do you hear me? If someone looks at your cane, you just chalk it up to curiosity. It's nothing to you. That cane is a tool, like your favorite pen, or that dreadful fringed purse you carry around."

"Hey. I like that purse!" Ellie laughed a little. Had she really flinched earlier? She hadn't meant to. But she'd seen the way Greg had looked at her, like she was pitiable. He hadn't said anything out loud, but he hadn't needed to.

"I'm not saying you can't complain," Roberta said gently. "Life can be hard, and we don't have to pretend otherwise. Especially among friends. But you have nothing to feel ashamed of. Period."

"I hear you, Roberta. I do."

Roberta's nostrils flared. "Good. Now, I have one more thing for you."

Stuart came out with lunch for two. He set the food carefully on the coffee table, refreshed the teacups from the small ceramic pot on his tray, and touched Roberta's shoulder. "I made that chicken salad you like," he said sweetly.

She looked up at him. "Thank you, my love. Will you fetch Ellie's contract from my office?" Stuart nodded and moved deeper into the suite. Roberta watched him go with a contented expression. She reached down to pick up a mini sandwich. She plucked the decorative toothpick out of the center and set it delicately on her plate. "When I was in New York I caught up with old friends. Theodora, my sorority sister, has clawed her way up the New York publishing ladder, and we got to talking. I told her about your novel. She agreed to read it."

"You let a stranger read my book? But it's just a first draft! I thought *you* were going to read it."

"I prefer historical biographies," she said flatly. "Anyway, Theodora read it, as a favor to me, and she said it has a lot of potential. You can trust her, by the way, she's not one to flatter a person unless she's being paid to do so. Anyway, she said it was good, so I read it the next day. Frankly, Ellie, I'm surprised. There was a lot of sex in that book."

"It's a romance novel."

Roberta took a file folder from Stuart when he returned. She fanned herself with it. "Speaking of which, how long are you going to keep poor Benji waiting? Although..." she bit her lower lip, "perhaps all your pent-up energy is doing your fiction some good? On second thought, Ben can wait a bit longer. Never let a man get in the way of your business interests. That's my motto."

Ellie laughed! Roberta talked a tough game, but she'd do anything for Stuart, that much was plain from the way she looked at him. "I'll take that under advisement."

Roberta held out the folder. "Anyway, here's an offer from the publishing house. They want two more books from the same historical period, but I told them you have your hands full on the ship and you'd get back to them in a month or so. They'll put you in touch with an editor after you sign."

Ellie flipped open the thin cardboard folder. The contract was full of small print, but the cash advance was bolded on the front page. Someone wanted to publish *The Captain's Kiss*! What a nice surprise this was! "Wow. Roberta! I hadn't even thought this far ahead! But thank you. Thank you *so much*."

"Bah. It was the least I could do. I can't tell you how many years it's been since I had a proper vacation, one without people hounding me over the phone. I wanted to thank you for keeping the wolves off my back for a while." She nodded once, as if to say the matter was settled. "But let's keep our eye on the ball. If we get in good with The Sugar Channel, we may get more business from the network, and thus, more publicity for the cruise line."

"And Secrets of the Dead? Where do they fit in?"

"If things go well, they'll join us once per year for a ghost cruise. Theme cruises are a growing segment of the market. Do you remember our last shareholder meeting? Charlotte Picklewick accused me of being set in my ways." Roberta rolled her eyes. "I am *not*, and I will not have Charlotte believing she's a better businesswoman than me. I knew that girl when she was in diapers, and she wants to out-business me?" Roberta's eyes narrowed. "I will *crush* her." Her expression softened, and she raised an eyebrow. "Can you handle Chryss Tiano on top of the baking competition, or do I need to assign someone else?"

Ellie glanced down at the contract in her hands. Roberta might be pushy, but she was also incredibly generous. Not to mention, a good friend. She looked up. "Like you suggested, I'll ask Violet to help me out. I'm sure we can handle whatever the oogly booglies throw our way."

"Good. We can't afford to let anything go wrong. Especially with camera crews crawling all over the ship." She glanced down at Ellie's shoes and wrinkled her nose. "And now that we've gotten our pressing business out of the way, tell me, where on God's green and glorious Earth did you get your footwear?" Roberta's lip curled. "Did you go shopping in a dumpster behind a nursing home while you were in Florida?" She leaned back and called out, "Stuart? Will you bring out my catalogs?" She looked at Ellie with a wicked smile. "I found some wonderful new stores in Manhattan. Shall we order a few things? If you won't do it for yourself, do it for me. Those shoes are giving me a tension headache." Her face screwed up and she turned away. "Ugh! I can feel them draining my life force as we speak. Stuart! Bring me a blanket to cover up Ellie's feet, please?"

Ellie shook her head. "Never change, Roberta."

Roberta took a dainty bite out of her sandwich, using her free hand to block out the sight of Ellie's white sneakers. "I don't intend to."

Chapter Three

AFTER DINNER THAT NIGHT, ELLIE met Violet on the balcony level for a stroll. The setting sun placed a fiery kiss upon the horizon, and the dusky blue sky darkened, moment by moment. Their departure from San Diego had gone off without a hitch, and the guests were abuzz with first-day energy. The lounges and restaurants were overflowing with conversation and bursts of laughter. All the while, the *Adventurous Spirit* slid through the ocean on a halo of light.

They walked along, breathing in the refreshing sea air, stretching their legs, and looking East toward California. A faint glow near the horizon hinted at cities and towns along the coastline.

Violet sauntered over to the inner railing above the pool. Ellie followed. "Will you look at that?" Violet peered down at the activity below. "Cora and her army of volunteers rearranged the entire deck in less than twenty minutes. I swear, if that woman weren't already gainfully employed, I'd hire her." Violet shot Ellie a playful look.

"Cora's on top of things, and you've got the baking competition handled. Why am I even here? I could be on a beach, right now, in my new purple bikini, looking for a girlfriend."

"Oh, I see. You'd leave me here to deal with these people alone? What if Chryss Tiano whispers the wrong thing into his magic orb? He might raise an army of zombies. If that happens, I'll need backup."

Violet tipped her head back and laughed. "Yes. I'm the one you'd want in a battle against the undead. Not Paul, head of security. Not Kameron, our combat expert. Me, a middle-aged lounge singer without so much as a stage to stand on."

Down below, the outdoor pool sloshed gently with the motion of the ship. The lights below the water cast eerie blue illuminations on the faces of those enjoying an evening soak. Steam floated up from the hot tubs. Bubbles formed and burst. The long rectangular lounge chairs were gone, and Cora's volunteers had set up round tables with black tablecloths all around the deck. At each table, a gaggle of paranormal enthusiasts leaned forward, roasting marshmallows on clever portable burners no bigger than two fists put together. In a shadowed alcove near the hull, two members of the security crew stood with stoic expressions, turning their heads left and right slowly, like human surveillance cameras. Bright red fire extinguishers rested at their feet.

"Paul wasn't too happy about the burners," Violet added, "but I love the way Cora thinks. They're roasting marshmallows and telling ghost stories!" She frowned to herself. "I wish I'd thought of that."

Ellie pointed down at a man with a camera resting on his shoulder. The back of his pastel blue shirt bore the stylized cupcake logo of The Sugar Network, but he'd aimed his camera at the guests roasting marshmallows. "Check that out. It looks like the paranormal enthusiasts are stealing the baking competition's thunder!"

"Oh, the camera crews have been all over the ship," Violet said. "Billy told me they're filming B-roll. They need cruise ship footage during transitions on the show."

Billy, the ship's head photographer, had been pressed into service by The Sugar Network to capture stills of the contestants and crew for a future coffee table book.

"Have you seen the captain?" Violet asked.

"Yes, we had a quick dinner, but he had to hurry back to the bridge. I spent most of the afternoon finding a new suite for Chryss Tiano and getting his belongings moved over. Thanks for helping me out with the convention. Normally I wouldn't ask, but—"

"Oh, deputize away. It's not like I have anything better to do." Violet leaned on the rail and put her chin in her hands.

"No luck finding a new karaoke venue?"

"Nothing so far. The library is free, but it's too small. Ditto the jazz lounge. Roberta wasn't kidding. We're booked up tight. If I wanted to host karaoke at seven a.m., sure, we could make that happen. But no one is drunk or happy enough that early in the morning to belt out the hits."

"We'll just have to keep looking." Ellie pointed down at one of the tables. At each table, one person wore a special name badge with a black ribbon attached. "What's up with the ribbons?"

"They're volunteer storytellers. Want to go listen?"

"I'm not sure."

"Oh. Come on! I want to try Manny's new appletini. And we can eavesdrop on the way over. I met one of Cora's guest speakers earlier. His name is Allister, he wears a tweed coat with patches, and he forgot my name, twice, during a ten-minute conversation. These people are delightfully bonkers." She raised an eyebrow. "Besides, it's been *forever* since I had an evening off. My salsa class was cancelled too."

Ellie nudged Violet with her shoulder. "Come on, then. Let's drink and eavesdrop. And if you want, you can teach me how to salsa dance later. When it comes to anything other than a slow dance, I've got two left feet!"

"Deal." Violet's green eyes were merry.

Down on the lido deck, the sweet scent of toasted marshmallows made Ellie's mouth water. "I wonder if Manny has hot cocoa," she said to Violet, thinking of campfires flickering in the dark of night. "When my boys were little, Ronnie and I would load up the trailer and go camping at a state park. We did a lot of fishing too. I wonder if Ben likes to camp."

"He told me he wants to take shore leave as soon as Roberta can arrange for someone to cover. Maybe you two could go glamping."

"What on Earth is that?"

"It's fancy camping. Usually there's a proper bed involved. As for me, I prefer a nice hotel with room service, but if you're going to hang out with bugs and bears, you may as well get a good night's sleep."

"That sounds promising," Ellie said. Ben wanted to take leave? He hadn't mentioned it to her. But they still had plenty to catch up on. "Before I forget, I've been meaning to ask you something. Do you think Paul has a thing for Kameron? I saw him looking at her during her promotion ceremony before I went on vacation. He looked so... in love. But maybe I imagined it?"

"Ah," Violet said, pausing at the bottom of the stairs. "That? It's not my story to tell."

"But there *is* something to tell?"

"There was."

"Was? Did he—"

Violet shook her head. "Ask him yourself! I'm sure he'll tell you all about it." She put her finger to her lips and pointed at the tables between the pool and the Seashell Bar.

They made their way through, slowly. At one table, a man in his thirties spoke with tight gestures of his open hands. His black t-shirt had a vicious-looking white wolf on it, and the dark orange light from the marshmallow burner illuminated his unkempt eyebrows with a devilish tint. "They say the Birch Man only shows himself when there's been a *tragic* death," he said in a hushed tone.

"Aren't most deaths tragic? I mean, unless you're super old?" That question came from a teenage girl with twin braids, and she sounded skeptical.

Smart child, Ellie thought.

"I suppose that depends on your definition of tragic," the man replied. "The Birch Man is what's known as a lost spirit. His wife and children disappeared in the woods during a hike, and they were never found. One year later, he hiked into the birch grove where they were supposed to meet him that day, and he was so overcome with grief that he ended his life right there." The storyteller pantomimed slitting his own throat, and the listeners jerked back in unison. "Now," he continued, "the Birch Man roams the Earth giving warnings to the cursed. If you see him, someone you love is about to die. He'll try to warn you. But chances are, it's too late. When you see the Birch Man, the body of the person you love has already gone cold."

"Woah," the teenage girl said. She looked so taken aback, so disturbed, that Ellie took a step toward her. If that child's parents weren't going to properly educate her, someone should! Something clamped on Ellie's shoulder before she could take another step. It was Violet's hand. Ellie turned to her, and Violet shook her head. "Come on."

"But—"

"I know." Violet guided her toward the Seashell Bar. "There's no such thing as the Birch Man. But do you really want to interrupt their fun?"

"Fun? That poor child was—"

"She's having the time of her life."

Ellie looked back. Violet had a point. The teenager had shaken off her unsettled expression, and now she was asking questions, smiling from ear to ear. Ellie sighed. "You're right."

"I don't know why you get so testy about this stuff. Aren't you friends with an actual psychic on St. John?"

"Madame Tiffany is a *shopkeeper*. She runs a small business."

Violet looked amused. "Come on. I'll buy you a hot cocoa."

At another table, a woman in a long purple dress was telling a story. "When they found her husband, he was hunched over his desk with his tongue cut out! But the door was locked from the *inside*, and so were the windows. There was no way a human murderer could have escaped. The policeman who was first on the scene saw a red-cloaked figure running out into the woods. But when he went to investigate, there were no footprints in the soft mud. In total, the red phantom took three lives that summer. And it was never heard from again."

Good grief, Ellie thought. *This is their idea of fun?*

After ordering at the bar, they carried their drinks to the only unoccupied table and sat down. Ellie sipped her sweet hot chocolate with pleasure. Violet asked to see photos of Cole's new girlfriend, and Ellie was glad to oblige. Before long, an older gentleman wandered up to the bar. His woolen newsboy cap sat atop his thick white hair, and his heavy cable-knit sweater seemed an odd choice for a warm evening. When he ordered a beer in a working-class British accent, Ellie thought back to the press packet that Greg had given her that morning. When the man looked around for a place to sit, she recognized his face. She waved him over and called out, "Excuse me, but are you Harvey Fleming?"

"Alive and kicking!" He came over, his steps slow and heavy. "And who would you two be?" Harvey Fleming had a round, chubby face and a bulbous nose that sat atop his easygoing smile like a fat marble.

Ellie made introductions. "Harvey is one of the Sweetie Pie Baking Competition contestants," she told Violet.

"Would you like to join us?" Violet asked. "We have an extra chair."

"Don't mind if I do." Harvey grunted as he settled his bulk into the plastic deck chair. "I was out for my evening constitutional and I thought I'd see what all the hubbub is about." He looked over at the ghost story crowd. "Those people seem to be having a cracking good time. When I was a lad, my mates and I would go down the woods like and tell terrifying tales. We aimed to scare one another! That was the whole point. But this is a much grander setting."

"I doubt they'd mind if you joined them," Violet said. "Not that we're trying to chase you off. Do you remember any of the ghost stories you told in the woods?"

He shook his head regretfully. "No. I'm afraid they're lost to the pages of history." He tapped his temple. "These days all I've got room for are recipes, flour ratios, doctor appointments, and the last place I parked my car. Manchester airport, terminal three, row K, number thirty-six." Harvey grinned.

"I watched a few episodes of your show," Ellie said. "Not *your* season, of course, as it hasn't aired, but a prior one. Are you enjoying the competition?"

He took a long drink of his beer. "Not at all. Don't get me wrong, I'm honored to be included. My wife adores the baking shows, and she was the one who pushed me to send in my video. Now, she's puffed up with pride, bragging to all her friends that I'm on the telly. I'm a hero to my wife again!" He winked at Ellie. "But as for the competition? There's too much primping and not enough baking. Everyone wants something. A best-selling cookbook, or some of those insta-clicks, or their own show on the telly. And do you know what I want?"

"What's that?" Violet asked.

"I want to know why Ariana's pie crust is so much better than mine!" He laughed, a low rumbly sound that reminded Ellie of a car engine starting up. "She's promised to show me her tricks, but only *after* the final showdown. That's more than fair." He scratched his nose. "I had a job, ladies. A good one, for nearly forty years. I kept the trains running on time. Baking is my hobby, and I don't much like it when my hobbies feel like *work*. And as for being famous? Well, that's work I have little interest in. Still, I can't complain. We've got a tremendous group of bakers, lovely people to have a pint with after a long day on set, and the crew certainly knows their onions."

He noticed Violet's name badge. "You work here? That makes sense. You don't strike me as ghost seekers. I was talking to your coworker earlier. Devon?"

Ellie nodded. "Our executive chef."

"Delightful bloke," Harvey said. "A real treat to speak with. He turned me onto a new kind of flour mixture. Chickpea. Says it makes the muffins stand up at attention! I'll give it a go as soon as I get home. Assuming the local ASDA carries it. I don't like going cross-town. Too much traffic."

"Who do you think will take the Golden Cupcake?" Violet asked, sipping her martini.

"Why? Are you running a pool?" Harvey leaned forward with an eager, toothy smile. "Because if so, I want in."

Violet laughed. "Who's the one to beat?"

"Well, if there's any justice in this cruel world of ours, the Golden Cupcake will go to Mindie or Ariana. Ari's got the most talent in my view, but she's less experienced than Mindie. There's not a single recipe that's been a challenge for our Aussie baker. But Ariana's creative. She's got the touch, as my mother used to say. Ari reminds me a bit of my oldest daughter, Patty. Brilliant, but she doesn't like to put on airs, if you take my meaning. Ari's husband Teddy is gunning for the personal fitness thing. He puts courgettes in everything. Blech!"

"Courgettes?" Ellie asked.

"Sorry. You Yanks call it zucchini. Never could stand the stuff, no matter what the language. Food should taste good, or why bother? Sweets should be sweet. Veggies should be savory. Call me set in my ways, but it's true." He lifted his beer in a salute.

"How old are you, Harvey?" Violet asked.

"Seventy-three," he said proudly. "It's hard to believe, I know! I blame my wife Samantha. She keeps me young."

Ellie caught the tenderness in his voice. "You miss her."

"I do. And I'm not ashamed to admit it! But at the end of the week, I'll be back on a plane eating those terrible hard pretzels and looking forward to a proper cuppa. Win or lose, Sam made me promise I'd do my best, and that's exactly what I've done. But don't let me chew your ears off, ladies. Devon tells me there's a special raspberry chocolate cake you serve here. Can you tell me where to get some? I was thinking I might be able to con young Devon out of a recipe or two, but it helps to taste everything first." Harvey beckoned them closer and spoke low. "If you ask a baker for their recipe they'll clam right up. But ask them for their opinion on how many eggs to use in that recipe, and they'll stumble over themselves to tell you the *correct* way to bake their masterpiece."

"You're a cunning man." Violet teased.

"That I am," Harvey said, wiggling his big white eyebrows for comedic effect.

"Usually, they only serve chocolate raspberry lava cake with dinner," Ellie said. "But there's a loophole."

"And what's that, darlin?"

"Room service! They don't have set hours. And they'll bring you *anything* you like. If it's not on the menu, just ask."

Harvey looked around the deck appreciatively. "You know, I could get used to this cruise ship thing. Maybe Samantha would like to come on a cruise someday. And if I won that Golden Cupcake, I could afford to fly her out, first class. She'd love that."

"Well, now you can't let Mindie and Ariana win," Violet said sternly. "You need to get your wife that first class ticket!"

They chatted with Harvey for a while longer. Over at the bar, Ellie saw that Manny had called in a second bartender to help him out, and guests were standing around, waiting for tables to open up. Violet nudged Ellie with her foot. Ellie nodded.

"We need to get back to work," Ellie said, standing up. "But it was nice to meet you, Harvey. Enjoy your room service tonight."

"I certainly will," he said. "Thanks for the tip!"

As soon as they moved away, one of the roaming camera operators walked right up to Harvey. The man crouched and aimed the lens at Harvey's head, almost at eye level. Harvey sipped his beer and looked out to sea.

Chapter Four

ELLIE GLANCED AT HER WATCH. She lengthened her stride, turning the corner to head down the long, gray-painted hallway on the crew level. She stepped to the side to make room for a woman pushing two huge laundry carts full of dirty linens destined for the ship's massive washing machines. When Ellie reached an unmarked door between two eight-foot-tall metal cabinets, she knocked three times.

The door opened a crack. Paul Gumb's eye peered out at her. "Password?"

"Don't make me say it."

"Then how do I know you're not an imposter?" The security chief's Jamaican-accented English betrayed his amusement.

"Paul, you know me."

"That's exactly what an imposter would say." The door started to close.

"Wait! Can I have a Scooby Snack?"

Paul opened the door the rest of the way. His bright smile flashed against his deep brown skin. "Welcome back, Ellie."

During their last investigation, she'd learned that Paul loved Scooby Do, the crime-solving dog. That's why there was a small stuffed Scooby in her suitcase. It would make a fun birthday gift if she could figure out when his birthday was. Paul was tight-lipped about the strangest things.

Victor and Violet were already inside the small room, leaning against opposite walls. Aside from a wooden desk and a solitary chair, the main feature of the room was a barred cell containing a simple cot and a shiny, stainless steel toilet. But the brig was private and rarely used, which was why the senior officers held their stand-up meetings there.

Victor lifted his golden pocket watch out of his vest pocket and peered down at it through his round spectacles. "The officer's meeting starts promptly on the hour, Ms. Tappet. This hasn't changed in the weeks you've been away."

"I apologize. Please don't let me interrupt."

"As I was saying," Victor said, tucking the watch back into place, "I've allowed the baking contestants to request additional foodstuffs from the kitchen, but *only* with Devon's approval, and not at the expense of the pre-planned menus. They seem to be under the impression that grocery stores float upon the high seas. That Australian woman got quite persnickety when I informed her that she can't raid our freezers and take whatever she wants. We already made space for their ingredients, but this is a cruise ship, not a Kroger."

Ellie thought back to what Roberta had said about keeping Greg happy. "Roberta wants us to accommodate The Sugar Network to the best of our ability. But I hear you, Victor. There need to be limits."

"When I was young, we had this little thing called inventory control," Victor said, glowering a little. "I will not be steamrolled by these television people." His shoulders dropped, then he straightened himself right up. "But as always, the housekeeping and restaurant departments are dedicated to excellence. We are here to serve."

Paul nodded, accepting Victor's pomp with all due seriousness. He looked at Violet. "And how about you? Have you had any problems with our new guests?"

"Nope. *The Pirates of Peking* is on hiatus because The Sugar Network commandeered the theater. Wynona is handling bingo all week, bless her. I'm helping Ellie wrangle the VIPs. So far, so good. How about you?"

"We received several complaints about people running in the halls late last night. Two guests reported people banging on their doors. When they looked, no one was there. And there were three calls about," Paul's expression went blank, "*ghost* noises."

Violet laughed. "Like what? Chains rattling? Or are we talking about an excess of vowel sounds?"

"We didn't ask for details. Normally, I'd counsel our guests about wasting the security team's time. But we investigated all the complaints, and we found no ghosts." Paul shrugged. "It's almost as if we have a few hundred paranormal enthusiasts on board. So long as it doesn't get out of hand, I say let them have their fun. My overnight crew doesn't have much to do except their usual security sweeps, so I'll let them chase ghosts for a few nights. It will keep them on their toes, and off the internet."

Violet pushed herself off the wall. She tugged her black pencil skirt down and checked to make sure her *Adventurous Cruises* polo shirt was tucked in evenly the whole way around. Was that a new shade of lipstick she was wearing? She'd taken extra care with her eye makeup too. "Well, unless there's more to discuss, Ellie and I have been invited to attend the morning shoot."

Ellie smiled to herself. Victor might not have been impressed by the television people, but Violet seemed excited. And who could blame her? It wasn't every day you got a behind-the-scenes view of a world-famous television show.

Victor nodded. "Very well. Let's touch base the day after tomorrow. Same time?"

Violet held the door open, but Ellie hesitated. "Can you give me a minute? I want to talk to Paul."

As soon as she and Paul were alone together, he turned to her. "I know what you want to ask me about. Violet told me."

"Violet can't keep a secret to save her life. Except yours, apparently." Ellie chuckled. "But yes, I'm dying of curiosity! At Kameron's promotion ceremony, I *saw* the way you looked at her! Don't even try to deny it. Now, you don't need to tell me anything you don't want to, but—"

Paul burst out laughing.

"What? Did I say something funny?"

"I don't need to tell you anything I don't want to, eh? That's cute. But if I don't answer your questions, you'll get curiouser and curiouser until your head explodes. And you will *not* let it drop no matter what you say. So, go ahead. Ask me."

"Fine. Are you in love with Kameron? Or are you making goo-goo eyes at her for no reason?" If Paul was going to be sassy, she could be too!

Paul leaned against the wall. He looked down and plucked a bit of lint off his white polo shirt. An embroidered purple mermaid was stitched into the fabric, the *Adventurous Cruises* logo. "Even if I were, it would not matter."

"Why not?"

"Kameron and I came aboard the *Spirit* around the same time and we just... clicked. We dated for eight months."

"I didn't know."

"I only intended to be here for a year or two, until I found a job with the Constabulary Force back home in Jamaica. Kameron had been working as an au pair for a wealthy family in Lagos, and she wanted a career in security. We were both far from home, and we worked long hours. We became close."

"What happened?"

"Well, Captain Spark offered me the Security Chief position when the previous chief retired. At dinner that night, I asked Kameron if she'd be interested in marriage someday. Not a formal proposal, you understand. Just a conversation. I was trying to make my decision. Should I take the job aboard the *Spirit* or return home to Jamaica? I wasn't sure that working on a cruise ship was what I wanted, long term. And I wanted to know what Kameron's intentions were. The Security Officer position is a five-year contract, and I did 'na want to make such a big decision without knowing where we were headed."

"And?"

"And she broke up with me."

Ellie's heart dropped an inch. "But why?"

Paul exhaled forcefully. "I cannot say. She said she needed to go her own way." He shrugged. "Ever since, we've been colleagues. But when you first came aboard, you asked us to attend an award ceremony." His mouth quirked up in a smile. "Your first case, I suppose. That horrible finger incident. Do you remember?"

Ellie thought back. Paul had come into the Moonlight Lounge with a beautiful woman on his arm. His "date" for the little ruse she'd concocted to flush out the criminal. And that night was the first time she'd met Kameron Achebe. "I do."

"We dressed up that evening, and I put her arm through mine. Everything I'd felt for her came rushing back. I won't deny it. But does she care about me in the same way? I do not believe so. And I am her superior officer. I will *not* insult her by pursuing her when she's made it clear where she stands." He smiled sadly. "Does that answer your question?"

Poor Paul! "I'm sorry if my questions caused you pain. I was just so *hopeful* when I saw the way you two looked at one another. Because I want you to be happy. Both of you."

He shrugged. "Tis okay. I don't mind talking about it. What's the saying? Don't be sad that it's over..."

"Be glad that it happened."

Paul nodded. "I don't regret anything. But speaking of regrets, I should get to work before the day gets too old."

"Me too." She tapped one finger on the radio at her waist. "Call me if you need me. I'll be around."

Chapter Five

ELLIE AND VIOLET WOVE THEIR way through the ship, dodging the crowds. Couples strolled along the promenade deck outside the big square windows, enjoying the fresh air. Women wearing sundresses as bright and varied as the flowers in a summer garden perused goods on the shopping level. Bursts of conversation echoed in the atrium, and the sharp scent of coffee floated up along with the notes from the piano below.

They stepped inside the midship elevators and Violet pressed the brass button for the lido deck. "So. You talked to Paul."

"I did."

"And?"

"And now I'm sad. Paul loves Kameron, but he won't pursue her. And maybe that's right, given their history. Still, it doesn't stop me from wishing things were different." She gave Violet the side-eye. "I don't suppose you know what Kameron has to say on this topic?"

"Nope."

"There's something you're not telling me."

"Listen: when *you* play matchmaker, you're adorable. When I try, Kameron threatens to hog tie me with my own microphone cord and set me afloat on an inflatable dinghy."

"You've already talked to her. Is that it?"

"If I did, I promised I would let it go." Violet looked over. "Granted, if *someone else* wanted to give it the old college try..."

"Someone," Ellie agreed readily. "Once a suitable plan is formed."

"Tread lightly," Violet warned. "Kameron's as prickly as a cactus on this subject. This won't be as easy as bum-rushing her with a cup of tea and that grandmotherly charm of yours."

Ellie shot her friend a smug look. "I could use a challenge."

They stepped outside. The lounge chairs were back in place. Sunbathers splayed their limbs out beneath the morning sun. A faint snore came from a chair near the pool. The sleeping woman had tented a fashion magazine over her face. Her sunblock sat next to her chair with the cellophane wrapping still in place.

They ascended the stairs. At the balcony, a stern-looking man with a blond crew cut stood behind a yellow rope barrier. "Sorry. This level is closed temporarily." He had the grudgingly polite tone of someone forced to say the same sentence over and over.

Ellie flashed her badge. "Greg is expecting us."

He unclipped the yellow rope and beckoned them through. From below, a woman's screechy voice called out, "Hey! Why do *they* get to watch?" The security guard reached into his pocket and pulled out a free drink coupon. He nodded briskly as if to say he'd handle this, and he descended the stairs, holding the coupon out like a peace offering.

The balcony was partially shaded by the massive smokestack jutting upward. Inside that fat shaded crescent, there were folding chairs for the baking competition contestants. The cloth backs of the seats were printed with names in blocky white text: *Ariana*, *Teddy*, *Harvey*, *Mindie*, and *Kitty*. A film crew stood around a sunny area near the back railing. There was a big camera on a tripod, operated by a fortyish woman with a long blond braid that hung down her back. She wore jeans and a baby blue t-shirt emblazoned with the stylized cupcake logo of The Sugar Network.

Off to one side, a woman held a shield-like object covered in reflective fabric. On the opposite side, a skinny young guy hoisted a furry-looking microphone on a cantilevered pole. At the railing, a man with a loaded utility belt applied makeup to a young woman while she looked up at the sky, holding still. The ocean stretched out behind her, an endless vista of deep blue beneath a sky dotted with puffy cotton-candy clouds. Waves sped backward behind the rail. Wind picked up the woman's curly red hair and blew it gently back off her pale shoulders.

Ellie leaned over to Violet and whispered, "Let's get a closer look."

They stepped over the cables snaking across the deck as they approached the waiting contestants. Harvey raised his meaty hand to cover a massive yawn. He leaned over to speak to the woman next to him.

Harvey grinned when he saw them. "Ellie. Violet! Welcome to the set! May I introduce my fellow contestants?" He gestured at the woman in green. "This is Mindie Burton, our resident genius in all things French."

Mindie wore an emerald green dress that coordinated well with her auburn hair, and thin gold bracelets danced on her right wrist as she reached out to shake hands. Her pointed chin and big green eyes gave her a faintly elfin look.

"Pleased to meet you," Mindie said, her Aussie accent sharp and upbeat.

Ellie pointed at her gold pendant. It was shaped like a bird and the center was filled in with multi-colored enamel. "Is that a Kookaburra?" Ellie asked.

"Good eye! You know your Australian birds."

"We get a lot of birders on board. And I've picked up a few things here and there." Ellie gestured at Harvey's getup. Like the day before, he was wearing a heavy sweater, a wool hat, and thick tweed slacks. "Also, I noticed they've dressed Harvey like a poster child for British men of a certain age. I figured they might have asked you to wear something from your country."

Harvey grinned. "She's a sharp one, isn't she Mindie? Don't get too close to me, Ellie. In this heat I'm starting to sweat like an old cheese."

"This is Violet Wolfe," Ellie said. "Our cruise director."

But Violet wasn't listening. She was staring at the woman getting a makeover in front of the camera. Her long red hair, milky skin, and scattered freckles easily could have placed her on the cover of a fashion magazine. Ellie nudged Violet and whispered. "I think she's a bit young for you."

"It's not against the law to look," Violet whispered back.

"Ellie and Violet work for the cruise line," Harvey was explaining. "Violet's quite the singer, and Ellie is the official matchmaker."

Ellie laughed. "That's *not* what I said."

"Yes. But that's what Violet said last night, and I think our friends know us better than we know ourselves, don't you?" Harvey's grin was unrestrained. He was in high spirits. Perhaps he wasn't as camera shy as he'd seemed the night before?

"It's nice to meet you all," Violet said. She looked over at the woman who hadn't spoken yet. "You must be Ariana?"

"I hear you're the wedding cake genius," Ellie added.

Ariana smiled at the compliment. She had a quiet prettiness that paled in comparison to the vivacious Aussie. Whoever had done her makeup had applied too much foundation, and it flaked around the edges of her heart-shaped face. She'd painted her fingernails the same coral color as her dress, and her matching scarf was tied around her neck at a jaunty angle.

"And who is that?" Violet asked, pointing at the woman getting made up in front of the camera.

"Oh. That's Kitty." Ariana's flat tone and flared nostrils seemed to say that she didn't care too much for Kitty Gilbert.

"She is quite a looker, isn't she?" Harvey said. He quickly added, "All of our female bakers are. We're surrounded by beauty. And carbohydrates! Temptation everywhere!"

"I need quiet on set!" The director called out, pointing at Harvey like you might call out a naughty child with a penchant for breaking the rules.

"Sorry, Linda!" Harvey called back. He made a lip-zipping motion, and the director grinned. She pointed from her eyes to him with two fingers, back and forth, to say she'd be watching him.

The crew filmed Kitty Gilbert posing prettily near the railing with the Pacific Ocean behind her. She posed with and without a straw hat. She posed with and without her tortoiseshell sunglasses. Kitty smiled. She pouted. She stared pensively out to sea. At last, they affixed a small microphone to the collar of her sundress and asked her a series of questions. Scones were her favorite thing, she said. The kind with butter and strawberry jam they sold at the state fair in Oregon. As soon as the director called "Cut!" Kitty's smile dropped like a puppet with cut strings. "Can I get some water here?" she called out.

Harvey covered up his yawn. Mindie scrolled through recipes on her phone. Ariana swung her legs back and forth like a child at the doctor's office, burning off energy.

Before long, a man from the film crew ran forward, holding out a plastic water bottle. Kitty took a sip and wrinkled her nose. "Can I get some *ice* for my water? If that's not too much trouble?" Her peevish voice seemed like the hallmark of a very spoilt young woman. Or at least someone who didn't care much about what others thought of her.

Violet leaned over to Ellie and whispered, "Well, I might have been in love for five minutes, but the spell is broken. You stay put and wait for Greg. I've got this." She strode forward toward Kitty, her hips swaying. "I can get you some ice."

Ellie turned to Harvey. "Have you seen Greg? I was supposed to meet him up here."

"I assume he went to find Teddy." He turned to Ariana. "Where's your young man? Usually he's first on set, doing push-ups to plump out his pecs before the cameras start rolling." Harvey held out his arms and flexed them. "Granted, if I were thirty again, I might do the same thing. But you can't unmash a baked potato, can you?"

Ariana smiled fondly at Harvey. "Teddy probably got overwhelmed picking out the perfect outfit for the shoot." Glancing at Ellie, she said, "We women are supposed to be the pretty ones, but that's not how it works in our house." She shrugged. "Not that I'm complaining. It takes the pressure off me."

Violet was headed down the stairs to get ice for Kitty's drink. The man at the top of the stairs opened the yellow rope for her, and as soon as she descended, Greg Norris stepped up onto the deck.

"Sorry, everyone! So sorry I'm late. I was on the phone with corporate, and you know how they can be. They've got questions, and I'm the answer man." He strode over to the waiting contestants. "Good morning, bakers. Ellie, I'm glad you're here. Maybe you can do something for me. I was thinking we should—" He halted, looking from the chairs to the railing, where Kitty waited with crossed arms. "Where's Teddy? Is he in makeup?"

"He isn't here," Harvey said. "We figured he was with you."

Greg frowned and strode over to the director. "How many segments have we gotten through? Just Kitty? Okay. I want you to get hers wrapped up, and let's get the rest done by noon, please. At this rate we'll be filming till three a.m." He turned back to the contestants. "Ariana, have you seen Teddy?"

She reached down to adjust the ankle strap on her shoe. "No. Not since yesterday. Maybe you should ask Mindie."

Mindie's mouth compressed into a thin line. She looked at Greg and shook her head. "I haven't seen him since dinner last night."

"Why don't I go get him?" Ellie interjected, noting the irritated expression on Greg's face. "Just tell me where to go."

He thought for a moment. "Check his suite, and if he's not there, go check the gym." He forced a smile. "It's no problem. We'll get this shoot done, on time, *and* on budget. Even if we need to be here all night."

Mindie let out a quiet groan. Greg noticed but pretended not to. Harvey's stomach growled loudly, and he reached into his sweater pocket, pulling out a puff pastry wrapped in a paper napkin. He offered a bite to Ariana, who shook her head.

Ellie headed for the stairs, stepping over the cables to avoid tripping. "I'll be right back. Have Violet call me on the radio if he shows up."

Chapter Six

AT LEAST I'M GETTING MY exercise in, Ellie thought. She tapped her crew badge at the entrance to *The Suites* and headed to Teddy's stateroom. When there was no reply to her knock, she knocked again, calling out, "Teddy McIntyre? Greg sent me." There was a muffled banging noise inside the room. She pressed her ear against the wood. Laughter followed, but it sounded recorded.

Her gut tightened. So what if he'd left his television on? It didn't mean there was a problem. Still, if he'd slipped in the shower...

She lifted her radio and pressed the talk button with her thumb. "Security desk, this is ET. Please come back."

"Security here." Kameron's tone was all business.

"I need access to room 1250 for a safety check. Can you code me in?"

A minute later, the radio crackled. "You're authorized, ET. Don't forget to come by and fill out the log."

Ellie clipped the portable radio to the waistband of her pants and used her crew badge to open the door. She pressed the door open slowly. "Teddy McIntyre? I'm coming inside. I hope you're decent."

The television was indeed on. And the volume was up high! The big wall-mounted screen showed a close-up of an apple pie. The camera panned out to show a long table set out with nearly identical pies. A few of them looked crooked. One of them was falling apart, the filling leaking over the sides like it had been stepped on. Raquel and Vick, the celebrity judges, stood behind the table as the voice-over described the details of the dessert challenge.

Ellie hurried to the coffee table and muted the television with the remote. "Teddy? Are you in here?"

There was an empty glass decanter on the table. And two crystal glasses. They held hints of amber liquid. One glass was broken; a big V-shaped chip was missing from the side. Something red ran along the edge of the glass and dribbled down onto the wooden coffee table. Ellie's heart did a double beat in her chest. Was that blood?

The suite had two big bedrooms. She went from one to the other, calling Teddy's name. One bed was laden with stacks of shirts and slacks; each garment was wrapped in a dry-cleaning bag. The second bedroom was untouched. Both bathrooms were clean, and the one connected to the master bedroom had a shaving kit on the counter. The air in the rooms felt cool. Cold, almost, despite the warmth of the day.

Maybe he cut himself and went to the medical office to get stitched up. I can call and check.

Ellie returned to the living room. Cool air rushed in from behind the closed curtains at the sliding glass door. She went over and pushed them open. The metal hooks made a swishing noise as they slid over the rail. The balcony door was half-open. She grabbed the handle to close it, and that's when she saw it: more blood.

Red spots spattered the ground. The balcony chairs were stacked to one side, along the right wall. She stepped outside, taking care not to step on the spots. A familiar shape caught her eye. A red handprint was stamped onto the half-wall facing the water. She held her hand over the mark, not touching. The thumb and forefinger were clear. The pinky was barely visible, as if someone had pressed themselves against the wall, staggering.

She took a closer look. To the right of the handprint, four red smears ran over the top of the rail. Were those finger marks? Her heart leapt into her throat. She danced a step to the side and stood on tiptoes to look over the rail. Connected to those four finger marks, a fat reddish smear wider than her palm ran down the front. Now that she was standing close, she saw more blood smeared on top of the railing. It gave the railing a pinkish cast.

Her stomach clenched. She didn't need to look overboard to know what she'd see below. But she looked anyway. She couldn't help it. Frothy waves broke away from the hull at the waterline. The water churned and curled along the edges, swirling down into the darkness below. There was nothing down there but the cold oblivion of the Pacific Ocean.

She searched the horizon. She looked across the waves. Bending down, she inhaled, and the coppery scent of blood was unmistakable. She stepped inside and snatched the radio off her waist. Every second counted now.

"Security team, this is ET. Code Blue. No visual confirmation. I repeat. Code Blue. No visual confirmation. Port side, Forward. Deck twelve."

ELLIE WATCHED PAUL WORK. HE'D already taken photographs of the suite, and now he was squatting on the balcony, frowning at the red spots on the white-painted floor. He'd left Kameron upstairs with the film crew, asking her to keep them there as long as possible. Paul rolled a clean cotton swab in the largest red droplet and put the swab in a plastic baggie. He held it out without looking up, and Ellie took it, gripping the plastic zipper carefully to avoid touching the contents.

Teddy was not in the infirmary, nor was he in the gym, or running laps near the Sport Court. No one knew where he was. A recovery crew was out with the silver shark, performing a grid search around the ship, starting with the surrounding areas and moving backward along the path.

Paul motioned her out onto the balcony and handed her a measuring tape in a silver metal holder. "Hold this tape against the wall, will you? I want to measure that handprint." She stepped over the red spots on tiptoes and did what he asked. He snapped several photos with his phone and nodded. "That'll do. Thank you."

Beyond the rail, the ocean waves bobbed gently. The ship was at a full stop while the search was underway. Paul had used the word *recovery*, not rescue. She understood why. Unless you were rescued immediately, there was little chance of survival in the open water. Even if you were lucky enough not to get knocked out, and if you didn't break your bones when you hit the water, and if you weren't sucked into the powerful turbines behind the ship, there was still the matter of how *cold* the ocean was.

The recovery team was looking for Teddy McIntyre's body, and they weren't likely to find it.

Ellie blinked. Her mind kept serving up images of the churning sea and the inky darkness below. She followed Paul back inside.

He stopped at the coffee table. "Ellie, what do you make of this?"

"If I had to guess, I'd say he cut himself."

Paul nodded, pointing at the carpet. "It's hard to see against the dark blue, but do you see those spots? I think that's a blood trail." He took a few steps toward the balcony. "It goes all the way to the slider."

"So, he cut himself, and he went outside. Maybe he didn't know how bad it was? And he felt weak from the blood loss?" She winced. Her suppositions sounded weak, but the alternatives were too awful to contemplate. And she didn't want to go there; not yet. Hadn't she just looked Ariana in the eye? "Maybe he did go get help. But not to the infirmary. There are first aid kits everywhere."

"That blood trail goes right over the rail," Paul said, grimacing. There's blood on the side of the ship."

She nodded.

"Here's what I think. Teddy McIntyre committed suicide. He cut his wrist, and perhaps he hesitated. Maybe he got squeamish, or maybe it was taking longer than he thought. So he went over the rail."

Ellie's heart sank. "We don't know that. You might be right, but we don't *know*."

"Agreed. But it's not looking good."

Wasn't all death tragic? That's what the teenage girl had said the night before. Ellie felt sick to her stomach. Ariana was upstairs, right now. Her husband was late. The ship had stopped moving. Did she suspect? Was she upstairs, afraid, right now? Was the dread creeping in? Poor Ariana!

Ellie took a breath to steady herself.

Paul made a call on his radio. "Safety team report."

The radio crackled and a faint male voice responded. "There's no sight of him, sir. Should we expand the grid?"

"Yes. You've got an hour. Make the most of it." He keyed the radio again. "Search team, report."

"No dice, sir. We checked the places on our list. We've begun a general sweep, and we made an announcement on the intercom."

"Good. Report back at twenty-minute intervals. Gumbs out."

"Help me search the room," Paul said. They set to work, and before long Kameron radioed. "Paul, you're going to have company in a minute. Greg Norris and the wife. They're headed your way. And before you ask, yes, I told them they had to wait with me. But unless you wanted me to cuff them..."

Someone banged on the front door, and Paul opened it. Ariana came in first, her hair streaming behind her, her eyes wild. Greg was hot on her heels, reaching out for her, asking her to wait. Ariana froze when she saw Paul standing in the open doorway to the bedroom. Her gaze went to the latex gloves he wore. She swiveled her head toward Ellie, and her mouth trembled. "What is this? Why are you in my husband's room?"

Paul stepped forward and put his hands behind his back. "Mrs. McIntyre. I'm sorry to say we haven't found your husband yet. I need to ask you to—"

She pushed past him, heading into the bedroom. He didn't stop her, but he held out a hand to prevent Greg from following.

"The ship stopped," Ariana's voice called out. "And I saw that boat out there, searching. Why aren't we moving?" She came out of the bedroom and went into the unused room on the opposite side of the suite. The bathroom door slammed. She returned quickly. "Have you checked the bar? He's probably there, signing autographs." Her voice went higher, spiraling up toward a breaking point. "He has to be. I'll never forgive myself if—"

Ellie had been backing up toward the balcony door, one step at a time. They'd shut the slider, but it wasn't locked. Ariana must have noticed because she made a break for the balcony. Ellie reached the handle first, and she held it fast, blocking the handle with her body. "Ariana. Wait. You shouldn't jump to any conclusions. It could be—"

But Ariana just ripped the curtains open on the other side. For a long moment she said nothing. Then she turned to Ellie, her face as white as the ship's hull. "Is that... Did he...?"

Ellie willed herself to speak. But the words didn't come. What could she possibly say?

Ariana crumpled to the ground. "No. He wouldn't. He's..." Her chest heaved. "He *has* to be okay. He..."

Ellie carefully got down on the ground and embraced her. Ariana's skin felt hot, and her body jerked as she sobbed, her hair streaming down over her face, her hands resting limply on her dress, her back hunched. "Sweetheart, I know this is scary. We're doing everything we can to find him."

Over near the entrance, Greg Norris was watching Ariana. He glanced at the sliding glass door, but he didn't move toward it. He asked Paul what was going on.

"We aren't done searching," Ellie said gently, speaking to Ariana. "I know, it doesn't look good. But we're checking the ship, and the water. We're looking everywhere."

Everywhere but beneath the waves.

Greg and Paul were speaking in low voices. A few minutes later, Greg came over and crouched down. "Ari. Please. Come with me. Let's sit in my suite. They've still got work to do, and there's no reason for you to be alone. We'll wait there until there's news." Ellie helped Ariana to her feet. Greg put his arm around her shoulders and led her toward the door.

"Mr. Norris," Paul said.

"Yes?"

"We will be with you as soon as we can. Keep her safe, will you?" He shot Ellie a knowing look. If Teddy McIntyre had indeed gone overboard, and if his wife were wild with grief, who knew what she might do?

Greg seemed to understand. "I won't let her out of my sight."

"Do you want me to contact your film crew?" Ellie asked. According to Greg's schedule, the camera crew would be setting up the theater for the first bake, right now.

Greg thought about it. "No. Let them get started without being... burdened by this. We'll talk to them after."

"Sir, I'll need to speak to your entire crew. To anyone who had contact with Mr. McIntyre." Paul sounded apologetic.

"Of course. Whatever you need. Please, just find Teddy." He led Ariana away, and shut the door behind them.

They continued their search. Ellie looked in the couch cushions, the small desk, and in the unused bedroom. She swept aside the shower curtain and opened the bathroom cabinets. Before long, Paul called out from the bedroom. He came over and held out a handwritten note. "I found this inside Teddy's dressing table."

"What does it say?"

He held it up. "It says, *I'm sorry.*"

Chapter Seven

GREG USHERED ELLIE AND PAUL inside his suite as soon as they arrived. "I gave Ariana a valium," he said quietly. "She's asleep in my spare room. *Please* tell me you found Teddy."

"I wish we could." Paul said. "But based upon the evidence recovered in his stateroom, I believe Mr. McIntyre went overboard. He's gone." His jaw muscle tightened as he glanced at the closed bedroom door.

Greg sat down on his sofa. He looked up at Paul, his expression doubtful. "But wouldn't someone have seen that? I mean, this ship is crawling with people."

"If it had happened in a public area, probably," Paul said. "But unless someone directly beneath his suite happened to be looking out the window, it could have gone unnoticed. Also, we don't know what time he went overboard. Was it dark out? There's still a lot we don't know."

"Could it have been an accident? Ariana said she saw blood on the balcony. I thought maybe she was imagining things, but..."

Paul waited while Greg's sentence expired unfinished. "We need to ask you a few questions about Teddy's state of mind," Paul said. "Had he been depressed lately?"

"Why? Do you think he—" Greg's eyes widened. He shook his head. "No. You're wrong. Teddy was chasing his lifelong dream. He wouldn't have... you know."

"What dream are you referring to?" Ellie asked, sitting down across from Greg.

"Teddy was starting a lifestyle brand. Workout videos, healthy cookbooks, and maybe even a television show. He pitched me his ideas during the flight to San Diego." Greg glanced at the closed bedroom door. "He had a real shot at success, especially with Ariana at his side. She's bursting with talent, and Teddy's got more hustle than a West Coast rapper. Best of all, they supported one another. Ariana only came on our show because Teddy wanted it so badly." He scratched his sandy brown hair above one ear. When he put his hand down, the spot he'd touched was pink and irritated. "Teddy wasn't the suicidal type."

"I'm not sure there is a type," Paul said cautiously. "It's hard to know what's going on inside a person's heart and mind. Speaking generally, what can you tell us about Teddy's mood lately?"

"He was wound pretty tight. But that wasn't unusual. Teddy always got anxious before a filming. Ariana said he was up at all hours, making plans, futzing with his wardrobe, watching old episodes of the competition."

"Is that why they were sleeping in different rooms?" Ellie asked. There had been no sign of Ariana's belongings in Teddy's room, and only half of the king-sized bed had been disturbed. There were nine suites booked for the Sugar Network party. Five contestants, Greg, and the two celebrity judges. None of them had doubled up.

"A suite was one of the perks we offered to our contestants this round. Ariana asked if they could have adjoining suites, so Teddy would have more space to spread out. I didn't..." He glanced away. "I didn't realize they were sleeping separately."

Was it her imagination, or was Greg pleased at that bit of news? His cheeks were flushed, and he'd dropped his gaze.

Greg caught her looking. He cleared his throat. "Anyway, we're screwed! I don't know how we can finish the show without Teddy." He scratched at his dark slacks with one blunt fingernail. "Should we take reaction shots of the contestants today? No. I can't do that to them." He was talking to himself now. "We could skip directly to the final showdown, as grim as that sounds. I guess Kitty Gilbert will survive another round after all."

"Mr. Norris—" Paul began.

Greg's face snapped up. "Forgive me. I'm babbling. The truth is, I'm gutted about Teddy, and I don't know what to say. So here I am, running my mouth about our show. As for Ariana, what am I supposed to do about *her*? She can't be expected to continue. But Nora's going to have my skin for a rug. We're already twenty percent over budget."

Paul took a small notepad and pencil out of his shirt pocket. He flipped to a blank page and rested it on his knee. The gesture seemed to focus Greg.

"Sir, I need to gather a few more facts for my report. When was the last time you saw Mr. McIntyre?"

"Last night, at dinner. We ate together in the captain's dining room. Everyone was there, me, the contestants, and the judges. That's a little tradition of ours, having a private meal together before filming."

"How was Teddy's mood?"

"He seemed upbeat. Eager. Typical Teddy."

"What time did you two part? And did you see where he went?"

"We finished dinner after seven. Teddy was talking to Mindie when I left the room. They were over by the big windows, chatting away as usual. Harvey said he was going to the bar. I don't know which one. Ariana and I took a walk around the promenade deck, and she said she was going to call it an early night. I dropped her off at her stateroom around eight? I didn't check my watch."

"And Ms. Gilbert?" Paul asked.

"Kitty was talking to your chef when I left the dining room. Pumping him for baking tips, I expect. Kitty's the opposite of Teddy. She's as cool as a cucumber, always, but she saves her prep work for the last minute. Raquel and Vick said they were going to the comedy show. I didn't see them after that."

Ellie nodded. "And where did you go after you left Ariana?"

"Oh, I walked all over. I went up to the balcony for a while, to enjoy the night air. I ran into Harvey down by the pool. We went upstairs and had a beer at the sports bar. There was a nice couple from Argentina there; we talked about soccer. Harvey followed me back to my room after. He gets lonely, I think. We talked until about one in the morning, and then he returned to his room. I went to bed after that."

"Was there anyone on board that Teddy was close with? A friend?"

"Mindie, for sure. They hung out a lot, which I thought was odd, given how different their temperaments are. Mindie's a peach. A total class act. I have no idea what she saw in Teddy." Greg shifted in his seat. "Socially, I mean."

"Did Teddy and Mindie have a romantic relationship?" Ellie asked.

"I don't think so. But there was some tension there, because of how Teddy treated Ariana."

"How did he treat her?"

Greg winced. "Teddy was sweet to Ari when the cameras were rolling, but aside from that, she may as well not have existed. Perhaps I shouldn't speak ill of the dead, but you did ask. Does any of that matter now?"

"Probably not," Paul said. "Do you think Teddy was feeling guilty about anything?"

"I doubt it. He wasn't the self-reflective type."

"But you said he was anxious?"

Greg moved his hand like a teeter-totter. "Teddy was great in front of the camera. A real natural. But he was obsessive about preparation. He'd have a million questions about the shoot. What camera angles we'd be using. What time of day we'd be filming. Which color of shirt would best showcase his skin tone. He was high maintenance."

"Did anyone want Teddy out of the way?" Paul asked. "Maybe to improve their chances at winning the competition?"

Greg recoiled as if he'd been slapped. "Wait. You don't think he was *tossed* overboard do you? I thought you wanted to know if he was depressed! Which one is it?"

He looked so upset! Ellie interjected, "Oh, Paul needs to write a report about what happened. For insurance purposes, you understand. There are certain questions we're required to ask."

"I see." Greg eyed her warily. "Well, to answer your question: no. Teddy wasn't going to win, so removing him would have been pointless. In editing, we make the competition look neck and neck until the end, but the man was no genius in the kitchen. Barring a sugar-frosted miracle, the fight for the Golden Cupcake is between Ariana and Mindie."

"Can you think of any reason why Teddy might have been depressed? Had he had a setback recently?" Paul asked.

"No, not particularly. Like I said, he was a bad husband, but—"

"Don't talk about him like that." Ariana had come out of the spare room, and she was wearing a thick white *Adventurous Cruises* robe. The hem of her coral-colored dress peeped out from the opening, and her feet were bare.

Greg looked chastened. "Ari. I didn't know you were awake. Sit. I'll get you some water." He hurried over to the kitchenette, putting distance between him and Ariana.

"Is Teddy dead?" Ariana stood with her arms wrapped around her middle, hugging the robe as if the garment might shield her from the terrible blow headed her way. But the truth was already in her eyes. *A wife knows*, Ellie thought. *Deep down in her bones, she always knows. No matter how much she wishes she didn't.*

"We believe so," Paul said gently. "It looks like your husband went over the railing of the balcony in his room."

"So he could still be out there, in the water."

"Ma'am. I'm so sorry, but I don't think so. We've searched the ship. And we've searched the waters."

"But Teddy's a good swimmer." Her lower lip trembled.

"Even so, the water is very cold. The average person–"

"Teddy wasn't average." She flung the words out like an accusation. "He's out there. He *has* to be."

Paul reached into his pocket and pulled out the note he'd found in Teddy's room. He held it out. "Is this your husband's handwriting?"

She snatched it out of his hand. "Where did you find this?"

"In his bedroom."

Ariana stared at the paper.

Ellie stood and maneuvered Ariana into the seat she'd vacated. "Sit right here, hon. You've had a shock."

"On the balcony," she said, "through the window. I saw blood. Did he..."

"There was a broken glass in his room. He may have cut himself with it," Paul explained.

"Why?" She stared at Paul. "Why would he...?" Her voice trailed away, and she looked down at the note.

"It's hard to say, ma'am." Paul took the note back from her.

"When did it happen?"

"We don't know yet. When did you see him last?"

"At dinner. I asked him to have breakfast with me today, but he wanted to work on his wardrobe. He said he'd see me at the shoot."

She sat, mute. The air conditioner came on with a faint whir. Greg came over with a glass of water, and he held it out. Ariana didn't seem to notice him.

"This is Hell," she whispered, her head hanging down.

Ellie felt the weight of Ariana's grief inside her own chest. A familiar, terrible heaviness. Greg stood near her, holding out the glass of water, frozen in place like a fool. Ellie snatched the glass from him and set it on the coffee table. She went and stood behind Ariana, resting a hand on her shoulder. "Officer Gumbs, I think that's enough questions for now. Don't you?"

Paul looked surprised, but he didn't challenge her. "Yes, we can continue this conversation later."

"I'll take Ariana back to her room," Ellie said. "And I'll stay with her for a while."

"I'll cancel the rest of the filming," Greg said suddenly. "We can't... we can't expect anyone to bake under these conditions. It's not right."

"Don't cancel." Ariana looked up at him, her eyes bright with unshed tears.

"What? Why?"

"I want to finish the show," she said, wiping her eyes. She stood and let the bathrobe drop to the ground. She smoothed her dress down.

Greg shook his head. "No one would expect you to. *No one*. We'll bring you back next season. You can have a fresh start."

"Teddy would finish. It's what he would want. And I'll... I'll bake his recipe for the final showdown." She blinked rapidly. "Teddy worked so hard to be here. He... he deserves his moment."

"Are you sure?" Greg asked.

"I am." She stood. Her expression crumpled, and she put her face in her hands.

Ellie reached for her hand. "Come on. We'll get you settled." She led Ariana to the door.

Paul could handle the rest. Her hands were full.

Chapter Eight

LATER THAT EVENING, ELLIE MET Violet at the Moonlight Lounge. She sank into the plush booth with a heavy sigh, and she smiled at the sympathetic look Violet gave her. Paul must have filled her in. "Is Cora all set for the evening show?"

"Everything's been handled. How are you holding up? And how is Ariana?" Violet waved down a waiter and ordered a martini with extra olives for herself and a pot of Earl Grey for Ellie.

From their vantage point at the back corner of the room, the lounge looked dim and gloomy. Pewter-colored curtains hung around the small stage, pulled closed like an iron curtain. The lounge was half-full, and more guests were streaming in through the central hallway by the minute.

"I'll be all right." Ellie said. "Ariana is resting, and Raquel is sitting with her tonight. Raquel's a widow, so she gets it. Ariana's made of strong stuff, but I wish she hadn't insisted on staying in the competition. Once the shock wears off, she may regret it."

Violet's eyebrows lifted. "Don't tell me they're still going ahead?"

Ellie nodded. "They're shortening the season by an episode and they'll have the four remaining contestants skip to the final showdown. Greg said they'll spend the next two days filming tributes to Teddy McIntyre's life. I don't know how I feel about that. It's nice, but it's also..."

"Commercial? Yeah. Well, I expect The Sugar Network is trying to turn lemons into lemonade. Still, it doesn't mean they're not sincere. How is the investigation going? Paul was a bit vague about what happened up there."

"I'm not sure what happened after I left. We found a note in Teddy's room. All it said was 'I'm sorry.'"

"So, it *was* a suicide."

"It seems like it. But I still have questions. Someone was in Teddy's stateroom, drinking with him, before it happened. And I can't get the television out of my mind. The volume was blasting. Why leave the TV like that? It doesn't make any sense."

Their drinks arrived. Ellie wrapped her hands around her mug and waited for the warmth to soak in.

"Maybe Teddy wanted someone to find out what happened before his wife did?" Violet sipped her martini. "It's hard to know what's going through a person's mind when they're in that much pain."

"It could be. You were up with the contestants when I went to find Teddy. What happened up there?"

"Well, you were gone for a long time. Greg kept saying that Teddy was holding the shoot up. They filmed Harvey, and Ariana, and Mindie. That all went pretty quick. Maybe ten minutes each? Then they filmed Kitty again.

"We heard Teddy's name over the intercom. They asked him to contact the security desk. The ship had stopped moving by then, and I turned up the security channel to listen in." Violet winced. "*That's* when we all heard there was a search team in the water. Kameron put everyone off for a while, but when Ariana asked where Teddy was, and Kameron didn't answer, Ariana freaked out. She demanded to be let downstairs. I can't blame her. Kameron doesn't have much of a poker face."

"Excuse me. I'm so sorry to interrupt, but I was hoping we could sit with you for the show? My sister doesn't want to sit too close to the stage, and you two have such nice auras." The stranger who spoke was pleasantly plump. She had long black hair down to her waist, a crooked nose, and her dark eyes were merry. Her companion could have been her twin, except that her nose was as straight as an arrow and she was a good six inches taller. Also, the taller sister had a long silver streak running down from each temple, like the bride of Frankenstein.

"Oh, we can leave," Ellie said automatically. "We're not—"

"Don't be ridiculous," the second woman said, dropping into the booth next to Violet and scooting inward. "There's plenty of room."

"We're happy to share," the woman with the crooked nose said, sitting next to Ellie and plopping her purse down on the seat.

Violet and Ellie exchanged an amused look. They were pinned into the center of the booth.

The woman with the crooked nose held out a hand. "I'm Rebecca Triumph, and this is my older sister, Josephine. This is our first time attending Secrets of the Dead. How about you two?"

Ellie shook hands. "I'm Ellie Tappet and this is my good friend Violet Wolfe. We work aboard the *Spirit*, which is why I was saying we'd be happy to give you the table. We can—"

"Nonsense," Rebecca said, peering over into Ellie's teacup. "You've hardly started your tea. Sit. Keep us company! It must be *fascinating* working aboard a cruise ship. Tell me, do you ever dream that you're a mermaid?"

Ellie stared. "Yes. Once or twice. How did you know?"

Rebecca grinned. "Just a feeling. This ship is magical. More than the sum of her parts. Wouldn't you agree?"

Violet's eyes widened with recognition. "Were you two at the ghost stories event? I swear I've seen you someplace before."

Josephine chuckled. Her laugh was creaky like an old staircase. The sound would have been off-putting if it weren't for the open friendliness she exuded. "Yes, Rebecca was dying to attend the ghost stories event, but I wasn't too keen. I told her I'd take part, but only if I could have a good soak at the same time. So, we did our ghost stories in the hot tub." She shot her sister a fond look. "It was fun. But I expect tonight's séance will be spectacularly stupid."

"Jo!" Rebecca chided. "You said you'd be a good sport. You promised."

"And I will." Josephine picked up the drink menu and perused it. Her heavily made-up eyes glanced at Ellie over the rim of the paper. "Becky *loves* Chryss Tiano. She has all his books at home. Personally, I think the man's a fraud, but I enjoy being out on the open water. When I agreed to come on this cruise, I didn't think I was agreeing to attend all these events with Rebecca. But my sister's a scaredy cat. She insists I tag along, everywhere she goes. It's been that way since we were children."

"I like spending time with my sister. Is that a crime?"

"No, it's not," Ellie said with warmth. "Although I'm afraid I agree with Josephine on the matter of Chryss Tiano. Ghosts aren't real. Therefore, anyone who claims to speak to them has something to sell you."

Josephine grinned. "Oh, I wouldn't go that far! My grandmama's ghost lives with us, I'll have you know, and Abernetha makes her opinions known when she isn't happy with how we're conducting ourselves. But I understand where you're coming from, Ellie. Why believe in ghosts if you've never seen one?

"Still, *this* fellow." Josephine fluttered the fingers of her left hand toward the stage. "I doubt he'd recognize a ghost if one smacked him on his well-toned hiney." She winked at Violet. "That's the real reason I agreed to come tonight. Chryss Tiano is ten pounds of sex in an eight-pound bag. I haven't seen leather pants that tight since the nineteen eighties." She frowned at the drink menu and waved at a waitress with her other arm. "Miss? I'd like your biggest margarita. With two umbrellas. And a virgin mojito for my sister."

Violet looked delighted. "Ellie, let's stay."

"I don't know."

"Come on! You have to be a bit curious about this séance business."

Violet's enthusiasm was infectious. "Well, I *would* like to see what all the fuss is about. And like Rebecca said, I haven't finished my tea." She picked up the cup and took a sip. The essence of bergamot and lavender floated up into her nostrils and hit the pleasure center of her brain. She felt her shoulder muscles loosen, and she let out a long breath.

"I'll give you ladies a hint," Josephine said, pointing at a camera set up discreetly on one side of the stage. "Cameras are useless for picking up spectral energy. If you see a camera, you can trust that you're not seeing ghosts."

"Chryss Tiano is a medium," Rebecca said, her tone exasperated. She tilted her head to one side, glaring at her sister. "We don't need to see the ghosts. He channels them."

Violet turned to Jo, "You said we have nice auras. What does that mean?"

"Well, yours is purple and kind of sparkly. And Ellie's is pink like cotton candy."

"Do the colors mean something?" Violet asked.

"Well, it's not like a mood ring, if that's what you're asking. But trustworthy people have nice smooth auras. They're stable, not shifting about like a chameleon trying to hide in a ball pit. And you both have that going on. Although, if I had to guess, I'd say that you're the extrovert, Violet. Sparkly auras are all about charisma. And Ellie here isn't like that, is she? She's the person you go to when you need someone on your side. A confidante." Jo patted Ellie on the hand. "But your aura is flickering at the edges, dear. There's some dark red in there. You've had an incredibly stressful day, and you should get a good night's sleep."

Ellie pressed her lips shut. Anyone with eyes in their head could have said the same, aura or no aura. What Josephine was doing was reading body language! Still, she seemed like a sweet lady, and she didn't mean any harm.

"And what about Chryss Tiano?" Violet asked.

Josephine squinted up through the crowded room. "I've only caught a glimpse of him, so I'm not sure. Fortunately, you can't see auras through the television."

"Why fortunately?"

Josephine grinned. "I prefer to lose myself in the story when watching TV. That's hard to do if you're concentrating on what kind of person the actor is!"

Rebecca said. "I bet Chryss Tiano sparkles too. He's so dreamy."

Her sister barked a laugh. "Dreamy? We're fifty-five years old, Becky. He's not some cute boy on the cover of Tiger Beat."

"You can be as old as you like," Rebecca said good naturedly. "I will choose my own age, thank you very much, and tonight I am seventeen on the cusp of eighteen." She brushed her hair back with her hands, primping. "Besides, if this were a NCIS convention, you'd be throwing your thong underwear on stage at Mark Harmon. So don't act so high and mighty with me."

"Mark Harmon wouldn't be at a fan convention. The man has dignity. And dignity is always sexy."

Rebecca laughed. "My sister's a weirdo. But she's right about one thing. You two do have nice auras. Thanks for letting us sit with you."

"Ellie's a devoted Christian," Violet said, after the waitress dropped off more drinks. "She doesn't believe in auras."

Josephine didn't seem surprised. "No biggie. We can talk about something else. Do you believe in ghosts, Ellie?"

"I believe in Jesus," Ellie said firmly. "And that's enough for me. The rest of this stuff... it makes me uncomfortable." She smiled at the sisters. "No offense intended."

"Well, I believe in ghosts." Violet said. "When I was twelve, I was playing with a Ouija board with my friends, and—"

"That's very dangerous," Rebecca interjected, her eyes wide. "But go on."

"And the board started saying the most horrid things to us."

"Your friends were pushing with their knees," Ellie interjected.

"Anyway," Violet continued, shooting Ellie a snarky look, "we cut the Ouija board up and burned it in the backyard. And for weeks, we found pieces of the thing all over the place. In our book bags. One time, in a locker at school.

"Another prank by your friends," Ellie said.

"Yes, looking back, I guess you can chalk it up to our overactive teenage imaginations. Still, I like being open to the possibility that we don't know everything. It keeps life interesting."

"Well, I certainly believe in ghosts," Josephine said, "because I've seen them with my own eyes. Still, I don't approve of Chryss Tiano and the television mediums." She lowered her voice. "Look, I say if you're fortunate enough to see beyond the veil, that's a gift. It's like..." she glanced at Ellie. "It's like communion. Like prayer. And you shouldn't be selling that gift for any price. It's sacred. Even if the guy is legit, and I'm *not* saying he is, he's like one of those television preachers. They say: Give me money and God will love you. Or, give me money and I'll speak to your dead loved ones. Either way, it's offensive."

Ellie nodded at Josephine. "On that topic, we agree."

Josephine sipped her margarita and shot Rebecca a superior glance. "See? Ellie the Christian supports me. Why can't you?"

"Hush. He's coming." Rebecca put her chin in her hands and leaned forward.

The curtains opened. A silver spotlight shone down on one of the leather chairs. A thin tendril of smoke wafted above the orb on the table. A scent like burning shrubbery filled the air. Ellie wrinkled her nose. "What's that?" she whispered to Rebecca.

"Burning sage. For purification."

"Yes, he's got to remove all common sense from the room," Jo whispered.

"Hush!" Rebecca whispered back.

A pre-recorded voice came over the speakers. "Ladies. Gentlemen. Formless ones. Spirits of the past and the future. We welcome you on this most dark and holy night, to join us as we join our hearts and minds together, as we reach out, and as we place ourselves under the spell of He Who Dazzles the Spirit Realm: The one and only, Chryss Tiano."

The crowd applauded, loudly at first, but the applause tapered off as the lights in the room flickered. Out from the shadows, a man in tight black leather pants and a loose white shirt stepped out onto the stage, resting one palm on the back of the leather chair. Several members of the audience gasped.

Chryss Tiano's shirt was open at the chest, revealing hints of his well-sculpted pectoral muscles and not a speck of chest hair. His lips curved into an arrogant smile. He posed, hips cocked, and then he thrust both hands forward like twin rockets before raising his palms up to the sky. His dark hair curled over his forehead and around his ears. It looked shiny beneath the spotlight.

He didn't skimp on the hair product, Ellie thought wryly. *And he's got Cora flicking the light switch back and forth. This is a high-quality production indeed.*

"Welcome, seekers! Tonight, we take a journey where the living dare not to tread. Tonight, we pull apart the veil between light and dark. Tonight, we open the gate, and we open our hearts to what comes through. I welcome you all to Secrets of the Dead."

The crowd breathed in and out as one. They seemed mesmerized. Even Violet, who should have known better, was staring at the man with shining eyes! Ellie sipped her tea and hid a smile. She couldn't deny the man had flair. He looked around the room, meeting the eyes of each person, one at a time, as if he were searching for something.

An easy mark, probably.

When Chryss Tiano's eyes met hers, she saw that they were shockingly blue.

"My name is Chryss Tiano, and I am a—" He flinched, turning his head to one side as if he'd been struck. He staggered back two steps, bumping against the table. The orb jumped, but it didn't fall. He bent over at the waist and groaned, gripping his middle.

Was this part of the act, or was he having severe gas pains? His face was reddening, and he seemed to be struggling to breathe. He flung himself upright, his back arched, his mouth wide open and his eyes staring up at the ceiling. "No! I did not call you! Wait! You must—" He fell to the ground with a thud and curled into the fetal position.

"Is this normal?" Ellie asked Rebecca.

She shook her head, her eyes wide with fear. To the right of the stage, Cora Wise came out of the sound booth. She was hurrying toward the stage, crouched low to stay out of sight of the camera. She shot a frantic glance back at the room, perhaps looking for help. Chryss Tiano wasn't moving. Ellie looked at Violet. Violet nodded. Ellie reached into her purse and fumbled for her portable radio. "I'm calling this in."

But Chryss Tiano was getting back up, slowly. He shook his head as if he were trying to clear it. "This is strong. I didn't expect..."

Ellie fumed. She put the radio back in her purse and set the purse between her feet. What a jerk! She'd been worried about him for a minute! Her face burned. Violet's eyes were glued to the stage again. Chryss Tiano had dropped to his knees, but this time he was in better control of himself. He swayed and moaned.

"I'm hearing someone," he called out, his voice an anguished rasp. "A man."

"Is it Robert?" a woman called out from a table near the front. Her voice was bright with hope.

Chryss Tiano's face twitched like he'd been pricked with an electric charge. "I'm hearing a T."

"Thomas?" a man's voice replied, almost too quiet to hear. "Thomas was my father."

The medium slumped, and when he looked back up, his eyes were bright with unshed tears. He looked straight forward, his eyes unfocused. "My name is Teddy. And I died today."

⚓⚓⚓

ELLIE'S CHEST FELT HOT. HER sweaty hands clenched beneath the table. How could Chryss Tiano be so craven? So cruel? Did he think this was funny?

Cora had stopped moving when Chryss had gotten up. Now she was retreating toward the sound booth. The light caught her face as she turned. She looked upset! And it was no wonder why. Someone had told her boss about Teddy McIntyre's death, and he was using it in his act!

"Teddy has a message," Chryss Tiano said, his voice deeper now. He squeezed his eyes shut and shuddered. "Someone's in danger. Someone..." Chryss stood and braced himself, one hand on the small table. As soon as he touched the surface, the orb lit up and swirled with a mixture of red and purple light.

"Hungry. He's always hungry!" Chryss Tiano convulsed, gripping the side of the table like a lifeline. He pulled himself up into one of the chairs. When he spoke again, his voice was higher than it had been before. His eyes were glassy.

"My name is Teddy, and I died today. Ask me what you will."

"How did you die?" Someone shouted from the back of the room.

"Rushing water. Cold. So cold!" Chryss Tiano shuddered.

"We need to stop this!" Ellie looked at Violet. "Sweet Jesus. If one of Teddy's friends is in here... Or God forbid, his wife..."

Violet's eyes narrowed. "I know! But what do you want me to do? Pull the fire alarm?"

"Who killed you?" That question came from a young girl.

"No. I..." He looked down at his wrists. "So much blood! I went outside and," he winced. "I was pushed! Ariana? Where's my wife? I must tell her. She's... She's in danger. She... She... She... She..." Chryss Tiano rocked back and forth, whimpering like a frightened child.

The crowd threw more questions at him, but he didn't respond to any of them. At last, he slumped over the table. The red orb shifted to gray, to white, and then it turned off entirely. Chryss Tiano looked up, and he straightened up in the chair. He smiled at the crowd, the same smug smile he'd used during his introduction. The crowd cheered, and he bowed his head. "Who else has a loved one they wish to commune with?"

Dozens of hands went up.

"That was the most disgusting thing I've ever seen," Ellie muttered.

Josephine leaned closer "What's wrong?"

Violet answered. "A man committed suicide today. Here, on the ship. His name was Teddy."

"Oh no! Someone should give his wife that warning," Rebecca said.

Josephine held out her margarita to Ellie. "Would you like something stronger than tea? Take a few deep breaths. You look like you're about ready to punch someone in the face."

Ellie glanced at Violet. "I need to go find Paul. Will you let me out, please?" She reached down for her purse.

Rebecca scooted out of the booth. "Of course."

"It was a pleasure to meet you both," Ellie said. She leaned over the table and whispered to Violet. "Keep an eye on Chryss Tiano, will you? Someone put him up to this. And I want to know who."

Chapter Nine

CORA UNCROSSED HER LEGS AND drank from her paper coffee cup. Sunlight streamed in through the big windows in the captain's dining room. This morning, it was doing double duty as a conference room. She sat across from Ellie and Paul like a witness in a tribunal. Ellie had wanted to talk to Cora last night, after the show, but Paul had insisted they wait until the next day. Ellie had tossed and turned all night, and now it was time for some answers.

"What exactly are you accusing us of?" Cora asked.

Paul shifted in his chair. "We're not accusing you of anything, we're just—"

Ellie interrupted. "Actually, I *am* accusing you of something. I'm accusing you of being heartless. A man committed suicide yesterday, and his wife is right here, on this ship, having the worst week of her life."

Cora was listening intently. "That's terrible. But I'm not clear what it has to do with Chryss."

"Ms. Wise," Paul began. "We understand that last night—"

"Chryss Tiano pretended to be speaking with Teddy!" Ellie interrupted. Paul's mouth snapped shut. "I'm sorry, Paul. But Chryss Tiano was up on stage pretending that he *was* Teddy. Just *hours* after his wife lost him. Do you realize how hurtful that was? How unethical? What if Ariana had been in that room? Her husband's death isn't fodder for their little freak show." She glared at Cora. "Did Chryss Tiano pause for one second to think about the impact on her?"

Cora nodded slowly. "Oh! I understand why you're upset. But I assure you that we meant no disrespect. Chryss doesn't control the spirits that speak to him. He merely—"

"Spare me your shock-jock spiritualism." Ellie crossed her arms. "I want your assurances that you will *not* exploit this tragedy for your own selfish aims. You will leave the McIntyres alone, or you will no longer perform aboard this ship. Is that clear?"

Cora's cheeks were pink. Was she embarrassed, or winding up for a fight? "Our contract clearly states that —"

"You can shove that contract right—"

"Ellie!" Paul's voice boomed. "Speak with me outside, please."

"Paul, you can't be—"

His expression was like granite. "I will speak with you outside. Right now."

"Fine." She followed him out, and he shut the door tight. "Paul. I'm sorry if I'm firm on this. It's just that—"

Paul Gumbs hugged her! Her cheek squished against his chest as he squeezed with his big arms. The buttons of his white jacket pressed against her face. Paul was as solid as a cliff and nearly as tall. "Ellie. It's going to be okay," he murmured. "But you need to stop taking this so personally." He released her and stepped back, looking down.

"How am *I* taking this personally?" His sweet gesture had knocked the vim right out of her, but he wasn't making much sense.

"Don't you see what's going on here? You're a widow. The fact that you love the captain doesn't change that. And from the moment you realized what happened yesterday, you've been in full mama-bear mode. You know *exactly* what Mrs. McIntyre is going through, and you want to protect her from everything. I hardly had a chance to interview her yesterday and you whisked her away and stood guard over her room."

"She needed to rest."

"I agree! And I'm not upset. But you can't let your empathy cloud your judgment like this. I need to question Cora, and I can't do that if you're shouting her down."

She sighed. "maybe you're right. But don't you agree their behavior is heinous? Ariana is our guest too. We must take care of her. I'm sorry if I got carried away."

"All is forgiven." His dark eyes held a hint of amusement. "But if I may ask, *where* were you going to ask Cora to shove her contract?"

"What?"

"You said she could shove her contract..." Paul made a continuing gesture.

Ellie's face felt hot. "Oh? I was going to say she could shove it right in the trash."

"Uh huh. I figured that must be it."

"Don't smirk at me, young man. I'll apologize to Cora for losing my temper. But they have to leave Ariana alone. No more channeling her dead husband. I don't care if Chryss says he can't help it. Cora can shoot him with a tranquilizer dart if he goes off script. I'm sure Kameron has something suitable in her weapons cabinet."

Paul snorted. "Actually, I have a better idea. But I need your help. Provided you can keep a cool head."

"I'm famous for my calm under pressure," Ellie insisted. "What do you need?"

"Cora was supposed to bring Chryss Tiano to this meeting. She didn't. I want you to go to his stateroom and have a chat with him."

"You want me to talk to *him*? Now?"

"Only if you think you can handle it. Cora said her boss couldn't come because he has a migraine. And maybe he does. But I want to know who put him up to that little stunt. Maybe you can lean on him a little, impress upon him that when there's an unexpected death, the police may get involved if there are too many unanswered questions. It would be *unfortunate* if he were considered a person of interest in a suspicious death. You're just doing him a favor by clearing things up."

"So, you agree Teddy's death is suspicious? It's not just my wild imagination talking? I couldn't sleep last night. I just kept thinking about all that blood. And the TV left on high."

Paul hesitated. "Teddy McIntyre probably killed himself. But Chryss Tiano made a serious allegation last night. He said Mrs. McIntyre is in danger. We can't ignore that. I have an obligation to find out *why* he said it. And I'm not taking "ghosts" for an answer."

"What do you want me to ask him?"

"Ask him about what he said. I want to know what the man has to say when Cora isn't speaking for him. Do you think you can you get him to talk? It won't go well if you break down his door and start reading him the riot act."

"I can handle it."

"Good. I'll keep Cora busy for a while, but you'll need to hurry."

⚓⚓⚓

CHRYSS TIANO LOOKED DIFFERENT BY the light of day. He'd traded his skintight leather pants for comfortable workout clothes and his curly hair was soft instead of greasy. Without his contacts in, his eyes were the pale blue of a February sky.

"Please, come in," he said in a soft voice. "What can I do for you?"

The big screen television was turned to children's programming. A cartoon cat strolled across the screen carrying a comically oversized mallet. There was an open box of sugar cereal on the coffee table. His clothes from the evening before were in a pile next to the couch, as if he'd stripped down the moment he'd gotten back to his room. His tanned bare feet looked pampered. The night before, he'd looked like a Las Vegas stage magician. Now, Chryss Tiano reminded her of a yoga instructor on his day off.

"My name is Ellie Tappet, and I'm here at the request of our Chief Security Officer, Paul Gumbs. We had an incident down the hall yesterday, and I was hoping to ask you a few questions."

"Of course! Can I get you anything? I have Count Chocula and Fruity Pebbles. And some fruit, I think. Cora's always trying to get me to eat better, but after a late night on stage, I crave something sweet."

Chryss sat cross-legged on the couch and pulled the cereal box into his lap. She sat across from him. Mindful of Paul's reminder to get the man talking, she asked, "How are you enjoying your cruise so far?"

He looked embarrassed. "I hate it here. Everyone's been great. And Cora was right, this is good for business. But I've always had a phobia of the open water. It gives me bad dreams. My therapist says that I may have drowned in a past life. All I know is, I won't rest easy until my feet touch dry land. Now that we're at port I figured I'd go for a walk. I'm just waiting for Cora to get back."

"She mentioned you weren't feeling well today."

"Did she?" He seemed surprised. "She knows how worn out I feel after a channeling." He rubbed his eyes. "And last night's session was particularly intense. But I'm okay. Thanks for checking in on me."

"I need to ask you about something you said at the séance last night."

"I'm afraid I'm not doing any private readings," he said, his voice tinged with regret. "It's not that I don't want to. Truly. But I need to save my energy for the evening shows. I simply can't do both."

"I have no interest in a reading," Ellie said.

"What can I do for you then?"

"We had a guest go overboard yesterday. A possible suicide. His name was Teddy McIntyre, and he was traveling on board as part of the Sweetie Pie Baking Competition."

His forehead furrowed. "How terrible!"

She saw nothing in his expression but dismay.

"Last night, after you came out on stage, you said you were speaking *for* Teddy. You made certain statements about his death."

"And you're from the security team. Ah. I think I understand now. You want a consultation. And I wish I could help, but I never do readings for the police. I'm afraid my gift is simply too imprecise to be held up in court. I've seen mediums go down that path, offering to help the police solve crimes, and it inevitably leads to heartbreak." He held out his hands, palms up. "It's too risky, for everyone. What if I interpret the spirits wrong and an innocent person is arrested? I couldn't live with myself if I made that kind of mistake."

Ellie hesitated. If she didn't know better, she'd swear that Chryss Tiano was completely sincere. It was extremely frustrating.

"I'm not here to ask for a consultation. But here's my problem, Mr. Tiano."

"Call me Chryss, please."

"Chryss, my concern is that last night you shared certain details about Teddy McIntyre's death. Details that no one knew. No one, perhaps, except for the person who was with Teddy right before he died. A person we're still looking for."

He nodded slowly. "You think I was involved because I knew things I couldn't have known. I suppose I'd feel the same way if I were in your shoes."

"I don't mean to be disrespectful," Ellie said carefully. "But I'm aware that sometimes a show like yours is based on things *other* than spiritual communication. Maybe you overheard someone say something, and you used it in your show. Or perhaps someone told you about Teddy's death, and you embellished it a little." Chryss was listening intently, so she added, "I know the dead man's wife, you see. And it wouldn't be fair to her if I didn't at least ask: Who told you about Teddy?"

Chryss Tiano uncrossed his legs and let them hang over the edge of the couch. "I see your dilemma." He reached inside the cereal box and pulled out a handful of pieces. He chewed and swallowed. "Ellie, if I open up to you about my process, will you swear to me that you won't share my secrets with the world? I don't like to discuss these things. It's bad for business. But a man is dead, and I can see your heart is sincere. I want to help."

"I'll need to share what I hear with our security chief. But only if it's relevant to our investigation. And aside from that, I'll keep your secrets."

He pointed at her gold crucifix. "I have your word. As a Christian?"

He wasn't going to make this easy on her, was he? She touched her pendant. "You do."

"Very well. Here's what my fans don't appreciate about the spirit realm. There are times, such as last night, when the spirits move me strongly. Think of spirits as being like impatient party guests. You unlock the door, and they come rushing in, eating all your snacks and turning up the music. Those are the moments I live for. I let the dead speak through me. But later, those moments are like a dream. The memories fade quickly. Sometimes, I remember bits and pieces afterward. But not for long. And that's too bad because I wish I could be a guest at that party."

What was she supposed to say to that? She didn't know, so she nodded to show that she'd heard him.

"Now, there's another problem. What happens when you unlock the door, and there are no guests waiting for the party? It happens more often than you'd think. Sometimes it happens when you've got a thousand paying customers, waiting for a show! The spirits don't work on a schedule. So sometimes I pad out my routine. And I try to keep those segments productive. Sometimes that means helping someone share a memory of a loved one. And you stick to the positive. You remind the living that they too are loved. You tell them that mistakes can be forgiven. You give them the razzle dazzle. And you wait for your next party guest."

He smiled ruefully. "Here's the thing. Not one seeker out of a thousand can tell the difference between a true channeling and the razzle dazzle. But I do my best to deliver the real thing. Channeling is hard on the body. I meditate daily, I sleep ten hours a night, and I take certain herbs to heighten my senses. I live a monk's life, Ellie. But there are rewards. From time to time, I can help bring closure, and peace." He bowed his head. "That is my purpose."

When he looked up, his smile was tinged with sadness. "You don't believe me. And that's fine. But I've spoken my truth, and you have listened. I trust you will keep my secrets. Now, on the matter of the man who died, how can I help?"

"When you spoke to Teddy, was that real to you, or was it the – um – razzle dazzle?"

"It was a true channeling. I remember very little of what I said, although Cora told me about it after the show. She was upset when I fell. It frightened her."

"You don't normally collapse like that?"

He touched the side of his head. "No. But I've had so many nightmares on this voyage. That can happen when a spirit experienced a violent death." He tapped his chin and looked upward for a moment. "Or perhaps it's my fear of the water talking. I can't be sure."

"Did anyone tell you about Teddy before your show? Or had you heard that someone was missing, or dead?"

"No. I spent the day in my suite, preparing for the evening show."

"All day?"

"I had a spa appointment after lunch, while my belongings were being moved, but otherwise, yes." He hesitated. "You mentioned the death was a suicide? Like I said, the details are hazy, but Teddy did *not* feel like a spirit who had taken his own life." He closed his eyes. "There was a flash of red, before it happened. Someone moving fast. And he'd been denied something. Something he felt entitled to." He squeezed his eyelids harder. Then he opened them. "I'm sorry. I wish I could tell you more."

"Had you met Teddy McIntyre before? Here. Let me show you his picture?" She took out her phone and opened the publicity photo Greg had given her.

He scrutinized the image. "No."

"Do you know any of the contestants or crew from The Sugar Network?"

"Not that I'm aware of."

They talked for a while longer, and when it was clear that Chryss had nothing useful to offer, Ellie got up and held out her hand. "Thanks for your help. I hope that we won't hear any more from Teddy during your evening shows. His wife is on board, and she's been through so much already. I just can't stand the thought of putting her through any more trauma. Don't you agree?" She fixed him with a hard stare.

Chryss Tiano bowed his head and put his hands at prayer position over his chest. "I will attempt to block his spirit should he return. But sometimes, when the dead speak, they scream. When this happens, I am powerless before them."

Chapter Ten

PAUL WAS IN THE SECURITY office when she arrived. Ellie shut the door behind her and sat down. "You were right. Chryss wasn't sick. He said that the séances wear him out; that's all."

Paul tidied the file folders on his desk into a neat stack. "And what did he have to say about Teddy?"

"Chryss swears that he was channeling him. And here's the craziest part: the man was completely sincere. Do you know how difficult it is to stay angry at someone who's genuinely deluded? It's like getting mad at a child for believing in the tooth fairy." She filled Paul in on the conversation, minus Chryss's confession about the "razzle dazzle." She'd promised not to share the medium's secret unless it was relevant to the case, and it wasn't.

"Mr. Tiano says Teddy was denied something he felt entitled to," Paul mused. "I wonder if it was the Golden Cupcake. Or something else?"

"You don't honestly believe he was speaking to Teddy's ghost?"

Paul smirked at her. "No, I believe in evidence. And there must be *some* reason he said those things. I'll circle back with him when we know more. In the meantime, we have another problem. Look at these." Paul opened his topmost file folder and took out two sheets of white paper. Each one held a big handprint in purple ink. "I think I'm onto something. But before I tell you what I think, look at this picture from Teddy's balcony."

Paul handed over an image he'd printed out. Ellie put on her reading glasses and peered down at it. The photo was of the bloody handprint on the balcony wall. Next to it, the ruler she'd held in place was partially cropped out. "What am I looking for?"

"Look at the handprint. Do you see those lines?"

She did. At the base of each finger, lines showed where the finger met the palm. In the corner, by the pinkie, a web of lines formed a mark like a crow's foot. The rest of the print was relatively smooth, and there was a small blank spot in the middle of the palm. "Okay."

"Now look at these two handprints. These are mine."

"What's the purple stuff?"

"Watercolor paint."

"You paint?"

"Kameron does. She let me borrow some supplies."

"Wow. Kameron's a martial artist, she's wonderful with children, *and* she's an artist too?" She smiled at Paul. "Honestly. What *can't* that woman do?"

Paul shot her a look that said he knew what she was up to. "Now, tell me how my handprints compare to the one in the photo."

She compared the three images. Paul's handprint looked bigger, for one thing. But the purple handprints looked quite different from one another. In one print, the texture of Paul's palm and fingers was imprinted onto the paper like a detailed stamp. There were lines running from left to right across the palm, thick ones and fine ones, and the texture of his skin was visible. But the other handprint looked like the one on the balcony. It had fewer lines and features.

She pointed from print to the other. "This one matches. That one doesn't. Why?"

"What would you say if I told you I made the matching handprint while wearing a latex glove?"

Her heart jumped in her chest. "You did?"

He nodded. "I was reviewing the balcony photos with a magnifying glass, and the handprint looked *off* to me. But I couldn't figure out why. So I made the first handprint as a comparison. At first, I thought maybe the difference was that my print was on paper versus the one on the wall. So I went out onto the smoking deck and—"

"You made purple handprints on the wall? The janitorial staff is going to *love* you."

"I did it for science! And I scrubbed most of it off, after. Anyway, my handprint still looked different than the one at the crime scene. So, I tried to figure out what had made the other one. That's when I realized that those little lines on the bloody handprint aren't like marks from lines on a hand. They look like crinkles in plastic. The surfaces are smooth, but there are marks at the finger joints."

"You're saying someone used a glove to put that handprint on the wall?"

"Not just the wall," Paul said, pulling out another photo. He held it facing her, pointing out features as he spoke. "Look at the finger marks going over the rail. They're completely smooth. *Too* smooth. Someone put that blood on the balcony. Someone who wanted us to follow the blood trail from the broken glass right over the side of the railing. They wanted us to believe Teddy went overboard, and they painted a picture, in blood, knowing we'd follow it."

Ellie couldn't hide her delight for one second longer. "Paul Gumbs. You are wasted working on a cruise ship! You should be leading up a crack team of detectives at Scotland Yard."

He flashed her a gratified smile. "But like I said, we have a problem. We've been operating under the assumption that Teddy McIntyre killed himself. But what if he didn't? What if it only appeared that he did so?"

"That means Teddy could still be alive."

"I like your optimism. But I have a different theory. What if someone wanted us to believe Teddy committed suicide, but they laid the evidence on a bit too thick? He cut himself, *and* he went overboard, *and* he left a note, all after leaving a trail of blood all over his stateroom? This is looking less like a suicide and more like a sloppy cover up."

"You think someone killed Teddy?"

"Perhaps. I'm not ready to say that. Yet."

Ellie mentally ran through what they'd heard so far. "Greg said Teddy wasn't the suicidal type. Maybe he was right? But what about the note you found in Teddy's room? The one that said he was sorry?"

"We'll compare the handwriting against what we have on file. But handwriting can be faked. Bottom line, there's something going on here. Something we're not yet seeing clearly. And I don't know what that is. All I know at this point is that someone is trying to pull the wool over our eyes."

She nodded. "What's our next move?"

"I've asked Doctor Strunk to identify the blood type from the samples I gave him. We can get Teddy's blood type from his wife. That won't tell us for sure who the blood belonged to, but maybe we can narrow things down. And we need to find out who was drinking with Teddy that night. I'll talk to room service about that decanter and the broken glass. In the meantime, I want you to keep an eye on the baking contestants and crew. We'll question them, *after* I hear back from the doc. Not before. Let's not tip our hand, yet."

"And Chryss Tiano? Where does he fit in?"

"I wish I knew. Maybe he's in on it. Or maybe someone asked him to shore up the story about the suicide."

Ellie shook her head. "I don't think so. Chryss Tiano didn't exactly back up the suicide thing, did he? He said Teddy was denied something he wanted. At the séance, he said Teddy was pushed! And today, he told me that Teddy didn't feel like someone who had committed suicide. Not that I believe he was talking to ghosts. Because that's nuts."

Paul thought for a moment. "Let's gather more information, and I'll take another crack at him. If I talk to him right now, he'll just deny the truth. I'd rather confront him when I have something solid to go on."

Ellie drummed her fingers on her knees. "Paul, during the séance, Chryss Tiano said that Ariana was in danger. Whoever did this thing, do you think they'd hurt her? Maybe to sell their story about what happened?"

Paul's expression was grim. "At this point, I'd say whoever did this is capable of anything."

Ellie sighed. "I figured you'd say something like that. The contestants are filming in the theater today. I'll go check in on them, and I'll keep an eye on Ariana while you talk to Tobias. Tell me what he says about that blood, will you?"

"I will. And Ellie, until we know more, keep this under your hat. Someone's lying, and so long as they think they've got us fooled, they're inclined to make mistakes."

Chapter Eleven

THE THEATER SEATS WERE EMPTY except for three figures sitting in the front row. Ellie walked down the left-side aisle, past dozens of rows of empty chairs. On the stage, The Sugar Network crew had constructed four miniature kitchens. At first glance, they seemed identical. There was an L-shaped counter, open to the front of the theater. Each station had a refrigerator with a baby blue door. Matching stand mixers rested on the oak countertops. The stainless-steel ovens looked brand new. Each kitchen had a small decorative detail unique to one of the bakers. One had a beautiful white wedding cake stand (for Ariana, no doubt). The one next to it had a porcelain reproduction of Big Ben with a real mechanical clock inside. A ceramic bird sat on a shelf on the rightmost kitchen, and the remaining kitchen was decorated with an old-fashioned film camera resting atop a yellow recipe book. Was Kitty a photographer? It hadn't come up, but certainly she enjoyed being photographed!

Huge portable video screens were set up to the left and right of the stage. They were made of many small monitors linked together into tall rectangular viewing areas. Two big black cameras rested on tripods on the front corners of the stage. They pointed inward, waiting.

Ellie recognized Greg's sandy brown hair and broad shoulders in the center seat of the front row. Harvey got up and slid over one seat when he saw Ellie approaching. "Hey. It's good to see you," he said in a quiet voice. On Greg's other side, Kitty Gilbert smiled politely before returning her attention to her phone. She scanned through colorful photos of tropical destinations with quick flicks of her thumb.

"How is the shoot going?" Ellie asked, sitting down next to Greg.

Greg nodded at the stage. "See for yourself."

Mindie walked out of the right side of the wings and went over to her assigned kitchen. Her dress was a sober gray, and she wore a golden pendant that looked like a bird in flight. Mindie looked tired; her head was tipped down and she didn't smile, but she put her shoulders back when she saw Raquel coming out from the opposite side of the stage. Raquel was followed by Linda, and the director held a shoulder cam, moving with smooth steps to avoid jiggling the frame.

Ellie leaned forward to watch. Raquel was known as the tough cookie, the judge that rarely gave praise unless the baking was exceptional. She was in her early seventies, with her iron gray hair in tight curls clustered around her scalp. She was wearing her habitual pink suit jacket and frilly blouse. Raquel dispensed the tough love. Her partner Vick softened every tough critique with his gentle smile and words of encouragement. But there was no sign of Vick today.

Once the trio was in position, Linda adjusted her position and the big screens to the left and right of the stage came to life. It was a clever setup! When the final showdown was filmed, even the viewers in the highest and most distant theater seats would be able to get a closeup of the action. Linda set her camera on the counter and began posing Mindie and Raquel like they were human-sized dolls, facing them the way she wanted them to stand. A little to the left. A half step back. She looked up at the stage lights and shook her head, then went over to the wings, leaving her camera behind.

Greg leaned over. "We've asked each of our bakers to share a memory of Teddy today. Post-production, we'll add some beautiful music, and footage of him from prior episodes. Plus clips from his audition tape. We'll do right by him. You'll see."

Ellie nodded. "That sounds nice. Where's Ariana?"

"She's in the test kitchen, working on Teddy's recipe. I thought she might want to watch us film our tributes, but she said she wanted to be left alone." He glanced down at his hands. "I think she might be mad at me. She hardly even looked at me when I invited her to breakfast this morning."

Ellie shot him a sympathetic look. "She's been through the worst day of her life. And she's probably furious at Teddy too. It has nothing to do with you, or the show." She'd spoken automatically, but in light of what Paul had discovered, her words felt flimsy and artificial.

"Ellie's right," Harvey said. "What happened isn't your fault. You've been a good friend to Ariana. To all of us. It's just a terrible, hard day, is all."

Greg looked miserable. "I keep thinking, if I hadn't insisted on filming at sea, maybe he wouldn't have... you know."

"I doubt the location mattered," Ellie said quietly, thinking of Paul's discovery. At some point, he'd need to question Greg and the crew. The way they reacted to the news would tell them a great deal. Until then, she'd need to bite her tongue. "If Ariana wants to remember Teddy by baking his recipe, that's what we'll help her do. What's the theme for the finale, by the way?"

"Pie," Greg said.

"Pie? Isn't that...?"

"Basic?" Greg smiled faintly. "Well, we had a snafu two seasons ago. We've been upping the ante for years — it makes things fun — and we had our contestants sculpt cakes in the shape of famous people from history. And the results were, let's just say, less than inspiring. One of our bakers made a rather horrific replication of Maya Angelou's head. She filled it with a delicate rose custard, but the custard didn't set properly, and as soon as Vick cut into the cake Maya Angelou's brains leaked out all over the plate." He grimaced. "We made a substantial donation to The Poetry Foundation, but the damage was done."

"So this year: pie," Ellie repeated.

"Exactly. Our bakers can make any kind of pie they like, so long as it's a recipe of their own design. I'm eager to see what they've come up with."

"You don't know?"

"Oh no. We like to be surprised. Just not brains-leaking-on-the-plate surprised."

Ellie chuckled. "Understood." She shot Greg a sidelong glance. Dare she ask the question that was on her mind? "Speaking of surprises, I was wondering if you attended the séance last night."

"The what?"

"Secrets of the Dead hosted a séance in the Moonlight Lounge. I was wondering if you attended."

"No. I wasn't there. Was it any good?"

"It was surprising. I'll say that much. Have you met the celebrity medium: Chryss Tiano? He's not at all what I expected."

"No, I haven't had the pleasure. Maybe you can introduce us if there's time."

Up on stage, the lights dimmed. Linda returned and hoisted her camera. Raquel and Mindie stood face to face inside the mini kitchen, waiting. Linda murmured something too low to hear, and Raquel's severe expression softened. She reached forward and hugged Mindie for a long moment. When Raquel stepped back, her expression was full of tenderness. "How are you holding up?" she asked, her voice clear enough to travel without a microphone. "I was so shocked to hear about Teddy."

Mindie's shoulders lifted and fell. "I'm okay. We're devastated, of course. And we're all so worried about Ariana. It's not fair what she's going through. But she's strong. She'll get through this. It's just..."

"It's very hard," Raquel said, when Mindie took a shaky breath. "You've all become very close, haven't you?"

"Yes. We've been away from our family and friends for months, sequestered for the entire season. It was only natural that we became like a second family to one another." Mindie smiled. "At the end of every challenge, we cook a big dinner together. No competition, just everyone in the kitchen laughing and getting in one another's way. Teddy always made a massive salad for us, and he'd lecture us about the importance of taking good care of our health. He believed that..." She blinked rapidly. "I'm sorry. I don't know if I can do this."

"It's okay," Raquel soothed. "Take your time."

"Teddy was passionate about life," Mindie said, her hands resting on the empty wooden counter. "Some people thought of him as a health guru, but in truth, he wanted to help people fulfill their dreams. When your body is healthy and strong, you can do anything. Teddy loved to help people. And that's what I'll remember most about him. But I'll try to forget those muffins of his from episode two! They were dreadful." She laughed weakly.

Raquel tilted her head with sympathy and touched Mindie on her upper arm. "We'll never forget Teddy. Thanks for speaking with us."

The women embraced again, and Linda pressed a button on her camera. She set the machine on the counter and peered at the small screen on the side, reviewing what she'd recorded.

Greg stood and walked toward the stage, looking up at them. "That was great, Mindie. Raquel, well done. You hit the mark beautifully. But can we do one more take? I'm sure the editing team will want as much footage as we can give them."

"No, we can't." Mindie snapped, turning to face him with flushed cheeks. "I'm not baking cinnamon rolls up here. And I'm not an actress." She took a shaky breath and wiped her right eye with one finger, trying not to smudge her makeup. "We're talking about what happened to Teddy, and I can't..." She turned away. "I can't *pretend* that I'm okay right now."

Greg's face fell. He stepped back, holding up his hands. "Of course! You are right. My apologies." He turned to the camerawoman. "Linda, I think we're good. Let's get reset for Kitty, shall we?"

Kitty stood and tugged her navy-blue sheath dress down. "I'm up for as many takes as you need." She shot Mindie a superior glance. "Of course, I wasn't as *close* to Teddy as Mindie was."

"Kitty, dear, you're not helping," Harvey said, his tone exasperated. "Mindie, come down and sit with me." He turned to Greg. "Maybe we should just speak from the heart? Let's get through this, and let's put it behind us. We should check on Ariana. She's been locked up in that kitchen all morning. And maybe we could go do some sightseeing at port? I need an anniversary gift for Samantha."

Greg nodded absentmindedly. His worried gaze was still fixed on Mindie. To his credit, he seemed embarrassed by what he'd said earlier. "Yes. That sounds fine."

Kitty went up on stage and Mindie came down. Ellie got up. "Here. Take my seat, hon. I'm going to go check on Ariana while you finish up here."

Chapter Twelve

ELLIE FOUND ARIANA WORKING IN the small kitchen attached to the ship's Teppanyaki restaurant. The Japanese eatery was closed for remodeling, and Devon had set aside the adjoining kitchen as a private space for the Sweetie Pie baking contestants to work on their recipes. Ariana's long brown hair had bits of white flour in it and her apron was stained with flour and water. She looked up when Ellie walked in, but she didn't smile.

"Do they need me for something?" Ariana worked a rolling pin back and forth over a wad of yellowish dough. She picked up the rolling pin by one end and bashed the dough with the other end. The wood thudded wetly into the dough with each stroke.

"No. They've got a way to go. I wanted to stop by and see if you needed anything."

"I could use some chocolate chips," Ariana said, rubbing her forehead. She held out her hand and frowned at it. Tiny bits of dough clung to her face where she'd touched it. She brushed them off with the back of her hand. "I went to find mine, and they're missing. I suppose I could have rummaged in the other boxes, but I wouldn't want to get between Harvey and his snacks. I might lose a finger." She smiled. "I adore the man, but if he isn't more careful with his diet his wife will be burying him before the year is out." Her smile faded and she stared down at the oval of dough on the kitchen island. It was surrounded by a faint halo of white flour.

"Are you making chocolate chip cookies for the show?" Ellie eyed the wooden rolling pin warily. A person didn't usually 'roll out' chocolate chip cookies, and Ariana was holding the pin like a weapon. *Probably she's working out her stress*, Ellie thought.

"For the film crew. They've been working so hard, I figured they could use a reminder that we all care about them. Besides, baking cookies is supposed to be relaxing. That is, when I can find my ingredients." She thwacked the dough with the rolling pin one more time. "I probably should have stopped when I saw my chips were missing, but I needed to do *something* other than stand around and wait for the final showdown to start." Her mouth worked like she was tasting something sour. "I nearly bit Greg's head off this morning. I'm sick of the way everyone is staring at me like I'm incapable of holding myself together. I don't need their pity."

"Let's handle one problem at a time," Ellie said, pointing at the kitchen telephone. She dialed a number and waited for the answer. "Hey. It's Ellie. Can you do me a big favor and have a bag of chocolate chips brought to the Teppanyaki kitchen? As soon as you're able. Thanks. I owe you one." She smiled at Ariana. "It pays off to have friends in the kitchen staff."

"I expect you think I'm a coward, hiding in here instead of listening to everyone praise my husband."

"There's no wrong way to grieve, dearheart. No matter what you're feeling, you're allowed to feel it."

"It was complicated. What Teddy and I had."

"That doesn't mean it was bad."

"You're trying to be nice, but you don't know what you're talking about. Here's the thing no one wants me to say: Teddy and I were getting divorced after the show was over. We had the papers drawn up a year ago, but he begged me to wait. I should have said no. If I had, we wouldn't be in this mess."

"Why did Teddy want to wait?"

"We were offered the show as a package deal. We'd be the first married couple to compete for the Golden Cupcake. But the good news came at a bad time. Still, it was important to Teddy, so I agreed to wait."

"That couldn't have been easy."

Ariana turned to the counter behind her and snapped the lid back on top of her flour container. "Do you know why most people don't bake well? They lack patience. Every ingredient needs to be handled with care. People don't take the time to sift their flour. They add butter before it's soft enough. And they crank up the heat too high because they don't trust the oven to do its job. You can't create anything good without trust. It's the ingredient no one talks about."

Ariana put her hands on both sides of the rolling pin and worked the dough again. Tears fell onto the dough, and she mixed them in.

She's putting up a tough front, Ellie thought. *And maybe that's what she needs to do, to get through the rest of this week. But I should make sure she has family waiting when we return to San Diego.*

"Did Teddy understand that?"

"I thought he did. But it turns out he was in a hurry too." She dropped the pin on the counter and left it there. "You've heard I'm good at wedding cakes. Well, the first time I ever made a cake was for my own wedding. And it was beautiful. After Teddy and I decided to split, I tried making the same recipe for a friend. But it didn't work. The ingredients were fresh, but it tasted rotten. I pushed it into the trash, and we bought one from a shop."

"I'm so sorry," Ellie said.

Ariana sniffed wetly. "I can't sit in that theater and listen to them talk about him. Everyone's been so kind to me. And they want me to cry for the camera. But they can't understand why I'm really crying. They don't want to see that I'm relieved. I'm so tired of pretending to be someone I'm not."

"And who is that?"

"The woman Teddy loved," she said.

"But you loved him," Ellie said gently. "I can see that much."

Ariana face twisted in despair, and she turned away to wipe her hands on a dishtowel.

"Do you want me to go?" Ellie asked.

Ariana turned back, in control of herself again. "No. I don't like baking alone. Stay, please. As soon as those chocolate chips arrive, we'll mix them into this over-worked dough. Cookie recipes are so forgiving. It's all that sugar. Will you preheat the oven for me?"

Ellie twisted the black and silver knob on the front of the oven. She pulled the oven door open to peek. The racks were as shiny and clean as the day they'd been installed. She stood straight and wondered: Did Ariana believe that her husband had committed suicide?

"Everyone describes Teddy as being so full of life. And so excited for his future. It's hard to make sense of what happened. Do you think he was depressed?"

"He'd been... behaving erratically for months. Teddy has taken Adderall since he was a teenager, it helps him focus, but he's been upping his dosage, and I was worried. Six months ago, I caught him buying extra pills from a friend. And he isn't supposed to mix alcohol and his meds." She wet a hand towel and used it to wipe down the stainless-steel counter opposite the kitchen island. "When we were together, I was able to keep an eye on him, to help him keep perspective when he got bent out of shape. But he's been shutting me out for months now." She threw the wet towel in the sink and leaned against the counter, folding her arms over her waist. "If you'd asked me yesterday if Teddy was okay, I would have said yes. He was anxious about the show. And he was stressed about doing well. But when wasn't he?" Ariana combed through her hair with her fingers, straightening it. "What if Teddy needed help, and I blew him off? He asked me to have dinner with him a few nights ago, in San Diego, and I didn't go. I figured he only invited me because everyone else was busy, and I didn't want to be his last choice. But what if he was finally ready to make things right, and I just..." She blinked rapidly. "What if I was too swept up in my own hurt feelings to notice when he needed me?"

Ellie took a step toward her, but Ariana wheeled away, wiping her face with her sleeve. "I'm fine. But I don't want to talk about this. I just want to get through the final showdown and go home."

Poor Ariana! She was stretched too thin, like an over-inflated balloon, one tiny pinprick away from losing all cohesion. It was time to change the subject.

The first cookies were in the oven when Mindie pushed open the door and walked inside. "Oh! You're still cooking. Sorry to interrupt." Mindie shot Ellie an anxious glance. Was she worried about Ariana? It was hard to tell. Mindie wrung her hands and stepped forward.

"It's fine." Ariana's voice was clipped.

"I need to talk to you. Ellie, will you excuse us?"

"Ellie can stay," Ariana said, crossing her arms over her apron. "I'm not going to claw your eyes out if that's what you're worried about."

"I wanted to apologize, again. I could have handled things better. I *should* have. But you know what Kitty is saying isn't true. It's not my fault what she's saying."

"What isn't true?" Ellie asked.

Mindie's ears were pink. "There's this... stupid rumor going around. People are saying Teddy and I were sleeping together. But we weren't. And when Ariana didn't show up at the shoot this morning, I thought maybe I was the reason why." She looked at Ariana. "Please don't stay away from the shoot because of me. If you're not comfortable with me there, I'll go. You shouldn't be alone right now."

"You lied to me." Ariana's voice was frosty. "You want to pretend that none of this was your fault, but you were lying to my face the whole time."

"I never lied to you. *Teddy* did. And all we did was hang out. I promise. He never touched me, Ariana. And I never moved in on your territory. I wouldn't do that to you."

"Is there anything else?" Ariana asked, bending to peer through the oven window. "Or would you like a trophy for *not* sleeping with my husband?"

"I'm sorry," Mindie said quietly. Her ears were bright red now. "Anyway, Harvey is looking for you. He's going sightseeing in Cabo in about an hour and he said he hoped you'll go with him. I told him I'd tell you."

"Points for effort," Ariana said. The oven door opened. It slammed shut.

"I was just trying to be nice."

"Mission accomplished." Ariana straightened up with one hand on her lower back. Her eyes narrowed. "Is there anything else?"

Mindie fled, leaving the kitchen door swinging in her wake.

Chapter Thirteen

AS SOON AS THE COOKIES came out of the oven, Ariana sprinkled them with coarse salt and set them out to cool on wire racks. She hadn't said much since Mindie had left, but the tension in the room was still palpable. Ellie hunted in the kitchen cabinets until she found a stack of paper takeaway containers. She carried the boxes over to the kitchen island and set them down next to the cookies. The air smelled like sugar and chunks of rich, dark chocolate.

"I suspect Mindie was trying to put your mind at ease," Ellie said tentatively, "but perhaps it wasn't the best time for that conversation." She snatched a cookie off the rack closest to her and bit into it. Still warm from the oven, it melted in her mouth. The salt had seemed like an odd choice, but it made the sweetness of the chocolate less overpowering. Perfection!

Ariana shot Ellie a small smile. "I'm glad you like them." Using a metal spatula, she lifted cookies from the rack, checking the undersides before placing them in a paper box. She closed the container with nimble motions of her fingers before setting an empty one next to the rack to repeat the process. "Mindie and Teddy were having lunch together behind my back. It was going on for a while."

"Ah."

Ariana's shoulders sagged. "Teddy told me he was using his lunch break to workout. He said he didn't have time to eat with me. But really, he'd just been hanging out with another woman. It shouldn't bother me, but it does. And Mindie should have known better. I knew Teddy wanted a divorce, but she didn't." Ariana grouped a batch of closed boxes in front of her and printed names on each box in looping cursive print. She shot Ellie a guilty look. "I'm sorry you had to see that."

"Don't worry about it. Have you eaten lunch?"

She shook her head. "I haven't, but maybe I will tag along with Harvey after all. He's a sweetheart, and I don't want him getting lost in Cabo." She smiled a little. "Maybe I'll get him talking about his wife. That way I'll be off the hook all afternoon." She sighed. "They don't make men like that any longer, do they?"

Ellie thought of Ben and her heart lifted. She turned to Ariana. "Do you want me to drop those cookies off for you?"

"Would you? Give them to Linda and she'll see that everyone gets some. Thanks for coming by, Ellie. You're a good listener. I'm sorry I wasn't better company."

"Nonsense. And come find me later if you want to talk. My stateroom is in *The Lofts*, and you have my extension."

Ariana hung up her apron on a hook and left. Ellie put the cookies in a big paper bag and carried them back to the theater. When she arrived, Linda was sitting on the edge of the stage, her legs dangling over the edge, and she was eating a sandwich. Next to her, Paul Gumbs sat in his uniform, taking notes. Paul saw her approaching, and he flipped his notepad shut and tucked it into his breast pocket.

"I'm glad I caught you," she said to Linda. "I have sea salt chocolate chip cookies for the crew, courtesy of Ariana. She's heading out with Harvey for some sightseeing, but she asked me to drop these off."

Linda reached for the bag. She had an attractively square jaw, and her blonde braid was casually tossed over her left shoulder. "See what I mean?" she said to Paul. "That's what kind of people they are. I've worked on a half-dozen reality shows, but I'll take a baking competition any day." She reached into the bag and pulled out a box of cookies, opening it and taking a sniff. Her eyes half-closed in pleasure. "Fresh from the oven. Bless her." She shot Ellie an impish look. "My last show was about do-it-yourself home improvement. And do you know what the cast of *that* show gave me?"

Ellie shook her head.

"Herpes. No one washed their hands before chowing down at the craft services table. My whole crew had cold sores for a month."

Paul looked aghast.

Linda chuckled. "Say what you will about bakers, but they know how to keep things clean." She took out a cookie and bit into it. "Want one?" she said, her mouth half-full.

"I already ate four," Ellie confessed.

Paul still looked disturbed. "No thank you." He hopped down from his seat on the edge of the stage and landed on the carpeted floor below, a feat that would have left a shorter person with a twisted ankle. "Thanks for answering my questions," he said.

Linda nodded. "I'm not sure how helpful I was, but no problem. I'm staying down in *The Lofts* if you need anything else."

"Ellie, I'm headed back to my office." Paul's expression seemed to say that she should come along.

"I'm headed that way myself," she said. "I'll walk with you." To Linda she added, "Don't eat *all* those cookies! She wrote names on the boxes for a reason."

Linda grinned. "And it's a good thing too. I end every season of the competition needing to go on a diet to lose my extra cookie weight!"

Ellie and Paul walked up the theater aisle together. Paul glanced sideways at her cane and slowed his steps a little. "Let's head to Strunk's office for an update. Stairs or elevator?"

"Elevator," Ellie said. "And why don't we walk along the promenade? The kitchen was stuffy, and I could use a breath of fresh air."

When they stepped outside onto the promenade deck, Ellie went up to the railing and looked out. The *Spirit* had dropped anchor a good half-mile from Cabo San Lucas, and small covered boats called tenders were ferrying passengers to and from shore. The clean sea air washed over her shoulders, cool and refreshing. Cabo's seaside marina was packed with boats. The tall white masts of the sailboats jutted upward like the stiff bristles of a hairbrush. Cabo was a fairly touristy spot full of seafood restaurants, shopping centers, and charter boats ready to make a cruiser's fishing, snorkeling, or sailing dreams come true. At least, that's what her guidebook said. She let out a quiet sigh and squinted, trying to catch a glimpse of *El Arco de Cabo San Lucas*, a famous rock formation also known as Land's End.

Paul nudged her gently with his elbow, breaking her reverie. "You can dream about shopping later. Come on. Strunk said his work wouldn't take long."

Ellie spotted two men and two women up ahead. They were walking stiffly, their arms and fingers out in front of them, their eyes closed tight, like they were pretending to be zombies on Halloween. They were blocking the promenade. As soon as a gap opened, a pair of joggers quickly darted through the opening, glancing backward with irritated expressions.

Paul quickly jogged forward and tapped one of the women on the shoulder. She jumped! Her eyelids snapped open and she staggered back, one hand on her chest. "You scared the stuffing out of me!" she screeched.

"I'm sorry, ma'am, but if you're going to walk outside on the promenade, you'll need to keep your eyes open. It's not safe to move about on the deck when you're not aware of your surroundings."

She tugged her black t-shirt down and hitched up her jean shorts. "Sorry about that, I got swept up in the moment." She called over to her companions. "Guys! Keep your eyes open."

"I think I'd notice if I'd hit the outer wall, Franny." The other woman replied peevishly. But when she turned and noticed Paul in his uniform her mouth snapped shut. "Oh! Okay."

Ellie smiled at her. "If you don't mind my asking, what are you doing?" She gestured them over to the side so other passengers could pass.

"We're practicing energetic sensing," the woman said. She was tall and slender with waist-length hair dyed a dark blue, and her t-shirt was decorated with a screen print of Chryss Tiano's blue eyes. "You activate your sixth sense and feel around for cold spots, electricity, pulses, or anything else that might represent spectral energy. And you have to visualize what you're searching for."

"I'm looking for the red phantom," her companion said. His hair was a normal shade of brown. But his right nostril was pierced with a black metal hoop that made Ellie's nose ache in sympathy.

"I see." Ellie said.

"According to what I heard," the man continued, "The red phantom is a vengeful spirit. He seeks out people with the blackest hearts, and he gives them a chance to redeem themselves. But if they refuse, he kills them on the spot. My friend Adrian saw the phantom last night! There was a bang on the wall, and when he went outside, he saw the creature racing down the hall, his robes flowing behind him. And word is that he killed that man the other night. The guy who went overboard."

Ellie glanced at Paul.

"And what will you do when you find this phantom?" Paul asked.

"Well, the class this morning didn't cover that part, but tomorrow we've got a session called *Exorcism 101*. That's the good stuff."

Paul pretended to consider this. "Perhaps you should take that class first? This phantom sounds dangerous. You wouldn't want to be unprepared."

"I told you!" the blue-haired woman said, slugging him lightly on the arm. "You need to be *ready*."

Paul cleared his throat. "By the way, where was your friend when he saw the phantom?"

"In his stateroom."

"What floor?"

"The tenth floor. Near the elevators."

Paul nodded. "That's good to know. If anyone disturbs your sleep, you can call the security office. We're here to help. But please *do* keep your eyes open. And I mean that literally."

"We will."

"Enjoy your day," Paul said smiling at the trio. "Ellie?"

She followed him, stealing a furtive glance at shore before they headed inside. They waited at the elevator to descend to the crew level. "I assume you have a reason for indulging in that claptrap?"

He shot her an amused look. "Did you notice how the ghost hunters have connected Mr. McIntyre's death to this myth of theirs? That could be coincidence, or it might not be. I'll send my team out to patrol the tenth floor tonight. If someone is running around the ship in a red cloak, we'll find them. Either it's a prank, or it's connected to what Chryss Tiano said on stage. Either way, I want to know."

She nodded.

"Maybe we should attend that class. In case we need to exorcise the phantom ourselves." Paul said, keeping his eyes forward.

"Very funny."

Chapter Fourteen

DOCTOR TOBIAS STRUNK LOOKED UP from his small brown desk with an eager smile. "Paul! Ellie! I have news. Come inside. I want to show you something." He stood up and gestured to his chair. He turned and picked up a stack of three-ring binders from his guest chair and set it precariously on top of a filing cabinet next to a box of tongue depressors. "Sit. Please."

Tobias had shoved his keyboard and monitor back against the wall to make room. His desk held a rack of test tubes, a bunch of scribbled notes on paper, and a large white microscope. A framed photo of an elderly couple — Tobias's parents, probably — rested next to an empty coffee cup. A glass slide labeled *Victim* was positioned beneath the microscope's lower lens; the slide glowed with white light.

One time, Ellie had asked Tobias what happened to a person's body if they passed away on a cruise ship. His answer, that dead bodies were stored in the big fridge between the floral arrangements and the surplus bananas, had put her off Devon's banana-stuffed French toast for well over a month. Perhaps there was an upside to not being in possession of Teddy McIntyre's corpse.

Tobias was practically bouncing with excitement, so she sat down at his desk and asked him, "What am I looking at?"

"Look in the microscope. Tell me what you see." She held the scope steady and peered in through the center lens. "I haven't used one of these since my boys were in school," she said, turning the focus knob. On the slide, masses of tiny purple blotches were spread out like confetti.

She looked up. "What are they?"

"Officer Gumbs, do you want to see?" Tobias grinned. "Come on. You *know* you want to."

"It's okay, doc. Just tell us what you found."

"Those are red blood cells."

"And?" Paul asked.

"And they're *not* human!"

Paul looked skeptical. "Don't tell me the blood is alien. We already have rumors of a murderous ghost. If you add flying saucers to the mix, I'm swimming for shore and starting a new life in Mexico."

"You don't even like Mexican food," Ellie retorted.

"What we serve aboard this ship is not Mexican food. It's hamburger meat inside a tortilla. I prefer *authentic* cuisine."

Ellie gasped. "What would Devon say?"

"You will *not* rat me out. Or I'll tell him what you said about his low-sugar cheesecake."

Ellie's mouth snapped shut.

Paul looked at Tobias, "Perhaps you can explain?"

"Well, I've had that sugar-free cheesecake. I get that he's trying to make food for diabetics, but it's not worth it. I'd rather eat an apple, because at least an apple won't make me flatulent. I could have powered one of the hot tubs, solo, after that particular dessert."

"I meant, maybe you could explain about the *blood*?"

"Oh! Yes. When you asked me to identify the blood group for the samples taken from the crime scene, I was intrigued. I keep a few typing kits on hand in case we ever need to do an emergency transfusion. I ran the sample myself, and it came up as inconclusive."

"What does that mean?" Ellie asked.

"Usually, it means the testing kit failed. So, I ran a second test, and a third. They all came back the same: inconclusive."

"And?" Paul raised an eyebrow.

"Well, I knew we had a mystery on our hands. And I called up my friend Wayne — we were in Boy Scouts together, believe it or not — and these days he's a hematologist at a cancer center in Milwaukee. Anyway, we got to talking, and—"

"Any day now, Doc," Paul interjected.

"Hush! Let him tell the story," Ellie said.

"No, no, Paul is right. To make a long story *slightly* shorter, we ran through some possibilities. And I think we're looking at blood type Z."

"Z as in Zombie?" Ellie turned to Paul. "I'm joining you in Mexico. Just give me ten minutes to pack a bag."

Tobias chuckled. "Z as in bovine! The sample you brought me is cow blood. It might be pig, but I'd put my money on cow. If you want me to pinpoint the specific species, you'll need to get Roberta to spring for some better lab equipment." Tobias tapped his microscope. "With the right materials, we could get a state-of-the-art crime lab in here. Just say the word. Please, say the word! I haven't dealt with anything more interesting than a sunburn in weeks."

"Well, let's hope this kind of testing isn't a regular occurrence," Paul replied. "But great work, Doc. That wasn't Mr. McIntyre's blood at the scene. Now that we can prove it, we've got something more to go on than my hunches."

"Unless your missing man is a cow-human hybrid," Tobias joked. "I'm kidding! A cow-human hybrid probably wouldn't have hands. Or a working brain, for that matter. But if any of your suspects start mooing, come get me and I'll run a DNA test, pronto."

Ellie tugged on Paul's coat sleeve. "Do you remember what Victor said yesterday at the officers' meeting? About inventory control? If there is beef blood on the ship, I bet Devon has it on one of his spreadsheets, somewhere."

Paul's eyes lit up. "Right! He also mentioned a certain Australian baker was taking ingredients from the kitchen without asking."

"Cruise ship crime team, activate!" Strunk held out his fist toward them.

Ellie fist-bumped him back, laughing. "It's always a pleasure, Tobias. Thanks for all your help."

The doctor looked pleased. "If you need more tests run, you know where to find me."

"LET ME MAKE SURE I understand," Roberta said slowly, leaning back in her chair. "We thought Teddy McIntyre killed himself after dinner the first night of the sailing. But Paul got a bee in his bonnet about handprints, and you asked Strunk to bust out his chemistry set. Now he says the blood in Teddy's room came from a cow."

"Yes," Paul said.

"Ellie, what do you think happened?" Roberta asked sharply.

"Don't mind me," Paul muttered. "I'm just the head of security."

Roberta shot him a flat look. "I'll get to you shortly. I figured I'd let Ellie unspool her wild theories and you'd tamp her down. Respect the process."

"Paul's already figured it out. Someone wanted us to believe Teddy went over that balcony. And did you hear what Chryss Tiano did during his séance last night?"

Roberta shook her head. Ellie filled her in. By the time she was done, Roberta's expression was pure exasperation. "So now you're telling me the medium is in on it? How far does this conspiracy go?"

"Paul thought it might be aliens," Ellie quipped.

He shot her a brief glare. "The drama at the séance might be relevant, or it might not. We stopped the ship while we searched for Mr. McIntyre's body, remember? Mr. Norris and Mrs. McIntyre knew what had happened, and they could have talked to anyone. Possibly some of the crew overheard details on the radio. You know how fast gossip moves on a cruise ship."

"I doubt Chryss Tiano was involved," Ellie said.

"You're defending him?" Roberta was incredulous. "The last time we talked, you could barely say his name without rolling your eyes."

"I'm not defending anyone. I'm just saying we don't know where he got his information. Chryss Tiano insists that he was channeling Teddy's spirit. The man may be a few crayons short of a full pack, but I don't think he's malicious."

Roberta winced. "So much for seeing our ship and crew on national television! I don't see how Greg can continue filming under these circumstances." She glanced at Paul. "I don't suppose we could just let this one go? If it weren't for your meddlesome curiosity, I'd be at my massage appointment right now and we'd be none the wiser about that bloody cow."

"Roberta," Ellie warned.

"I know. I just needed to say it out loud, once. Sit, you two, you're making me nervous." She crossed one leg over the other. "Tell me what you've learned so far. I presume whoever made a mess in Teddy's suite knew him, or else, why bother? Did any of Teddy's companions have something against him?"

Ellie nodded. "Apparently Mindie and Teddy were having lunch every day behind Ariana's back. They had an argument this morning in the Teppanyaki kitchen."

Roberta pursed her lips. "Are we looking at some sort of sordid love triangle?"

"Mindie swore up and down that she and Teddy were just friends. And there's something else. Ariana and Teddy were planning to divorce when the show was over. I got the sense that the divorce wasn't Ariana's idea."

"So, Ariana was jealous of Mindie," Roberta mused, tapping her chin. "Perhaps she offed her soon-to-be-ex? Vengeance for being dumped for the pretty Aussie."

"She did no such thing," Ellie said firmly. "I know heartbreak when I see it. Ariana loved Teddy. And Mindie looked genuinely broken up when she was doing her tribute to Teddy on stage today. She was barely holding it together. As best I can tell, they *all* cared about Teddy."

Paul shifted in his seat. Roberta leaned forward. "What is it?"

"This morning, while Strunk was running that blood sample for me, I sent Ellie off to keep an eye on the Sugar Network contestants. By the time I went to find her, the contestants were gone, but the director and her crew were packing up their gear for the day. I asked Linda to tell me about Teddy."

"Did you tell her what we'd found?" Ellie asked.

"No. I asked her about Teddy's state of mind. For the most part, her answers confirmed what we'd already heard. Teddy was anxious and high strung. He drank a bit too much. He was obsessive about being presented in the best possible light. And in her opinion, he'd seemed entirely normal in the days leading up to his death."

"Assuming he's dead," Roberta said. "Maybe Teddy strapped on a fake mustache and he's up on the lido deck right now, looking for a new side piece. Stranger things have happened."

"Yes, when *you* make them happen," Paul said, raising an eyebrow. He might have forgiven Roberta for her involvement in the Picklewick affair, but he wasn't about to let her forget it. "Here's the thing. According to Linda, everybody hated Teddy McIntyre's guts. Well, everyone except for Mindie Burton, that is. The two of them got along okay. Linda told me about a time when Teddy ruined another contestant's entry. It was early in the season, and Teddy tripped and knocked the guy's cupcakes over. The whole display came crashing down. They fixed it in editing, but everyone believed Teddy had done it on purpose."

"That's why they hated him?" Roberta asked.

"There's more. Linda said that Ariana followed Teddy around like a lovesick puppy, but Teddy wouldn't even look at her. The camera would turn on, and he'd be all lovey-dovey, but as soon as the red light went out, he'd turn away and walk off like she was nothing more than a stage prop."

"Greg said something similar the morning Teddy disappeared," Ellie said.

"And Ariana denied it," Paul replied.

There was a soft knock on the door. Stuart went to answer it.

Devon stepped inside, holding a thin stack of paper in his large, meaty hands. His chef's jacket was double buttoned, and he walked forward with his head bowed. He handed the papers to Paul. "Sorry to interrupt, Roberta. Paul said this was an urgent matter. You'll find what you're looking for on page six." He stepped back and waited with his hands behind his back.

Paul flipped the pages and scanned down the sixth page with one finger. His lips compressed. He looked up at Devon. "You're sure this was the only one in inventory?"

Devon nodded. "We don't use blood products aboard the Spirit. There are trace amounts left over from preparing meat, but nothing in the quantities you asked about. And before you ask, I went to the freezer and looked. It's not there."

"Was anything else missing?"

"I didn't check. Would you like me to?"

Paul nodded. "Please do."

"I'm on it. Come by my office later today and I'll have a list for you." Devon took off, nodding at Stuart as he passed by.

Paul cleared his throat. "This is an itemized list of the supplies Devon stored for the Sweetie Pie Baking Competition. It's organized by contestant." He pointed at the page. "Item eighty-four is ten ounces of frozen beef blood."

"Who does it belong to?" Ellie asked.

Paul let the papers drop to his lap. "Ariana McIntyre."

Chapter Fifteen

ACCORDING TO THE SECURITY LOG, Ariana was still away at port. While they waited for her to return, Paul and Ellie went to ask Victor about Mindie Burton. Victor was in his office staring at his computer with a blank expression when they arrived. He nodded in recognition when they asked about the incident with Mindie.

"Yes. I remember quite well. One of our sous chefs mentioned that the Australian woman nicked a basket of zucchini from his workstation. She was quite brazen about it too! The fellow turned around and asked her what she was doing, taking her for a guest who had gotten lost on her way to the buffet. She told him that she needed the vegetables for a recipe, and she stormed off like he was the one at fault!"

Ellie nodded. "Do you know where the supplies for the baking competition are kept? Are they stored along with the rest of our food?"

"No. Devon and I arranged for the bakers to have their own space. All of their supplies are stored in the Teppanyaki kitchen." He inhaled, puffing up like a bullfrog about to croak. "Has there been a complaint? I know Roberta wants us to be accommodating, but I won't have our kitchen crew bullied for doing their jobs. We have an obligation to *all* our guests, and—"

Ellie smiled. Victor, even with all his rules, could be vociferous in defending his crew. "There's no complaint. We're following up on an unrelated matter."

Victor huffed out his breath. "Well! I hear Mr. McIntyre was murdered by a ghost. Is that what this is about?" He fixed Paul with a stern look. "Did your team ever find those hooligans running up and down the halls, making noise? I know you laughed it off, but this is what happens when you don't maintain decorum, my young friend. Chaos begins slowly. Always. But the next thing you know, you're under siege and guests are flying off their balconies like popcorn!" Victor's ruddy cheeks were flushed. He clenched his fists atop his thighs.

"Victor, are you okay?" Ellie asked. "You seem... passionate today."

"Am I?" He seemed to shake his frustration off like a dog shakes off water. "I am quite well, Ms. Tappet. But thank you for your concern."

"Is this about Wynona?"

"I'm sure I have no idea what you mean. It's true that Wynona hasn't returned my calls this week. But that's of no consequence. She's under no obligation to communicate with me socially."

Paul was taking slow steps backward, toward the door. Ellie gave him a quick nod and he stepped out into the hall and shut the door behind him.

"If Wynona didn't call you back, I'm sure there's a reason. Why don't you go find her?"

"I'm sure she's very busy," he said, turning back toward his computer. "And if she wanted a gentleman caller, no doubt she'd return my messages. How am I supposed to know what she's thinking? Am I psychic, Ms. Tappet? No, I am not. Perhaps there's a reason I've remained a bachelor all these years. I lack the sixth sense about women that other men seem to possess."

This wasn't good! Either Wynona was intentionally blowing Victor off, or he'd wildly misinterpreted. Knowing him, it was probably the latter.

"Well, I *never* call Wynona on the phone," Ellie said. "It would be pointless."

"And why is that?"

"Because her quarters look like a bomb went off inside, and her phone is probably buried under a pile of underwear. You couldn't have picked a less organized girlfriend if you tried."

"Buried under..." Victor's eyes widened, almost as if the existence of Wynona's undergarments had never occurred to him before.

"If she went on a date with you, she likes you! So maybe drop the formality? Find an excuse to bump into her. The flimsier the excuse, the better."

"I don't enjoy games."

"It's not a game, it's... *tradition!*"

She could tell she'd piqued his interest. But he said, "What on Earth does dating have to do with *tradition*?"

Ellie thought for a moment. She wasn't prepared for this conversation, so she'd need to wing it! Finally, she said, "In nature, the male almost always woos the female. If you were a blue footed booby, you'd show Wynona your feet. If you were a pufferfish, you'd draw her a beautiful pattern in the sand. But you're a man, so you'll show Wynona you're interested by going out of your way to see her. You'll make time out of your day to run into her. Think of it as a dance. She has her moves, and you have yours. That's tradition." She waited to see if Victor was buying what she was selling, and her heart lifted when she saw the furrow in his forehead smooth out.

"When do I get to see her moves?" Victor asked. "Or does the male have to do *all* the work? That hardly seems fair."

"Since when is life fair?" She smirked at him. "Anyway, I need to run. But if I wanted to look for Wynona..."

Victor leaned forward to listen.

Ellie smiled. "She has a sweet tooth, and she usually stops by the crew mess for a snack around three o'clock."

Victor checked his pocket watch. "It just occurred to me; I could use a coffee break." He opened his office door for her, shut and locked it behind them, and then strode down the hall, nodding curtly at Paul as he passed. "Officer Gumbs."

"Officer Vasquez," Paul replied, his expression neutral.

Men, Ellie thought. *What would they do without us?* Once she and Paul were alone in the hallway, he turned to her. "I say we talk to Ariana, and then Mindie. Do you agree?"

"I do." She sighed.

"What is it?"

"I was just thinking, if that beef blood was stored in the Teppanyaki kitchen, any one of them could have gotten access to it."

"I'm not too worried. Whoever messed up that crime scene did a poor job of it. They're no match for us."

"Cruise ship crime team, activate?"

Paul chuckled. "You and Strunk are two peas in a pod, did you know that? This is what happens when you watch too many murder shows on television. Everyone wants to fight crime and bring in the bad guys."

"So? Where would you be without your loyal side-kicks?"

"Oh! You're my sidekick, now?" Paul considered this for a moment. "I can live with that."

IN THE EARLY EVENING, ELLIE and Paul headed to Ariana's suite. She'd re-embarked about thirty minutes earlier, and when Paul knocked, they heard her light footfalls approaching the door. Ariana's hair was damp from the shower, and her skin was blotchy and pink from too much sun. She stepped back to let them in. "Ellie! Mr. Gumbs. Please come in. So sorry to keep you waiting. I was just getting dressed, and I ordered room service." She headed toward her bedroom, turning back to say, "Harvey told me about your loophole, Ellie. And he managed to get his hands on menus from all your restaurants too. I'm trying out a few new dishes."

"How was your day at port?" Ellie sat in the living room and indicated with a nod of her chin that Paul should do the same. Paul Gumbs had two modes, comforting and serious, and whenever he had bad news to share, he seemed twice as stern and half again as tall. Ariana asked them to wait for a moment, and when she came back out, she was wearing makeup and a clean sundress. She looked more at ease.

"The walk did me good. I'm sorry you had to see Mindie and me scrapping like that. Harvey and I took a long walk through the shops in Cabo. They have these tiny juice carts all over the place, and they squeeze whatever kind of fruit you want, while you wait! It was so delicious." She closed her eyes for a moment as if steadying herself. "I'm trying to keep things in perspective. Mindie might be a crappy friend, but she didn't kill Teddy. I can't blame her for everything I'm feeling right now." She sighed. "And Harvey's right. After the final showdown, I never need to see her again. It's only a few more days."

"We're here because we need to talk to you about developments in your husband's case," Paul said abruptly.

"His *case*? Is that cruise ship lingo for something?"

"I'm afraid not. Mrs. McIntyre, it appears your husband didn't kill himself, as we first thought. We believe he was murdered."

Ariana goggled at Paul. "You can't be serious." She looked back and forth between them. "Wait. That blood in his room..." Her face flashed with fear as the implication hit her. "You're saying someone hurt him, and they pushed him over that balcony? Oh my God." Her hands clenched in her lap and she squeezed her eyes shut. When she opened them, she asked in a strangled voice, "Who did it? Tell me."

"We're still trying to figure that out," Paul said. "At the moment, I need to ask you a couple questions. First of all, I need you to tell us about the beef blood you brought aboard the ship."

Ariana did a double take. "Beef blood? Why would you—" Her expression relaxed. "Oh, you mean for my shepherd's pie recipe! But what does that have to do with Teddy?"

"You brought beef blood for a pie?" Ellie prompted, "Isn't that unusual?"

"Not too unusual, I think. It was for the final showdown. I was going to make spicy shepherd's pie with homemade black pudding. Fresh blood sausage. Raquel keeps hinting that my scope is too narrow, and I wanted to give my final entry an international flare. Black pudding tastes best with fresh pork blood, but pork blood doesn't freeze very well. The beef blood was my backup in case I couldn't find fresh pork blood at port before Friday."

"But you changed your recipe for the final showdown, is that correct?" Paul asked.

"Yes." Ariana looked confused. "I decided to make Teddy's recipe instead."

"To honor his memory," Paul said.

"Yes."

"Even though you believed he was sleeping with Mindie Burton. And even though he rejected you at every turn. You chose to honor him in the finale."

Ariana flinched like she'd been slapped. "Ellie? Why is he talking to me like this?"

"Mrs. McIntyre, please answer my question. Other than honoring your late husband, was there any other reason why you switched recipes?"

"No!" Ariana's cheeks were pink, and not just from the sun.

"Have you inventoried your supplies for the finale?"

"I've had other things on my mind." She looked away, toward her stateroom's balcony. Her mouth tugged down. When she looked back, her eyes shone with tears. "Will you *please* tell me what this is about?"

"Just one more question, dear," Ellie said. "When you saw that note we found in Teddy's room, the one that said he was sorry, did you believe it to be genuine? Was that his handwriting?"

"I'm not sure what you mean. The note was from me. I'd tucked that note into his packet from the Sugar Network. He was mad at me for being clingy. I needed to apologize... But I knew he didn't want to hear from me."

"Why didn't you tell us that?" Paul asked.

"Why didn't I tell you it was *my fault* that Teddy killed himself? Oh, I don't know. Maybe because it was none of your business. Teddy was moving on. That much was obvious. He didn't love me anymore. But I kept trying to work my way in, didn't I? I kept begging. Apologizing. Trying to get him to take me back. And it didn't make one bit of difference. I figured maybe I'd driven him to it. If I'd just left him alone..." She shot Paul a rueful look. "You never asked me about that note. You just shoved it in my face. I figured... I thought maybe you were just too polite to say it was my fault."

Ellie watched Paul. He was taking it all in, running Ariana's words through that big brain of his. She turned to Ariana. "The blood we found in Teddy's room wasn't his. It was beef blood."

The effect on Ariana was electric. She stood right up. "What? Then you're telling me Teddy could still be okay!" She paced back and forth, pressing her hands together in front of her face. "He could be... Wait." She turned. "Why would someone do that? Do you think *he* could have done it?" Her forehead furrowed. "No. This is ridiculous." She sank back into her chair. "If this is some sort of prank..."

"Or a cover-up for the real crime," Ellie said softly.

Ariana's head snapped up. "*That's* why you're here! You think I hurt Teddy? But that's crazy."

"Ariana, think it through," Ellie said. "You need to consider how this looks. Your husband betrayed you. You brought that blood aboard the ship. And you had easy access to his room through the communicating door."

"Oh. Did I?" Her voice was brittle with pain. "Go ahead. Open that door."

Paul went over to the door that connected the two suites. He unlocked the bolt and tried to open the door. It held fast.

"I was the one who asked for connected suites. Teddy locked his side up as soon as he checked in, and he wouldn't even answer my knocks. But sure, blame me because I had the audacity to experiment with British cuisine. Why not?" She burst into tears and covered her face with her hands.

"We're not accusing you of anything," Paul said. "But we needed to—"

"I think I know an accusation when I hear one," Ariana said, wiping her streaming face with the palms of her hands. "Please don't patronize me. It's time for you two to leave."

"I'm sorry if we made you feel attacked," Ellie said. "We're just—"

Ariana stood. "If you won't go, I will."

She walked right out of the suite and closed the door. Paul watched her go with a bland expression. "Well, so long as we're here, what do you say we do a quick search?"

"Do you believe her?" Ellie asked, her heart heavy in her chest.

Paul looked at Ellie. "Do you?"

Chapter Sixteen

THIRTY MINUTES LATER, THEY CLOSED Ariana's stateroom door and walked out into the hall. "Well, that was awful," Ellie said quietly. "Not only did we terrorize the poor woman, but we also violated her privacy. And there was nothing at all suspicious in her room."

Paul shrugged. "I don't buy what she said about that note. I might not have said 'here is your husband's suicide note' out loud, but I thought the meaning was clear."

"She was in shock," Ellie said. "You can't expect people to have their wits about them when their world turned upside down."

"I suppose not."

"Where do you think she went?"

Greg's stateroom was just a few feet down the hall. Somewhere nearby, a woman's laughter rang out like a friendly haunting.

They reached Greg's door and Ellie knocked. The brass anchor below the peephole gleamed softly in the light from the sconces nearby. "Hang on a minute!" Greg's voice called out. Two minutes later, he still hadn't opened the door.

Paul knocked again. "Sir? We need to speak to you."

Greg opened the door a crack. "Ah. Officer Gumbs. I'm afraid I'll need to speak to you later. I'm on the phone with my attorney, but I expect we'll have plenty to discuss in the morning." He slammed the door shut. The metallic click that followed was the privacy lock flipping into place.

⚓⚓⚓

"DO YOU KNOW WHAT FRUSTRATES me most?" Paul asked, once they were back in his office and sitting knee to knee. Ellie rested her cane against one of the desks and leaned back in the office chair. To Paul's left, a large rack of portable radios rested in their charging station, their orange-tinted displays luminous, their antennae tall like the masts of the sailboats she'd seen in port earlier.

"Uncooperative witnesses?" Ellie stretched her arms overhead and yawned. "I suppose we should have anticipated Greg's reaction. When you ask an average person to help you with a murder investigation, they're excited to help. Unless they're the perpetrator, that is. But of course someone like Greg would lawyer up. Ariana probably went straight to him, and now he's circling the wagons. Now we'll never find out what really happened."

"It's not like you to give up so easily."

"Maybe we should ask the ghost hunters to help us," Ellie mused. "They're so eager to solve a mystery that they're making up bad guys out of whole cloth. Like that whole red phantom business."

Paul rubbed his eyes. "Teddy McIntyre is dead. We would have found him by now if he weren't. But without a body, we can't prove anything. We don't even have time of death."

"Could the blood tell us?"

Paul stared.

"Not literally. I meant—"

"I know what you meant. And maybe. When you walked in, was the blood wet or dry?"

Ellie thought back. Mostly she'd noticed the blaring television, and that broken glass on the table. "The blood on the glass looked fresh enough. But the spots out on the balcony were partially dried out."

He nodded. "That's my memory as well. The handprint was dry around the edges and damp in the middle. It was the same with the larger spots on the ground. How long does blood take to dry? Less time indoors than in the wind outside." He bit his lip. "I need a chart. Maybe I could recreate the conditions if I got my hands on some blood. Assuming the temperature hasn't shifted too much, we could narrow things down."

"You should write a book about cruise ship forensics," Ellie said, smiling.

"With no body, there's nothing I can use to hold these people. You understand? I can fill out a report, and I can deliver it to the authorities back in San Diego, but I don't have enough for an arrest."

"Now who's giving up?" she said, poking him in the leg with one toe. "Let's get to work! You can do your disgusting blood chart thingy, and—"

"Let's call it a forensic analysis."

"Fine. You do your *forensic analysis,* and we'll build out a timeline. We'll try to account for every minute between when Teddy was last seen and when he didn't show up for the shoot the next morning."

"Most of them were asleep. That isn't much of an alibi. And if they won't talk to us..."

"They'll have to. We have an open murder investigation, and you have the right to detain all people of interest until they can be transferred to the correct authorities. Correct?"

"Technically. But I don't think they'll all fit inside the brig, even if Roberta let me detain them, which she won't. There isn't enough evidence."

"Our suspects don't know that, do they? Let me deal with Roberta. We should work through your suspects one at a time. We can do the whole good cop, bad cop thing."

"I suppose you want me to be the bad cop?"

She shook her head. "No. You're not scary enough. I suggest we bring Kameron along. When she glowers at me, she makes me want to pee my pants."

Paul barked a laugh. "If she's the bad cop, and I'm the good cop, what will you be doing?"

"I'll be on the side of the poor misunderstood suspects, of course." Ellie fluttered her eyelashes. "I'm sure there's a very reasonable explanation for what's happened. All they need to do is tell you about it."

"Roberta wants to impress the Sugar Network. Do you really want to risk making them mad?"

Ellie shrugged. "They're already furious. But let's make some tea before we bring them in. I have a feeling it's going to be a long night."

⚓⚓⚓

MINDIE BURTON LOOKED ANNOYED WHEN Kameron brought her to the security office. Mindie's arms were crossed over her waist, and her eyes were hard and flinty. Kameron was dressed in head-to-toe black. She wore her gold Sergeant-at-Arms insignia proudly on her shoulders. A pair of shiny silver handcuffs hung from her belt. Ellie's eyes widened at the sight. Where had she gotten those things? They were huge!

Kameron nodded curtly at Paul. "Ms. Burton, as you requested." She glared at Mindie and indicated with a jerk of her chin that she should go inside. As Mindie stepped through the threshold, Kameron followed, shutting the door behind herself and pressing her back against it. She stared at the back wall of the security office with a bored expression.

"What is this about?" Mindie asked. She was dressed for an evening in. Her stretchy leggings were a soft gray, and her oversized fleece sweatshirt had the outline of the Eiffel Tower on it.

Paul gestured to the empty chair across from him. "Ms. Burton? There's been a security incident and we need to talk. You've met my Sergeant-at-Arms, Officer Achebe. And Ellie asked to come along, as your representative from the cruise line. Please, have a seat."

"Paul, I'm not sure how necessary this is," Ellie said, as Mindie sat down. "If she knew something, I'm sure she would have told us."

Mindie watched them apprehensively. "I got a phone call from Greg. I don't know why you brought me here, but he recommended that I not speak with you this evening. He said you frightened Ariana."

Paul nodded as if he expected that answer. "If you aren't willing to speak to us, we can escort you to the brig where you can wait for your attorney. I'm sorry to be so firm on the matter, but we have a murder investigation on our hands. We can't afford to let a person of interest wander the ship unescorted." He glanced at Kameron.

Kameron, who had been waiting by the door, rested one hand comfortably atop her shiny handcuffs. "Ma'am? If you'll come with me, please."

"Hold on! Just wait a second." Mindie looked at Ellie. "What does he mean, a murder investigation?"

"Mindie. It's terrible!" Ellie leaned forward and spoke low. "Teddy's death was no suicide. In fact, we have reason to believe his suicide was faked. Someone killed him, and they tried to cover it up. I told Paul you had nothing to do with this, but he needs to gather some information before he can clear you."

"Ms. Burton," Paul asked. "Do you have knowledge of any such cover up? Do you know who put the blood in Teddy's room?"

Mindie looked shocked. "You have to be kidding me. Someone offed Teddy?" She blinked twice and muttered a profanity under her breath in her sharp Australian accent. "No. I don't know anything about it." She glanced at the door, and her eyes grazed right past Kameron. "Greg can shove it. I want to help." She blew out her breath. "Ellie, are they *sure*?"

"Unfortunately, yes. The blood we found in his room? It was cow blood. The signs of a struggle were planted. I'm so sorry, hon. I know you two were close."

Mindie looked at Ellie, a question in her eyes.

"You're not a suspect, dear. But you were close to Teddy. We need to know exactly where you've been since you came on board, and what you saw."

She nodded. "Okay."

"We understood you spoke to Teddy after dinner the first night of the cruise. What did you talk about?" Paul took his notebook out of his shirt pocket and flipped it to the last page."

"Teddy asked me about meat pies. He wanted to know how to bake them without the crust getting soggy on the bottom."

"That's what you talked about?" Paul sounded skeptical. "Pie?"

"Yes. He told me he was positive that he was going to win the Golden Cupcake. That he knew it in his bones." She smiled at the memory. "But that was just Teddy being Teddy. I know he rubbed a lot of people the wrong way. But he had a real passion for getting things right. Not everyone can keep up with that sort of energy. It intimidates them."

"But you weren't intimidated," Ellie said.

"I guess not. Have you ever had a friend who makes you see the world in a different way? Maybe they drive you up a wall, but they bring a perspective you lack? Teddy was like that. He was obsessive about reaching his goals. I appreciated that because he brought out my A game. And I told Ariana the truth earlier today. I was *not* sleeping with Teddy. I believe Kitty Gilbert had that honor." She frowned. "I won't lie; I might have been interested if Teddy was single, but I don't sleep with married men. Besides, I like Ariana. She can come across as standoffish. But she's a brilliant baker, and it's not her fault that Teddy was a crappy husband to her."

"But you did have lunch with Teddy behind her back." Ellie said.

"So? We liked to eat lunch together. But Teddy swore that Ariana was blowing him off. I had no idea what was really going on." Her face reddened. "Should I have guessed? Maybe. Teddy was the kind of man who went after what he wanted."

"What happened after you discussed meat pies?" Paul asked.

"We listened to jazz, and we had a few drinks. Then we walked back to our rooms. I stopped at Teddy's door to say goodnight, and he invited me in for a nightcap. I saw what he was driving at, and I said maybe another time. After he went inside, Ariana's door opened. She looked at me like I was the devil, and she said she knew exactly what game I was playing." Mindie frowned. "I told her that she was imagining things. She asked me why I was dating a married man. I followed her inside her room, and we..." She glanced away. "We argued. I tried explaining my side of things. She didn't care. Ariana let me have it with both barrels. She said Teddy wanted a divorce, but she didn't. And I guess she thought she was winning him over? But then she told me about his drinking, and the way he'd been abusing drugs." Mindie sighed. "At the time, I thought maybe she was just trying to ruin my friendship with Teddy. But in truth, I think she needed someone to talk to. You know Ariana by now. She's very controlled. She keeps everything buttoned up. But people like that have a way of letting things come to a head. She blamed me for a lot of her and Teddy's problems."

"What time did you leave Teddy at his stateroom?" Paul asked.

"It was close to eleven."

"When did you leave Ariana's suite?"

"It was late. After midnight? I ran into Harvey in the hallway. He was leaving Greg's suite. We said goodnight, and I went to bed. I didn't sleep well, though." She frowned. "I had nightmares."

"Did you see Teddy after he went into his room?"

"No."

"Not even the next morning?"

"No."

"Did you happen to hear any sounds coming from his stateroom?"

She shook her head. "If he heard Ariana and me arguing, he stayed out of it. I was annoyed about that, to tell you the truth. Ariana was calling me a homewrecker and pouring her guts out about what a mess he was, and he was probably next door, hearing every word. But did he step in to own *his* part of the mess? No."

"It sounds like Ariana was angry," Ellie said.

"Wouldn't you be?" Mindie sighed. "I don't blame her."

"Do you think Ariana would have hurt Teddy?" Paul asked.

"Not in a million years. Why do you think she blamed me for the way he'd been treating her? To Ariana, Teddy could do no wrong."

"And how about the rest of the cast and crew? Did any of them have a problem with Teddy." Paul asked.

"Not that I know of."

"You mentioned that Kitty and Teddy were sleeping together. How do you know that?"

"Kitty told me. I think she was proud of herself for having gotten to him first."

"Did you mention that to Ariana?" Ellie asked.

"No. Maybe I should have told her. At first, I figured it was none of my business. And later..."

"Yes?" Ellie asked.

Mindie looked embarrassed. "I felt sorry for her."

Chapter Seventeen

KITTY GILBERT RESTED ONE ARM high on the door frame and leaned against it. Her red curly hair rolled down her shoulders like ocean foam, and her big blue eyes were bright with curiosity. "I hear you're looking for me, Officer?"

Kameron grunted and nudged Kitty forward with one hand. She slipped past the shorter woman and went over to an empty chair, pushing it toward her. The casters whirred against the hard floor. "Sit down," Kameron said curtly. "Officer Gumbs has a few questions for you." She returned to her spot by the front door and stood, glancing at Kitty over the top of a book she'd picked up off a shelf nearby. It was titled: *The Complete Guide to Knife Fighting*.

Ellie felt a surge of delight. Was Kameron still playing bad cop, or was that jealousy? She hadn't missed the way Kameron's expression had hardened at Kitty's flirtatious posture and babyish voice.

Don't worry, sweetheart, Ellie thought in Kameron's direction. *She can't hold a candle to you.*

Kitty's flirtatious smile fell away, and she sat down in the chair, swiveling it to face Paul. Her eyes went to the security procedure clipboards hanging on the walls above the computer stations. She glanced at Ellie, then back at Paul. "What do you want?"

One point to Officer Achebe.

Paul got right to the point. He told her that Teddy's suicide had been faked.

Kitty's eyebrows shot up. "Shut the front door! I knew it! I told Greg the suicide thing was crap, but he was too busy patting poor Ariana's head to listen to me. What really happened? Do you know who did it?"

"How did you...?" Ellie hesitated over finding the right words. "How did you come to the correct conclusion so quickly?"

"Oh, I know Teddy," Kitty said. "He wasn't depressed, like, at all. And before you ask, no, I didn't kill him. We did have sex once, but that was just a stress reliever, you know? It didn't mean anything."

Paul nodded. "You doubted the suicide story."

"Yes. Because Teddy is a lot like me, and that means he wouldn't do anything like that. Teddy knows what he wants out of life, and he isn't afraid to ruffle some feathers to get it. That's why we were both outcasts on the show. I used to joke that we were on Outcast Island together."

"How were you outcasts?" Ellie asked.

"Oh, none of the other contestants wanted us around. They'd make plans for the post-shoot dinners, and they didn't even ask me to bring anything! Look, I know what the other contestants say about me. They think I can't bake. And they're jealous of how much attention I get. That's why they grouch and moan about how my aunt got me this job."

"Did she?"

Kitty smirked. "Totally! Well, she got me an audition. But after that, everything was one hundred percent *me*. Maybe I'm not the world's best baker. Fine. But neither are the rest of them. If you were really good at baking, you wouldn't be trying to get famous for being on television. You'd be working on your baking business. That's only common sense." She grinned. "Now, me, I'm *incredibly good* at being on television. I'm developing my own talk show. And not just a show. I'll have recipes, fragrances, and a fashion magazine. I'll be Oprah, basically, but younger and way cuter. My aunt says being famous is all about having a consistent brand identity."

"Will your show be on The Sugar Network?" Ellie asked.

Kitty laughed. "No way! Cable TV is dead-dead-dead. This show is just a steppingstone to raise my profile. But everyone else acts like the baking competition is life and death." She rolled her eyes. "I mean, we bake cookies. We're not solving the moon. Ugh!"

Paul compressed his mouth like he was trying to seal it shut. "Indeed," he said in a strangled voice.

Ellie's eyes watered with suppressed laughter. Solving the moon? Who was this woman and where had they found her? She'd seemed like such a pill on set, but the more she talked, the more her charisma shone through. Kitty Gilbert was beautiful and kind of hilarious. But was it all an act?

Paul cleared his throat. "Perhaps you can tell us if Teddy had any enemies."

"No. He wasn't important enough to have enemies."

"Was he fighting with anyone?"

"His wife, I assume. She was depressed that he was divorcing her."

"And how did he feel about that?"

She shrugged. "He didn't love her. That's a tough break, but sometimes you need to accept things and move on. Like this one time, when I thought I was going to get a contract with Maybelline, but they said my eyes were too far apart for print. I can change a lot about myself, but I can't change the space between my eyes. Not without surgery that might mess up other parts of my face, anyway. So, I moved on. That's what you need to do. Move on, already!"

"When did you last see Teddy?" Paul asked.

"At dinner the first night. He was eying me up and down like he was up for round two, if you know what I mean, but I wasn't feeling it. I listened to the ghost stories for a while, but they were kind of dumb. So I went to bed."

Paul nodded. "Can you tell us your movements after dinner and the next morning?"

Kitty clapped her hands. "This is just like a police show on television! Yes, I'll tell you everything. First, I said goodnight to Raquel and Vick. It's important to maintain good relations with those who will be judging you. Personality matters just as much as talent and hard work, that's what Aunt Nora says. Then, I went to the Spa to ask them if I could get a free facial because we're like promoting the cruise line or whatever. But they were closed, so I went upstairs to look at the water because the water is pretty at night. But there were all these people telling ghost stories, and..."

Paul shot Ellie a weary look. Was Kitty going to give them a detailed blow-by-blow of every thought that had fluttered through her brain? It seemed like it. Ellie shrugged. At least the woman was thorough?

By the time the interview wrapped, Paul was out of coffee and the moon outside was high in the sky.

⚓⚓⚓

KITTY WAVED AT THEM WITH her fingers as she left. "I'm glad I could be of assistance. Any chance I can get a selfie with Officer Gumbs? I'm not allowed to post on social media until after the show airs, but I bet my followers would *love* to hear about this later on." She looked down at her blue dress. "Besides, this color will really pop next to your white uniform."

Kameron cleared her throat. "Come along, Miss Gilbert. I'll escort you back to your stateroom." She shot Paul a questioning look. "I was wondering, should we go have a conversation with Mr. Norris and follow up on what we've heard? I could pick him up next."

Paul glanced at Ellie. "Well, we were going to talk to Greg last, but..."

Kameron's eyes narrowed slightly. "That's fine. Although if you two don't need me, perhaps I'll clock out? I had dinner plans that I canceled to be here tonight."

Paul looked at Ellie. "Um. I suppose we could—"

"Good!" Kameron said brightly. She rested one hand on the doorknob. "Unless you *need* my help."

Paul swallowed. "No. We can take it from here. Have a nice evening."

Before Kameron shut the door, Kitty could be heard asking, "Are those real handcuffs? Do you know how to get out of them? Because one time, I—"

The door shut with a click, and Paul turned to Ellie. "What do you think?"

"I think we hurt Kameron's feelings. You shouldn't have sent her away."

He looked startled. "I didn't send her anywhere! Leaving was her idea. Besides, what I meant was, what did you think about Kitty Gilbert? Do you think she told us the truth?"

"I suppose so. She's one of those people who lets every thought that flits through their brains come stampeding right out their mouths. I suppose it's possible that she's a criminal mastermind, but if so, she didn't try to hide her relationship with Teddy. If you could call a one-night stand a relationship."

Paul nodded.

"Kameron was jealous when you gawked at Kitty."

Paul scoffed. "I did no such 'ting! I don't gawk. Where was I supposed to look when she walked in? At the floor? I was making eye contact."

Ellie framed her eyes with her hands. "Sure. But the eyes are up here, sweetie."

Paul's phone rang. He picked up the receiver and listened. "Yes, sir. We'll be there in a few minutes. Thank you." He looked at Ellie. "That was Greg Norris. It sounds like he's ready to talk."

⚓ ⚓ ⚓

HARVEY WAS SITTING ON GREG'S couch when they arrived at the suite. There was a soccer game on the television, and a room service tray rested on the coffee table, well picked over. "Please come in," Greg said amicably. "Can I offer you something to drink?"

Greg Norris had changed his tune. But why? Harvey patted the seat next to himself. "Ellie, sit with me. Would you like some dessert? Tonight, we're sampling the cherry pie, lemon meringue, and three types of biscuits. But don't worry; I'm pacing myself. I try four different desserts per night, so I don't ruin my girlish figure." He chuckled at his own joke. "Officer Gumbs, feel free to have a bite. Sit down. I have a feeling you had a busy day while we were off gallivanting at port."

"Did you find a gift for your wife?" Ellie asked Harvey. Greg was in the kitchenette pouring sparkling water into glass tumblers, his back to them.

Harvey beamed. "I did at that! We found a talented jeweler with a small shop not too far from the marina. I bought Sam a beautiful set of bracelets. Ariana helped me pick out something nice. That poor child; it was good to take her mind off things for a little bit."

Greg came over and set the glasses on the coffee table. He sat down in the upholstered chair across the table from Harvey. He turned to Paul. "I understand you've spoken to Ariana, Mindie, and Kitty so far," he said pleasantly. "And I expect you'll be wanting to interview us as well."

"I got the impression you weren't too keen to speak with us," Paul said.

Harvey cleared his throat. "On that front, Greg has something he'd like to say."

Greg looked uncomfortable. "Indeed. I owe you an apology. Ariana came to see me, and she was in tears. She said you accused her of murdering her husband."

"That's not what happened," Ellie said.

"I know. Once I calmed her down, we went through everything and she told me what you found. The blood planted in Teddy's room. My God! Of course, you'd have questions. I talked to the legal team for The Sugar

Network. It's all agreed. We're to cooperate. Fully." He shot Ellie a rueful look. "I'm sorry that I jumped the gun. It's just that Ari was..."

"She was a mess," Harvey said. "She's been through more than any person should need to cope with. Anyway, I suggested we wait here and talk to you together, so you don't have to run from room to room. If you like, we can call Raquel and Vick and ask them to come by. We haven't told them what happened yet."

"I sent Ariana back to her room," Greg added. "And we've canceled the rest of the season. I was a fool to assume we could continue under these circumstances. When it looked like Teddy had killed himself, it was bad enough, but..." He shook his head. "If someone did kill him, we owe it to Ariana to get to the bottom of this."

If Paul was surprised at Greg's change in attitude, he didn't show it. He just said, "At this point, we need to establish where everyone was, and when."

Harvey nodded. "Right-O. Well, we all had dinner in that posh dining room the first night of the cruise. Devon served us four courses, and I was stuffed to the gills. I said goodnight and came back to my room to check for messages."

"What time was that?" Paul asked.

"Seven thirty? I could check my email and tell you for sure. Samantha emails me a letter every day, and I send her one back. After that, I decided I wanted a beer. So, I went for a walk and I ended up on the big deck with the pool. That's where I ran into you," he looked at Ellie. "And your friend, the singer."

"What time was that?" Paul asked.

"Perhaps around eight? Eight fifteen isn't out of the question."

Paul looked at Ellie. "That sounds about right," she said.

"I stayed up there for a good while. The night was warm, and I wasn't sleepy. Greg came by later, and I talked him into a game of gin rummy. Oh! We had a beer at the sports bar first. We came here to relax, and I went back to my room sometime after midnight."

"And did you run into anyone on your way back to your room?" Ellie asked.

"Oh. Now that you mention it. Yes, I saw Mindie out in the hallway. She looked upset, and I asked her if she was okay. She said she was tired, and she was going to bed." He frowned to himself. "I doubt it matters, but there was one other thing. I heard someone running in the halls. Much later. After I'd gone to bed."

"Do you know who it was?"

Harvey shook his head. "I woke up when I heard thumping. I thought someone had knocked on a door nearby, then I realized I was hearing footsteps. Someone running back and forth. I got up to ask them to keep it down, and when I looked outside, I saw someone turn the corner down to the left. A skinny bloke in a red jogging suit. Strange time of night to be running, but I suppose it takes all kinds to make the world go round. Anyway, that's when I went to sleep."

"And the next morning?"

"I was up at seven, eating breakfast in my room at seven-thirty, and in my chair upstairs by eight-thirty. Linda runs a tight ship, doesn't she?" Harvey glanced at Greg.

"That she does."

"And what about your night, Greg?" Ellie asked.

"Like I told you before, I had dinner with the group. Teddy wanted to talk to me about his chances at winning the Golden Cupcake, but like I'd told him a dozen times before, it's really up to the judges."

"You told us earlier that Teddy didn't have a chance. That it would probably go to Mindie or Ariana," Ellie said.

"Oh. That's how you play it!" Harvey teased. "And here I thought I had the competition in the bag."

Greg's shoulders slumped. "The show is over. What does it matter now? I told Teddy it was up to the judges because I didn't want to talk to him. I was tired, and I wasn't in the mood to deal with him."

"And you said Teddy was speaking to Mindie when you left the dining room?" Paul asked.

Greg nodded. "Raquel and Vick invited me to go to the comedy show with them, but I told them I was going to walk around the promenade deck and get some air." He glanced at Ellie. "Ariana and I took a walk, and I dropped her off at her stateroom around eight. I wasn't tired, so I wandered around the ship, met Harvey, had a beer at the sports bar, and he and I played cards in here for a while. He left, and I went to bed."

Ellie glanced at Paul. Greg hadn't changed his story since the first time they'd questioned him.

"And the next morning?" Paul asked.

"I had breakfast in my room. Then I was on the phone with Nora for a good ninety minutes. She had ideas for the new season, and she didn't want to wait until I got back to Los Angeles. You're welcome to check with her secretary; I can get you that number."

Paul nodded.

"Then I went upstairs to check in on the shoot. Linda, God love her, had started things without me. And that's when I noticed Teddy wasn't there. Ellie went to look for him, and, well, you know the rest."

Harvey picked up his fork and used the side of it to cut a bite of lemon meringue pie. After he swallowed, he said, "Now, here's what I don't get. Ariana said the blood you found was from a cow?"

Ellie nodded. "Beef blood."

Harvey frowned. "That sounds like a waste of good sausage to me. Why would a person do something like that?"

"We don't know," Paul said. "But given that someone worked so hard to make us believe Terry went overboard in his room, I have to assume he did not."

"Could he have hidden himself away? Or escaped by dinghy?" Greg's voice was tinged with hope.

"None of our lifeboats are missing," Paul said. "And our search was extremely thorough. But the nature of the crime scene seems clear to me. Our perpetrator wanted to blame Teddy's death on Teddy, so we wouldn't look elsewhere. To me, that suggests he was killed somewhere else and dumped overboard."

"Did Teddy have any enemies?" Ellie asked Harvey.

"Teddy wasn't that popular among the cast and crew. We're all very fond of his wife, and he could appear... heartless at times. But there was no reason to hurt the man." He sighed and looked down at the fork in his hands. "I wish we could help you. I truly do."

"Ariana mentioned that her husband had been abusing drugs and alcohol. Were you aware of this?"

"The Sugar Network performs routine drug testing of *all* cast and crew," Greg said defensively.

"He may have been abusing a drug he was prescribed, mixing it with alcohol."

"Ah. Well, I can't say I knew about that," Greg replied. "I had seen Teddy intoxicated a time or two, but none of us are teetotalers. So long as he fulfilled the terms of his contract, and he did, it wasn't my business."

Harvey nodded. "I've seen him in his cups a time or two, usually after filming had ended for the day. Never at work."

"One more question," Paul said. "The night after Teddy disappeared, the Secrets of the Dead convention hosted a séance in the Moonlight Lounge. Chryss Tiano channeled Teddy. He claimed that Ariana was in danger. And he said that Teddy had been denied something he wanted. What do you think about that?"

"It's disgusting," Greg replied. "He obviously heard about what happened to Teddy, and he's trying to capitalize on it for his own fame."

"That's what I suspected," Ellie replied. "The medium also said something about being hungry all the time. Chryss said, "He's always so hungry.""

Harvey put his fork on the table. "What an odd thing to say!"

"You don't believe he was really talking to Teddy, do you?" Greg asked.

Ellie shook her head. "No. I don't. But we were concerned about what he said about Ariana."

"Did he say her name?" Greg asked.

"Yes. He asked where she was."

They all looked at one another. But what was there to say? Chryss Tiano's statement was inexplicable.

Greg exhaled forcefully. "Well, is there anything else?"

Paul leaned forward. "Harvey mentioned someone in a red jogging suit in the hall that night. Did you see or hear anyone outside your room that night, Mr. Norris?"

"No. But when I fall asleep, I'm dead to the world. You could knock on my door with a battering ram and I wouldn't hear you."

Harvey looked troubled. "I don't like what that medium said about Ariana. Do you think she'd agree to bunk with Mindie for the rest of the cruise? I'd feel better if she weren't by herself."

Greg frowned. "That might be a hard sell." He looked at Ellie. "Maybe you could suggest it?"

"I don't think she's very happy with the two of us," Ellie said, glancing at Paul. "But I'll bring it up if I get the chance. You two should do the same."

Chapter Eighteen

WYNONA SHOVED A CUP OF coffee under Ellie's nose. "Drink that," she said. "I know you don't like coffee, but if you keep yawning, *I'll* start yawning, and then I'll feel tired all morning."

Ellie looked at the white mug dubiously. Despite her late night with Paul, she hadn't wanted to miss breakfast with Wynona. One day a month, they met in the crew mess for what was colloquially known as Waffle Madness. The kitchen crew always came through with three unique varieties, and waffles were Wynona's favorite food. Ellie pointed at the waffle on Wynona's plate. It was piled high with what looked like green soft-serve ice cream. "And what's that one?"

She sipped her coffee. With the heavy cream and sugar that Wynona had put in it, it was almost drinkable. And her friend was right, the caffeine might do her good.

"This is a mochi fusion waffle," Wynona said, cutting herself a bite. Thin, hot pink hoop earrings as big around as dessert plates hung from her ears and disappeared into her masses of curling brown hair. She gestured at Ellie's strawberry waffle with her fork. "I don't know why you bother with Waffle Madness if you stick with the normal flavors." She chewed her mochi waffle experimentally and made a face like she'd just bitten something sour. "Well, maybe I *understand*, but like my momma used to say, variety is the spice of life." She lifted the rest of the green topping off her waffle and set it on the side of her red plastic tray.

"Oh, this is amazing!" a woman cried out from a nearby table. Her fork was loaded up with green foam. "It reminds me of the summer I taught English in Japan." Her two companions, young women in housekeeping uniforms, were taking bites of their own waffles. They'd chosen the safer chocolate-dipped option. They exchanged a look that seemed to say their friend was nutty. The murmur of conversation in the busy dining hall was punctuated with the clink of silverware on plates, and occasional bursts of laughter. The overnight shift had ended, and the late-night crews were having breakfast for dinner.

Ellie pointed to the dark black dot Wynona had put above her lip, probably with the tip of her mascara wand. "Are you trying out a new look?"

Wynona nodded. "I've been giving some thought to our next production, and I'm *feeling* the eighties lately. I want something sultry. A musical like *Flashdance*, maybe. The Pirates of Peking is a crowd pleaser, so I'm in no hurry, but I think my dancers will be ready for a palate cleanser. Fewer wigs and corsets. More Spandex and hip thrusts." She raised her skinny arms up and pumped her hips once, making the table shake and her bosom jump.

"That sounds fun. But I didn't invite you to breakfast to talk about work. I want to hear about you and Victor." She speared a piece of fruit with her fork and let it hang in the air. "I hear you two are an item?"

Wynona blushed! "Gosh, Ellie. Let me tell you, dating Victor was *not* on my radar. I mean, the first time I met him, he berated me for not wearing my name tag. And the second time, he wanted to complain about one of my dancers. She'd spilled something on her sheets, and she didn't put a note in with the laundry. As far as I was concerned, Victor Vasquez was a stuffed shirt wearing a stuffed shirt from a planet full of stuffed shirt people."

"I have no idea what you mean. I've always found Victor to be the very spirit of laid back."

"Shut your face," Wynona said cheerfully. "Anyway, one minute we were talking about staffing levels, and the next minute he suggests we go out for a walk because the night was fine. So I thought: sure, I've been cooped up all day, why not? And we were walking, and talking, and he offered me his jacket. He was *so smooth*. I wasn't even cold, but I said yes because he was so sweet about it. I've been having hot flashes – damned menopause – and I probably left my lady sweat all over his coat. But he was so sweet! He asked me about how I got into acting, and the theater, and he actually listened. Not like most men, who just ask because they know they're supposed to." She smiled.

"Anyway, we finished our walk, and he asked if I'd like to have dinner with him. And I said yes!" She cut into her waffle with a butter knife. "Dinner was wonderful. He's an excellent conversationalist."

"You like him."

"I do. But it's early. So don't you go smothering us with your matchmaker vibes. I know exactly what I'm doing."

Ellie sipped her coffee. "Oh, is that why you haven't returned his calls?"

"Can't a lady play hard to get?"

"I suppose she can. But do you really want to hurt his feelings? He's so sensitive."

Wynona winced. "How much trouble am I in?"

Ellie smiled. "It's nothing that you can't fix. But I spun him a tale about you never checking your voicemail, so I bought you some time. Assuming you're still interested."

"I am." Wynona's mouth quirked up on one side.

"Well, he's not a player, hon. Don't treat him like one. Treat him like... a coconut. He's hard on the outside, soft and squishy on the inside. You've already cracked that shell, so there's nothing left in your way."

"It's mostly his hard parts that I'm interested in."

Ellie laughed out loud. "You two are the strangest pair!" She stabbed her fork in the air. "You best treat him right. He's a good friend of mine."

"Oh, I'll treat him well." She batted her fake eyelashes. "Don't you worry."

"Speaking of matchmaking, I wanted to ask you something else. Do you know if Kameron is seeing anyone? She mentioned she had dinner plans last night, but she was vague."

"That girl doesn't know what she wants."

"What do you mean?"

"She was at our crew meeting two weeks ago giving us our security briefing. And we got to talking afterward. Kameron told me she wants a big family, like she had growing up in Lagos. And I asked her: what in the heck is she still doing on a cruise ship? We have no facilities for crew members with children, and even if we did, this is no life for a young'un. The long hours, and the stress, and being surrounded by strangers all the time. And where are the men?"

"We have plenty of men on board."

"Sure. We have men who chose a life at sea. Do you think they'll give up their careers because their significant other wants to have a family?"

"It probably happens all the time," Ellie said. But as she spoke, she realized she'd never actually heard of it happening. Most of the crew members with families experienced long months of separation. They worked hard, and they sent money home to their children and spouses. Trips home lasted weeks, and they only happened once or twice per year. Heck, Violet's last relationship had fallen apart because of the time apart.

"Well, I'm just saying, Kameron's a catch. And she'll make a wonderful mother. If her kids misbehave, she'll just karate chop them into submission. But those eggs of hers won't keep forever. If she wants to be a mama, she should leave this ship and go somewhere where she can find a husband."

"Do you have kids?"

Wynona laughed. "Lord no! I had a goldfish once, and it died because I forgot to feed it. So I got another one. It also died. I took that as a sign. But not all women are like me." She pointed at her pelvis. "Tick-tock, Ellie. That's what I told her. Tick-tock goes the fertility clock. She'd best get knocked up soon."

"Well, she still has plenty of time. But you never answered my question. Is she dating someone?"

"I have no idea. But if she is, it's because of *my* good advice." She sipped her coffee with a smug expression. "You're not the only one making magic happen. Love is in the air. And I'm going to sing it from every perch and deck on this ship!" Wynona frowned. "Speaking of which, I'll go find Victor once we're done here. Just in case he's gotten any foolish ideas about me not being interested."

Ellie smiled. "Before I forget, I have something for you."

"What's that?"

"Well, when Ben and I started dating, it was hard to find privacy. We didn't want to be stuck in our rooms the whole time, and—"

"But that's the best part."

Ellie smiled. "Anyway, we talked to Devon, and he said he didn't mind if we used the captain's dining room when it wasn't booked for official events."

"Ben's the captain. Can't he use his dining room whenever he wants?"

"Technically, the captain's dining room is under the purview of the executive chef. They just call it that to make it sound fancy."

"And how does one get this magnificent privilege?"

"Devon says if you two promise to leave the place pristine when you leave, you're welcome to have dates in there. Just check the calendar first. And when you two are ready, let me know and Ben and I would like to have dinner together. A double date."

"Oh. You've been talking about us, have you?"

Ellie shrugged. "It's hard being the captain. His friends aboard are also his employees. But maybe when we double date, we can let the titles drop? I think Ben would like that."

"Victor could use some loosening up," Wynona said with a conspiratorial smile. "This will be good for him. I'm in!" She ate another bite of waffle. "So, tell me about the baking competition. Is it true that it's been canceled? Roberta called to ask if we can put on the Pirates of Peking the last night of the sailing. I would have loved to, but I gave half my performers the week off. We'll come up with something, I suppose."

"Let's talk to Violet. She's got a cupcake karaoke show ready to go. I'm sure she'd love to hold it in the big theater." Ellie sighed. "And yes, I hear the show is canceled. Because of the contestant who passed away. It's all very sad."

"It's always heartbreaking when someone ends their own life. I was supervising bingo the other day – dreadfully dull, by the way – and a few of those ghost hunter people told me the dead man was pushed overboard by the red phantom. Apparently, he's a mean ghost." She compressed her lips. "I sprinkle salt across the threshold of my room now, just in case."

"Why? Are ghosts afraid of seasonings?"

"You joke, but there are things in this world beyond our understanding," Wynona's curls bounced as she nodded her head. "The day Victor asked me out on that walk, my horoscope said that Venus, the Goddess of love, was smiling on me. And the week I applied for this job; can you guess what my horoscope said?"

"Something vague about new opportunities?" Ellie teased. "Something that might apply to just about anyone?"

"I love you, but you're like Scully on the X-Files. Always pooping in the punch bowl. But let me just say, if there is an evil spirit on board this ship, it's best not to be alone in the dark. Better safe than sorry, am I right?"

Ellie finished her coffee in three big gulps. "On that part, we agree."

Chapter Nineteen

ROBERTA DRUMMED HER FINGERS ON her dining room table as she listened to Paul describe what they'd learned the night before. Sunlight streamed over her forearms. She looked from Ellie to Paul to Violet, and she cleared her throat. "So, Greg isn't going to interfere with the investigation? Good. I was willing to fight him if I needed to, but I'm glad he came around. The Sugar Network might circle the wagons to cover up a mere scandal, but I'll guarantee you that they want no part of a murder investigation." She glanced at Paul. "What else did you learn?"

Violet covered her massive yawn with a freshly manicured hand. She'd painted her nails a bright red, and she ran her fingers through her shiny black hair like a comb and blinked sleepily.

"I'm sorry, are we boring you?" Roberta's tone was grouchy.

Violet raised an eyebrow. "No. I was up until two a.m. watching that silly séance while you were asleep in your comfy bed." She glanced at Ellie. "Those séances get later and later every night. And in case you're curious, the ghost of Teddy didn't make an appearance. But there was an especially tender moment when Chryss Tiano comforted one of his fanboys by claiming that his long-dead father approved of his decision to open an Etsy shop specializing in rare *Pokémon* dolls."

"That's a very specific kind of comfort," Paul said, smiling a little. He turned to Roberta. "In addition to interviewing all the Sugar Network guests, I checked the security logs for their staterooms to see if their stories matched up. And they do. "Teddy entered his room shortly before eleven that night. That lines up with what Mindie told us. And that was the only keycard entry in the system. We don't track every time a door is opened, only keycard entries. Perhaps Teddy let someone in, they drank together, and then Teddy went over the balcony. Then his killer planted the mess to make sure we believed it was a suicide."

"Ariana could have gone into his room," Ellie said. "Through the connecting door."

Paul shook his head. "I doubt it. First, we saw that Teddy had locked his side of the communicating door. But even if she'd been clever, and she'd locked that door from Teddy's side before exiting, how did she get back into her room without triggering another key card log? Our system shows one entry into Ariana's room. It happened when she returned to her suite after dinner."

"Maybe she used a doorstop," Violet said. "Then she could have round-tripped it without triggering our system."

Roberta barked a harsh peal of laughter. "Remind me never to cross you, Violet. You're too clever by half. But consider this: whoever left that blood in Teddy's room was hardly a criminal mastermind. A suicide note *and* a bunch of blood? It was overkill."

"Ariana says it wasn't a suicide note," Ellie reminded her. "She says we misunderstood."

"Very convenient." Roberta's hooded eyes narrowed even further. "I say the wife did it. She's got a tidy answer for everything. And the beef blood was hers. Most tellingly, the moment her husband bites it, she insists on baking *his* recipe? She's either a saint with extremely bad luck, or she knew that her beef blood was no longer available." She crossed her arms. "Besides. I've seen Masterpiece Theater. It's always the wife. Or the butler."

In the kitchen, out of sight, Stuart made a faint noise of disapproval. The oven door opened and closed with a slam. Roberta's mouth quirked up on one side.

"Ariana is a suspect, for sure," Paul said. "But where's the motive? Jealousy? Would she have tossed her husband overboard for having lunches with Mindie? That seems like an extreme reaction."

Ellie shrugged. "People have killed for worse reasons. And her husband did sleep with Kitty Gilbert. Maybe it was a crime of passion. But if so, when did she do it? Ariana was with Greg after dinner. And then she had that fight with Mindie. No one entered Teddy's room after that unless he let them in through the front door. And then, why didn't we see logs of the killer going back into their own room?"

"Maybe Mindie lied," Violet said.

"But Mindie and Teddy were friends," Ellie retorted. "When she was filming her tribute, she was having a hard time holding herself together. Mindie admired Teddy. So why would she give Ariana an alibi? That makes no sense."

"Ariana could have killed Teddy the next morning," Roberta said. "Maybe he let her in, and she killed him, and then she returned to her room."

"But the communicating door was locked from Teddy's side," Paul reminded her. "And there was no keycard entry back into Ariana's room. Or Teddy's for that matter. Even if he let her inside, there was no way she could have locked the communicating door from *his* side without leaving his room and re-entering hers. And there's no entry log. Do you suppose Ariana crawled from balcony to balcony like Spiderman?" He rubbed his forehead. "We're talking in circles."

"Maybe someone else killed Teddy," Violet said. "Was there a financial angle? I get that the guy was annoying, but you don't kill someone for being irritating. If you did, there would be dead people all over this ship and I'd be in handcuffs."

Ellie snorted, inadvertently inhaling hot tea into her nose. It burned! She sniffed, her eyes watering. She set her teacup down. "Paul, is there a money angle we haven't found? Was the Sugar Network upset with Teddy?"

"Not that I've been able to find. But I do have an update on the timing of the cover up. Early this morning, I was able to obtain a packet of beef blood from a butcher in Puerto Vallarta. By applying the blood to several surfaces and using a stopwatch—"

Violet's nostrils flared. "Gross!"

"Based on the viscosity and drying time of the blood —"

Roberta glared at him. "Skip to the good part."

Paul huffed out his breath. "Whoever put that blood in Teddy's room did it about an hour before Ellie went inside."

Ellie's heart did a double beat. "But the cast and crew were upstairs by then! Everyone except for Greg Norris."

"I believe a male hand made the handprints on the balcony," Paul said. "Based upon that, and the timing, Mr. Norris does seem like the most likely perpetrator."

"So why aren't you interrogating him?" Roberta asked.

"I spoke to his boss's secretary. She says Mr. Norris was on a call for two hours that morning. She gave me the names of two other people on that call and invited me to verify with them. Our telephone records also confirm that phone call. And again, Teddy's room wasn't unlocked from the outside. So how did Greg get inside? Also, by all accounts, Greg will be in trouble with the network for not completing this season of television. Teddy's death doesn't benefit him. It hurts him."

"You're saying we've got nothing," Roberta said, flatly. "Nothing except an expensive suite with ruined carpet, a missing contestant who chased women like a tomcat on the hunt, and a batch of stolen blood smeared around the room at a time when no one could have possibly been inside except for the dead man."

"The killer was like a phantom," Violet said, rubbing her arms despite the warmth of the room. "I talked to a few people at the séance last night. They told me the red phantom murdered people inside a locked room. Three people, during the summer of 1994."

Ellie turned to Paul. "Did you ever hear back from the kitchen about the decanter we found in Teddy's room?"

"They have decanters, but they use them for special occasions, and even then, only in the private dining rooms. There's no record of a decanter being delivered to *The Suites*."

"Could someone have taken it from the captain's dining room at dinner?" Roberta asked.

"That's a good question. I'll check. There's also the matter of what Harvey told us last night. He heard banging in the hallway the night before Teddy disappeared, and when he looked outside, he saw someone in a red jogging suit running down the hall."

Roberta held up a hand. "But you said the blood was placed just an hour before Ellie went into the room. Not the night before."

Paul nodded. "Yes, but that only gives us the time of the cover up. Whatever happened to Teddy, it could have occurred any time between eleven at night and nine in the morning. Given that Ariana and Mindie were having a shouting match in Ariana's suite, and Teddy didn't reply to them, I suspect that he was killed in the evening, shortly after returning to his room. Either that or Mindie lied about dropping him back off in his room."

Violet tapped her finger on the shiny wooden table. Behind her, the panoramic windows showcased the back of another cruise ship. Now that they were in port, Roberta's million-dollar view was decidedly industrial. "Have you heard any other reports of a jogger in red?"

Paul pulled out his notepad and jotted something down. "My department has received a few calls about noise in the middle of the night, but we've yet to find the culprit, or culprits. I didn't think it was all that important, but we'll redouble our efforts. I assume they're pranksters, but maybe one of them saw something? It's a long shot, but it's what I've got." He looked around the table. "I'm open to other avenues. What am I missing?"

"I wish I knew," Ellie said. Maybe whoever did this will make a mistake. In the meantime, I suggest we keep our eyes peeled."

Violet crossed her arms. "Until we figure it out, I'm taking a page from Wynona's playbook. I'll be putting salt across my threshold tonight, and I suggest that you all do the same.

Ellie glanced skyward. "As for me, I'll be using pepper. That way when our perp sneezes, I'll catch them. Because *ghosts aren't real.*" She looked at Paul. "A human being did this. And you're going to figure out who. We just need to be persistent."

Violet chuckled. "No pressure, Paul. Do you want me to keep surveilling—" She caught Roberta's eye. "Ahem, *liasoning* with Secrets of the Dead?"

Roberta shrugged. "Do what Paul wants. I don't see how we could possibly make things worse at this point."

"Thanks for the vote of confidence." Violet winked at her.

"While we're on the topic of events," Ellie said. "We have a big hole in our Friday night schedule. The final showdown has been canceled, and Wynona doesn't have enough performers to pull off *The Pirates of Peking*. How would you feel about putting on Cupcake Karaoke in the big theater?"

Violet sat straight up at that suggestion! She looked at Roberta like she expected her to argue. "Well, we *do* have a ship full of baking enthusiasts who were promised a show. And it would be such a disappointment if we didn't give them one." She looked imploringly at Roberta. "Don't you think?"

"Stop fawning at me." Roberta scowled. "It's not like I had a vendetta against karaoke. I swear, you act like I'm here to vex you, but I'm trying to run a business here. Occasionally, you need to share your toys." To Ellie she said, "It's a good idea. Make it happen."

Violet grinned. "I have so many songs! *Pour Some Sugar on Me,* obviously. *Strawberry Fields Forever* by the Beatles." She ticked items off on her fingers. "*Tutti Frutti.* I love some Little Richard! Oh, and didn't ABBA have a food song?"

"*Honey Honey,*" Stuart called from the kitchen.

"Yes!" Violet nodded. "That's the one."

Paul stood and pushed his chair back beneath the table. He rested his hands on the engraved wooden cross bar. "I should get back to it." He shot Ellie an inquiring look, and she knew he was inviting her to come along.

Ellie thought back to Kameron's face from the night before. She'd looked so hurt and frustrated when Paul had batted her suggestions away. *I wish I could go with you*, she said silently. *But it would be a mistake. I might not have understood, before. But I do now.*

Ellie stayed seated. "I'll help Violet get the theater ready for Cupcake Karaoke. And we need to write up a notice for *Cruise News You Can Use*. There isn't much time before tomorrow's edition goes to the printer."

"I don't need your h—" Violet's eyes widened as Ellie's toe lightly kicked her on the shin beneath the table. "I don't need help writing the notice. But I *definitely* need your help getting the theater ready. There's just so much to do!" She nodded emphatically, looking at Paul.

He looked confused, so Ellie quickly broke in, "Good hunting, Paul. I'll check in with you as soon as I can break free."

After he was gone, Violet turned her head on the swivel to stare at Ellie. "And what was *that* about?"

She looked in the direction Paul had gone. "There's something I need to fix. Two things, actually. Wish me luck." She stood and picked up her cane. "Because I'm going to need it."

"What about Cupcake Karaoke?" Violet asked.

Ellie smiled at her. "You're on! Make your plans and we'll touch base later today."

Chapter Twenty

ELLIE FOUND CORA WISE WORKING in the Moonlight Lounge. In her left hand, Cora held a tiny bottle made of brown glass. In her right hand, she carried a small cotton cloth. Ellie walked down the central aisle and paused, resting her hand on the side of the booth Cora was standing at. Cora wiped the table with circular motions of her arm.

"Good morning," Ellie said. "Would you like me to have the cleaning crew take care of that for you?" The lounge was empty, and the stage lights were off. Ellie's voice echoed faintly in the distant corners of the room.

Cora looked up and smiled. "Thank you, but no. I'm using essential oil of rosemary. It's a very weak formulation, but it creates a welcoming atmosphere for the spirits. Also, it smells nice, and Chryss likes it." She held out the bottle and Ellie sniffed.

"That's lovely. It reminds me of baking Thanksgiving dinner. My daughter-in-law likes rosemary in her stuffing." She smiled. "I don't care for it, but occasionally I manage to remember that not everything is about me. I wanted to apologize for how I treated you during our last meeting. I was so upset about what happened that I came out swinging."

"Oh, it's water under the bridge. Chryss and I would never intentionally cause anyone distress, but that particular channeling was very poorly timed. The fact that it was an accident didn't make it any less hurtful. And we haven't had any other incidents."

"I hope you won't let my bad manners reflect on the cruise line."

She smiled. "It's behind us now. Oh, and I wanted to tell you, we'd love to come back next year if you'll have us. Our attendees are having a fabulous time on board the ship. And our revenues are twice as high as what we can get at a convention center. I'd call that a win-win."

"How is Chryss holding up? He told me that being at sea gives him bad dreams."

Her eyebrows shot up. "You two spoke? He's doing okay. We've added a bit of valerian to his evening tea, and he's been sleeping like a lamb. Still, he'll rest easier once we're back home. He's at port today, on one of your packaged tours. Maybe if things continue to go well between us, you'd allow us to add ghost tours to your itineraries?"

Cora was very forward! Then again, a woman needed to be forward sometimes, to get what she wanted. "Let's discuss it next year, assuming all goes well."

"Of course," Cora said. "I wanted to ask you for a favor. We're thinking about canceling tonight's séance. Chryss is dog tired, and he could use the night off. We were wondering if you and Violet could help us fill in the blank spot on our schedule. I'd considered trying to put together another event, but I'm short on time. What do people usually do on cruise ships when they aren't hunting ghosts. I thought about doing ghost themed bingo, but I actually don't know how to play."

Violet, dear, when it rains it pours. Ellie put her hand on Cora's shoulder and pointed at the stage. "Let me tell you about our most popular show. It's called Karaoke Crush, and it's always a crowd pleaser."

"Karaoke?" Cora sounded skeptical.

"Let's do ghost-themed Karaoke," Ellie replied. "We'll fit it perfectly in with your convention. Bingo is okay, but there are winners and losers. With karaoke, everyone wins."

"Do you think people will participate?"

"With Violet running the show, they won't be able to help themselves. How about this: We'll get Wynona, our theater manager, and see if her dancers can put on a little show. Maybe they could do the *Thriller* dance? And then we'll have a dance lesson to loosen everyone up. And afterward, karaoke. Depending on your budget, maybe we could wrangle some prizes?"

Cora bobbed her head up and down. "That sounds like so much fun! And best of all, poor Chryss can bow out. He's been so exhausted lately. I wish I knew why."

"I saw how worried you looked when he fell down on stage. Is he doing okay? We could get him an appointment with Doctor Strunk for a checkup."

"I'm sure it's nothing some rest won't fix," she said. "Let me get my clipboard. We'll plan out the entire evening, and brainstorm some prizes, and then we need to get the word out. Do you have a way of doing that?"

Ellie smiled at Cora's eagerness to get down to business. "How's this for an idea? You should take a few hours and enjoy yourself at port. Or go get a massage at the spa. Call it customer research if you like. Meet me here at five and we'll go over the plan for the evening. Shall we say a nine o'clock showtime?"

"Are you sure?"

"Absolutely. This is what we do best. Cruises are supposed to be about having fun. And when you work hard, you need to make some time for yourself. I bet Chryss isn't the only one who could use some down time."

"You're an angel! I take back everything I ever said about you," Cora blurted. Her face turned crimson. "Oh, I didn't mean—"

Ellie laughed out loud. "Oh, sweetie, maybe I had it coming. Don't worry about it. But there is something I wanted to ask you."

"Sure."

"We have a bit of a mystery on board, and I thought perhaps you could help us solve it? We've been getting complaints about ghost noises in the hall. People banging on walls. And reports of figures in red running through the hallways."

"I see," Cora said cautiously.

It's like I thought. She knows! But I can't spook her.

Ellie smiled. "Normally, it would be no big deal. We assumed some of your guests were having a spot of fun with one another. And like I said, isn't that the whole point of a cruise?" She lowered her voice and leaned closer. "But between you and me, there's been a terrible crime on board. That young man who we thought killed himself? He didn't. He may have been murdered."

"Oh God! That's horrible."

Ellie nodded. "One of the people in red was seen in the area where it happened. Now, we have no reason to believe that this mystery person was involved. They were probably just a bystander. But we do need to talk to them, to ask if they overheard anything. Now, our security team can go on a tear, hunting those folks down, but I had a feeling that you might be able to help." She met Cora's gaze evenly. *Come on, little fishy. I did you a favor. Now do me one.*

Cora didn't reply at first. Her silence seemed telling. But at last, she nodded. "You're right about that. Now, I hope you won't be mad, but I asked a few volunteers to spice things up for our attendees."

"I'm not mad," Ellie said, crossing her fingers behind her back. "You're just trying to keep things fun. I completely understand."

Cora looked relieved. "Exactly! At our ghost stories event, I went around and took some notes. The red phantom's story was especially popular. Everyone was talking about it. And after Chryss channeled Teddy..." She winced. "Well, you know all about that. Anyway, I asked a few of our volunteers to create some phantom sightings. I gave them red tablecloths to wear, and a hundred bucks cash, and I asked them to make some noise." She held up a finger. "I insisted that they stick to the areas where we'd booked staterooms! I wouldn't want to inconvenience your other guests."

Ellie nodded. "I thought it might be something like that. Can you introduce me to those volunteers?"

"Let me give you their names and room numbers. I had two volunteers on red phantom patrol, and one volunteer representing the lost spirit of Carina McGee, a bone eater." She went over to a table and opened her purse, pulling out a sheet of paper. "If you have any trouble reaching them, let me know. And please, don't yell at them. It was my idea, not theirs."

Ellie's ears felt hot. "Believe it or not, I'm not usually the yelling type."

"Okay."

"Cora, if you don't mind my asking, I'm terribly curious. Do you believe in what Chryss Tiano is doing? I mean, if you're sending people out dressed as ghosts..."

Cora quickly wrote three names and numbers on the sheet of paper. "It's a fair question. Between you and me, yes, I do believe. I've seen too much not to! Chryss is a medium, and by some miracle he's also an all-around decent guy to work for. But Fantastical Events LLC isn't just one man and his gifts. We're an entertainment company. Chryss does his part, and I do mine." Cora handed over the piece of paper, folded in half. She leaned against one of the booths, letting her arms hang loosely at her sides. "When I was a little girl, my Aunt Dot read tea leaves. But what made her special wasn't the fortunes. She helped the people who came to her. She listened to their problems, and she told them what to watch for, and she gave them loving advice. There was a lot of heart in those readings of hers. And I wanted to be just like her when I grew up."

"Is she still around?"

"She is! She retired to a small island in the Greek isles. She said I should go to business school, and so I did. I may not be like my Aunt Dot, but I can help people like she did. That's why I chose to work with Chryss. The man's got all the talent in the world and no idea how to turn it into a proper business. That's where I come in."

Ellie peeked at the names and tucked the sheet of paper into her pocket. "Thanks for this. I know Officer Gumbs will appreciate it. Not to mention, Violet was so disappointed that her karaoke show was canceled. She'll be thrilled to bring her talents to Secrets of the Dead."

Cora's forehead creased. "Please tell me we don't need to put those curtains up just for one show. We can, but I'd need to—"

"Cora."

"Yes?"

"You're off the clock! Go enjoy your day. I'll check in with you later."

She looked pleased. "A day off, eh? Well. I've never been to Mexico."

"Me either. You can tell me all about it when you get back."

Cora packed up her purse and headed out the door, pausing to wave on her way out. Ellie looked around the empty lounge. She headed toward the crew staircase, gripping her cane to take the pressure off her hip, settling into the rhythm of her walk, already thinking about her next destination.

Chapter Twenty-One

ELLIE WAITED OUTSIDE THE CREW gym, out of sight of the tall glass panels next to the door. If Kameron saw her waiting while class was in session, she might invite her in to throw some punches.

"Kyaaah!" a dozen voices shouted in unison. Faint thuds followed, the sound of elbows or fists hitting focus mitts with measured intensity. Kameron Achebe taught a mixed martial arts class six times a week. Fifteen minutes later, Ellie smiled at the crew members walking out the door, some of them rubbing their sore shoulders, others bright-eyed with the exhilaration of a good workout. "Don't forget to hydrate!" Kameron's voice called out.

Ellie went into the gymnasium. The room was a large windowless rectangle with low ceilings. Half of the space held cardio equipment and free weights. The other half was open, the floor covered in thick blue mats. The wall next to the matted area was a big mirror. Kameron wiped her neck with a hand towel and tossed it in the bin for dirty laundry. Her karate uniform looked crisp and bright white against her deep brown skin. Her black belt was tied in a square knot in front of her waist, and her long hair was in a braid to keep it away from her face. "Hey, do you have a minute?" Ellie asked.

"For you? Of course." Kameron eyed Ellie's cane. "How is your mobility?"

"Aside from my bum hip I'm as fit as a fiddle."

"Will you help me wipe down the mats?" Kameron asked, her tone measured, as if she were assessing something.

"Hand me one of those spray bottles and I'll take the right side of the room."

"You should be in my class. Given how often you get yourself into trouble, it might benefit you to know how to throw a grown man across the room." She sprayed a section of blue sports mat with bleach solution and bent at the waist to wipe it with a clean towel.

"You're probably right," Ellie said. "Has Paul caught you up on the McIntyre case?" She sprayed a section of the floor, and after setting her cane against the mirrored wall she carefully got down on hands and knees to wipe down the floor.

"No."

"We've hit a wall," Ellie said. "But I was hoping you could help." She reached into her pocket and straightened up, stretching her back as she moved from her hands and knees to a kneeling position. "Here. These are the names of the volunteers Cora Wise paid to run around the ship pretending to be ghosts. One of these folks may have been in *The Suites* shortly after Teddy McIntyre was last seen alive. Can you track them down and find out what they know?"

"Why me?" Kameron took the paper and opened it. "I thought you and Paul were handling this one."

Ellie sat back on the ground. She rested the towel in her lap and stretched one arm overhead. Arthritic hip aside, her back muscles had screamed in protest when she'd gotten down on the floor. "Paul has that "I'm the head of Security" energy. And he's so danged tall! He's intimidating, even when he tries not to be." She shot Kameron a wry look. "Also, it recently occurred to me that I don't need to be doing double duty as a junior security officer when we've got you on board, the woman who actually knows how to do these things." Kameron looked skeptical, so she added, "Besides, I just told Cora that Violet and I would put together a ghost karaoke and dance party for her. For *tonight*. I'm busy."

She got back on her hands and knees and shuffled forward. The spray arced out from the bottle. She wiped down the next section of the mat with big strokes of her arm. "Feel free to assign it to someone else if you're too busy."

She didn't dare look at Kameron. What she'd said was true. Every word! But she wasn't saying the one thing that might make Kameron bristle up like an angry porcupine. Kameron and Paul had been avoiding each other, and she'd been playing right into their hands. So long as she, part-owner of the cruise line, was butting her nose into

Paul's investigations, he had an excuse to freeze Kameron out. Those two had been dancing around one another for too long, and a bit of togetherness might bring the matter to a head, one way or another.

"I'll take care of it." Kameron said.

"Thank you." Ellie said. She finished wiping the next section of the mats, and she stood up carefully, wincing as her right leg straightened out. She hobbled over to the wall and grabbed her cane. "I should go check in with Violet. Be sure to tell Paul what you find out."

"Hold up." Kameron's voice was a command. Her brown eyes were serious, and she was regarding Ellie like she was a problem to be solved. Ellie's gut tightened. Kameron had seen right through her!

"Your hamstrings are tight. That's just making your problem with your hip worse. Come over here. I want to show you some stretches."

"Don't you think you should find those witnesses first?"

Kameron's mouth quirked up in one corner. "No. I think you should demonstrate these three stretches first. Show me that you can do them properly and without injury. And *then* I will go interview your witnesses."

"But I'm not wearing workout clothes."

"Ellie, those pants have plenty of stretch in them. Come!"

Great. Now she's using her karate instructor voice on me. Ellie went over to obey. "Someday, you'll make a very good mother," she said as she planted her feet on the two spots Kameron pointed at. "You're a very difficult woman to say no to."

Kameron chuckled. "So long as I'm Sergeant-at-Arms, I expect all of our crew to be in top condition. After we complete your stretches, I will give you the updated workout schedule. I want you to take two classes per week, minimum. And bring Violet." She placed one hand on Ellie's hip joint, touching lightly. "Bend from here. Go slow. Stop when it hurts."

"Ow!" Ellie protested almost as soon she as tipped forward.

Kameron touched a spot on the back of Ellie's leg. "See? Your muscles here are tight from too much sitting. We need to stretch that *ow* right out of you."

Ellie straightened up, breathing harder. "Why do I feel like I'm being punished?"

"I have no idea." Kameron's mouth quirked up on one side. "Why do I feel like you're trying to force Paul and me into the same room? But don't worry. I'm sure we're *both* imagining things."

Ellie's face burned. She did the stretch again, dipping her head toward the floor, feeling the stretch in her legs. "I think I'm getting the hang of this one."

"Give me ten more. And then we'll do the harder ones."

Chapter Twenty-Two

ELLIE RESTED HER ARMS ON the outer rail of the lido deck and watched the shore recede into the distance. The sun was sinking below the western horizon behind her, and the lights of Puerto Vallarta brightened into pinpricks of light as the sky turned a deeper blue. Ellie closed her eyes and felt the sea air brush past her face and skim along her arms. Tomorrow they'd arrive at Mazatlán, the last stop before returning north to San Diego. She hadn't stepped off the *Spirit* once since she'd come aboard. So much for the Mexican Riviera! And despite everyone's efforts, they were no closer to figuring out what had happened to Teddy McIntyre.

According to Paul, Kameron had questioned Cora's volunteer ghosts at length. None of them would admit to being in *The Suites* the first night of the cruise. They swore that they'd only haunted the areas that Cora had specified.

Well, one of the men *had* admitted to streaking through the atrium, pants-less, at three in the morning. Manny's spectral sangrias were too potent, perhaps. Kameron had extracted a promise that he'd keep his clothes on in public areas, moving forward.

For his part, Paul had spent over an hour with Raquel and Vick, the baking competition judges. And at first, Vick had refused to be interviewed. He'd insisted that his contract required him to be at the filming, and that was it. Greg had intervened, and Paul got his interview. The judges had heard nothing useful, although Raquel confirmed that Teddy had knocked over his fellow contestant's food earlier in the season. She'd asked to have Teddy booted, but Greg had declined. It would be bad for business, he'd said.

Ellie glanced at her watch and sighed. Violet and Wynona would start setting up the Moonlight Lounge soon. Cora had returned to the ship hours ago, happily laden with bags from shops in port. *Everyone went to Mexico but me*, Ellie thought. She held out a hand toward the shore as if she could grasp it and pull it close again. *Maybe next week won't be so busy. Besides, you told Roberta you'd take care of the VIPs. You might as well do your job.*

Even if one of them might be a murderer.

"Ellie Tappet?" A familiar voice grabbed at her from behind. She turned and saw the two dark-haired ladies she'd met at the séance. The Triumph sisters looked tanned and happy, and they wore matching sundresses in a multicolored dot print. Rebecca's dress still had the price tag attached. It dangled off the neckline like a pendant made of paper.

"Rebecca and Josephine! How nice to see you." She took a closer look their new garments. "Oh my! Are those skulls?"

Rebecca pulled her skirt out with two hands, holding the fabric flat for Ellie's scrutiny. "Aren't they pretty? You think they're just polka dots, and then when you get close – POW – they're spooky!" She came up alongside Ellie and leaned on the rail. "It's a beautiful night. So why are you standing out here by yourself feeling sad?"

"I'm not sad. I'm just getting some air."

"You don't need to pretend with us. We aren't going to judge you."

"Becky, mind your own business." Josephine went to Ellie's other side and leaned against the rail. She tipped her head back to let the wind toss her hair. "Just because you're an empath it doesn't give you the right to go rummaging around in her emotions. For Brigit's sake! Remember what Priestess Carla said."

"Sorry," Becky said meekly, shooting Ellie a guilty look.

"Did you enjoy Puerto Vallarta?" Ellie asked, dodging the subject of Priestess Carla for the moment. The Triumph sisters were a peculiar pair. She liked them, but they had an odd way of speaking. And an unsettling way of looking right through a person like they knew all their secrets. Even when you had none!

"Yes," Josephine said. "It was a fun town. Touristy, but that's to be expected. We went to the botanical gardens, and they had hundreds of cacti. I love cacti! They know how to take care of themselves. They aren't needy. My mother grew orchids, and I swear, those things had no will to live. I prefer a hardy plant. One that isn't constantly trying to off itself when you turn your back."

"Mama did have a black thumb," Rebecca agreed. "Daddy said that when she walked into the plant aisle at the hardware store the plants would point at one another and scream, 'No! Don't take me! Take her instead!'"

"Your father sounds like quite the character," Ellie said.

Rebecca smiled. "He was. I hope we find him, someday."

"He's missing?"

Rebecca nodded solemnly. "Oh, for years now! But it's fine. He and Mama said they'd be back once they were done traveling. And Daddy doesn't do cell phones. He says they impede the root chakra and give you erectile dysfunction."

Ellie opened her mouth and shut it again. What was she supposed to say to *that*? Thankfully, Rebecca kept on going.

"The woman that Chryss Tiano mentioned, is she okay? I've been so worried, ever since he did that channeling. That was *scary*."

Relieved to be back in familiar territory, Ellie said, "It's nice of you to ask. She's doing okay. She's still reeling at the loss of her husband, of course. They've canceled the baking competition, and we've had to move a few things around. But I'm bringing all the bakers to ghost karaoke tonight. They've had a hard week, and I figured they could use some cheering up. You two should come too. There's going to be dancing and singing tonight."

"Okay," Rebecca said, her voice quiet.

"You sound disappointed."

"It's just that we're four days into a ghost cruise, and I haven't seen a single ghost! I know they can't *force* ghosts to attend. But still, I was hoping for something more than stories."

Josephine had been watching her sister prattle with the indulgent expression of someone watching a child tell a story. She turned to Ellie, her forehead furrowed. "Do you know why they canceled the séance for this evening?"

"Chryss Tiano needed a night off."

"I can't say I'm surprised. That man is *not* well."

"Why do you say that?" Ellie asked.

"Did you see his aura, Jo?" Becky asked.

Josephine inclined her head. "I did. And it was muddy, that's all."

"What does that mean?" Ellie asked.

Josephine's mouth quirked up on one side. "You believe in auras now? This must have been quite the week."

"Well, I may not believe in auras, but there are things I do believe in. Intuition, for example. A person's ability to read body language and tone, and to make informed guesses. You call it what you like."

Josephine studied Ellie's face for a moment. Then she nodded. "Chryss Tiano is sick."

"Sick how?"

"I don't know. All I know is that there's something getting in his way. It's like... when a person is ill, and they can't think clearly? Have you ever tried to solve a problem, but the whole thing feels foggy, like no matter which way you turn, you'll end up lost? That's what's happening to Chryss right now. If we were friends, I'd ask him about it. But it's impolite to rummage around in someone else's emotional sock drawer. Right, sis?"

Becky stuck her tongue out at Josephine, and Josephine cackled like it was the funniest thing she'd ever seen.

⚓⚓⚓

ELLIE SIPPED HER CLUB SODA and looked across the table at Ariana. She looked small and pale, and the big pink frozen daiquiri Greg had ordered her sat untouched on the table. Condensation ran down the side of the glass. Greg was looking at her with his forehead furrowed, but he turned his attention to his drink when she looked in his direction. Harvey was reading the bar menu with interest, running his finger down the text. "Do they serve pub grub in here? I'm feeling peckish."

"Didn't you already eat dinner?" Mindie shot him a disapproving look.

"Yes."

"It's your funeral," Mindie said, flinching as soon as the words came out of her mouth. "Sorry. I didn't mean—"

He patted her forearm. "It's fine, darlin. I know it's just an expression. And I'll be back on the rabbit food as soon as my feet hit the tarmac in Manchester. Think of this cruise as my dietary stag party. My final nights of freedom before I'm back to peas and carrots."

"What's a stag party?" Ellie asked.

"A bachelor party," Ariana said, smiling faintly. She turned to Harvey. "Your wife loves you. That's why she feeds you so well."

"Sam's determined to keep my ticker pumping," Harvey said. "But she boils every vegetable until it screams. And she keeps feeding me rocket. Says it will keep me alive longer. I appreciate it. I do! But is that a life worth living?" He chuckled and flipped to the next page on the menu.

"Remind me to get an American English to British English dictionary," Ellie said to Kitty in a stage whisper. "I have no idea what he's talking about. Eating rockets? That sounds painful."

Kitty looked up from her phone, her expression blank. "I'd pretend to care, but honestly I don't."

Greg winced, "What Kitty meant to say was—"

"Don't do that," Kitty said flatly, putting her phone away. "You might not like what I said, but those are my words, and I meant them." She turned to Ellie. "Did I offend you? If so, I apologize. My honesty sometimes gets me into trouble." Kitty tossed her long hair over her shoulders. "It's a flaw. But sometimes our biggest strengths are also our biggest weaknesses. That's what my Aunt Nora says." She fixed Greg with an icy glare.

"Don't worry about it," Ellie said, looking around the table. "I hope you all enjoy the show tonight." She spotted a familiar face headed their way. "Chryss Tiano's event coordinator was so excited to meet Greg that she reserved this table for you all. Here she is, now."

Cora was dressed up in a slim black suit with a blood-red shirt beneath. Her heavy green eyeshadow gleamed softly like the scales of a serpent. She paused in front of the table, smiling. "I hope you're all enjoying your evening. Chryss and I are so glad you could attend."

"Greg, may I introduce you to Cora Wise from Fantastical Events? She's Chryss Tiano's manager, and she's running the Secrets of the Dead convention. Cora, meet Greg Norris, executive producer at The Sugar Network."

"It's such an honor to meet you," Cora gushed. "I've been following your work ever since The Haunted House Diaries, and what you've done with the Sweetie Pie Baking Competition is phenomenal. The volcano episode? Genius."

"Thank you." Greg sounded pleased. "I look forward to seeing your show. I've never been to a paranormal convention before."

Cora nodded. "Tonight will be fun. But you should see Chryss Tiano in action before you go. He's our superstar." She plucked a silver business card out of her pocket and handed it to him. "If you'd like to meet Chryss, let me know. I'll set you up." The stage lights flickered, and she looked up at the pewter-colored curtains. "It's showtime! Enjoy."

Ellie glanced at Greg. "What was that about Haunted Houses?"

Greg winced. "That was my first job as a producer, nearly twenty years ago. We locked teenagers inside haunted houses with some cameras and other equipment. This was around the time of the Blair Witch craze. The show was terrible. But my boss was great, and it was a good learning experience."

"Did you ever see a ghost?" Ellie asked.

"Not a one. But I did see a nineteen-year-old guy pee his pants on camera. That was our highest rated episode, believe it or not. There's reality TV, and then there's *reality TV.* Thankfully, I've moved past the ghost circuit. But hey, we all start at the bottom, right?"

Poor Cora, Ellie thought. It was good she wasn't around to hear that! No doubt she was excited about the possibility of getting Chryss on television. But Greg didn't sound interested, at all.

The curtains opened, and Violet and Wynona came out on stage. They were wearing long white dresses and oversized chandelier earrings, like victims from an old vampire movie. Ellie laughed as the crowd cheered. Where had they gotten those outfits? They looked ready for prom.

Violet introduced Wynona, and Wynona stepped forward into the spotlight. "For the last several nights, you've waited for the spirits to come to you! But even a ghost can appreciate a good party. So I say: Let's dance! Let's sing! And by the end of the night, the spirits won't be able to keep away!" She snapped her fingers. Purple light illuminated the small stage. Six dancers in head to toe black came out, and Michael Jackson's *Thriller* came over the speakers. The dancers jerked and swayed to the music. They moved like zombies. They moved their hips to the music. And they ended with their heads tipped down, one hand on their black hats, just like the king of pop himself! Ellie cheered along with the crowd.

"Now," Wynona said. "We're going to teach you the dance. Come on up! I have room for some of you on the stage, and the rest can stand in the aisles. I want at least two dancers per table. Move those tushes!"

Kitty slid out of the booth and ran up the center aisle. She faced the audience and posed, hands on hips, smiling wide like a first grader in a school play. Greg looked at Ellie. "Don't even ask! I've already been to the gym today."

"Come on," Harvey gently pushed Mindie's arm. "We may as well humiliate ourselves properly."

Mindie slid out of the booth, and she let Harvey out. As soon as she headed back to sit, he looped his arm through hers and spun her around, *do-si-do*. She shook her head and took her position next to him.

Wynona called out the moves like a cheer coach, and before long, the music started up. "Okay! Let's do this for real," she called out. She pointed at Violet, and Violet sang!

"Is she going to sing Michael Jackson?" Ariana asked. "That's a difficult song."

"Violet can do anything," Ellie said, clapping her hands along with the beat. She nudged Greg with her elbow. "It's okay to relax! This is what cruising is all about. Food and music and good friends."

Violet was in her element! She twirled and sang. The dancers all around the room jerked from side to side with their zombielike movements. Mindie was a natural, and Harvey looked like a chicken with two broken wings, but his smile was bright. Violet's arms went from one side to the other in time with the music. She froze in place, staring at the back of the room, and her voice faltered for a moment. Wynona's smile faded, and she stood on tiptoes to see over the crowd, shading her eyes from the spotlight.

Hundreds of steps thundered forward up the aisle. A woman screamed! The dancers in the aisles rushed forward and to the sides, clearing the center of the lounge.

Ellie's heartbeat doubled. Whoever was scaring people was walking forward, toward the stage. It was a man wearing pale blue pajamas, his dark hair messy as if he'd just climbed out of bed.

It was Chryss Tiano.

Ellie slid out of the booth and pushed her way toward the center aisle, weaving around the dancers who seemed frozen. Someone moved the spotlight back toward the commotion. Chryss's cheeks were smeared with blood. The terrible red liquid had dripped down his chin and stained the front of his pajama shirt. He held his blood-tinged fingers in front of him, as if trying to grab the frightened dancers fleeing toward the front of the room. "Cora?" he called, his voice full of bewilderment. "I killed him. Oh, God! I killed him!" He touched his face, then held his hands palm up, looking down at them. He showed his hands to a woman backed up against a nearby booth. "This is Teddy's blood," he said. "He went over the balcony in his room. I saw it! I was there. And..."

"Don't touch me!" The woman scrambled to the side and ducked down a side aisle.

"I'm sorry," Chryss said to her. "I am so so sorry." He staggered back two steps before his knees buckled. His head hit the floor with a sickening crack.

The room fell silent.

Ellie keyed her radio. "Medical emergency in the Moonlight Lounge. Bring the doctor." She stepped closer to the center aisle, and as she reached it, she saw Cora pushing her way through the crowd. She looked ready to start a fight with anyone who got in her way.

Cora dropped to her knees beside Chryss and grabbed his shoulders. She shook him, hard. "Chryss! You need to wake up! Now!"

Ellie gently pulled her back. "The doctor will be here any minute," she said gently. "Let's not move him."

Cora turned around, and for a moment it looked like she might swing a punch! But her angry expression crumpled, and all that was left was anguish. Ellie knelt and folded Cora into her arms.

Chryss stared up at the ceiling, not blinking. Only the slight movement of his chest showed that he was alive.

Up on stage, Violet and Wynona were speaking in comforting tones. Ellie wasn't listening. She kept one arm around Cora, whose body shook with sobs. She watched Chryss and waited until the back doors banged open.

Chapter Twenty-Three

CORA PACED BACK-AND-FORTH WITH LONG strides of her short legs. The medical office was closed up tight. White light filtered through the drawn blinds, leaving lines on the floor. Two crewmen had carried Chryss Tiano inside on an orange plastic backboard, and they'd left twenty minutes ago. Ellie had caught a glimpse of Tobias's assistant, Trina, resting her hand on Chryss's shoulder as the door closed, her blond hair shining beneath the bright overhead light. Chryss's face had looked even more ghastly inside the exam room. It was smeared with blood from cheek to chin as if he'd rubbed it all over himself.

"I should be in there," Cora said, eyeing the closed door like she was about to make a break for it.

Ellie stood with most of her weight on her good leg. "The doctor will be out soon," she said. "They've been in there for a while, and I haven't heard him get on the phone. That's a good sign. Chryss must be stable enough to stay on board until we get to port. Otherwise, he would have called for a helicopter." Oh, how she wanted to ask Cora about what Chryss had said! But poor Cora looked traumatized, so she stuck to easier topics. "Has Chryss ever collapsed like that before?"

"No."

"Why did you ask him to wake up?" The question slipped out before she had a chance to catch it. That was the problem with questions. They brought their friends along.

"What?"

"When you ran up to him, you told him to wake up. But his eyes were open, and he was staring at the ceiling."

"Chryss has night terrors." Cora tried to look through the medical office window. She crouched down, peering upward through the closed blinds. She made an irritated noise and came over to the opposite side of the hallway to stand next to Ellie. "He must have been sleepwalking."

"I thought night terrors mostly affected young children." Ellie thought back to Chryss Tiano's cartoons and sugar cereal. Perhaps the man was a child at heart? Not that it explained what he'd confessed to.

Strunk stepped out into the hall and shut the door behind himself. He ran a hand through his black hair, and Ellie saw that he was wearing house slippers on his feet. He must have been in his stateroom when the call had come in. "Mr. Tiano is okay," Tobias said. "He has a laceration on the back of his scalp, which I've stitched up, and some bruising. The blood on his face and hands came from a cut on his chin. It looks like he nicked a capillary while shaving. That wound didn't need stitches, just disinfectant and a bandage."

"So he *was* having a night terror." Cora's shoulders sagged. "Poor Chryss! He's been having bad dreams all week, but I kept pushing him to perform. I should have known better."

Tobias shot Ellie a look that she couldn't interpret. He wanted to say more, but he wouldn't do so with Cora standing there.

"Can I see him?" Cora asked.

"He's asleep. I'm keeping him under close observation tonight. In the morning, we'll have him escorted to his stateroom.

"I'll stay with him tonight," Cora said firmly. "I don't want him waking up alone in the dark, not knowing where he is."

"I'm afraid that won't be possible. I've asked Officer Gumbs to assign a security officer to this room. For everyone's safety. Trina and I will take turns observing him until morning. I don't believe his head wound is serious, but if his vitals deteriorate, I'll have him flown to a hospital."

"Why do you need a security guard? I already explained what happened. It's not like Chryss actually hurt that man. He wouldn't hurt anyone!"

The doctor held up his hands to stave her off. "You may be right. My only concern is Chryss Tiano's health. But he made certain statements while in my custody, and for that reason, there will be a security guard nearby at all times. I will *not* leave our crew alone with someone who just confessed to a murder. I'm sure you can understand why."

Cora turned to Ellie, pleading with her eyes. "He'll feel better if I'm in there with him."

Ellie looked at Tobias. His expression was firm. She turned to Cora. "Come on. I'll take you to your room. And first thing in the morning, we'll come check on Chryss. You don't need to worry. He's safe."

They headed toward the elevator. Ellie looked back, but Strunk had already gone back inside.

⚓⚓⚓

ELLIE'S PHONE RANG AT SIX a.m. sharp. She yawned and stretched before answering. Paul's tone was all business. "Strunk is moving Chryss Tiano to his suite. I'm headed there to question him. Will you meet me there in thirty minutes?"

"I can. But are you sure you wouldn't rather have Kameron there?"

"Not this time. Oh, and bring Cora Wise with you."

Ellie collected Cora from her room (thankfully, she was already awake), and they walked over to Chryss's suite together. Paul opened the door on their first knock.

"Ellie. Ms. Wise. Please, come in and have a seat." Paul stood back while they entered the room. Chryss was sitting in a lotus position on the floor, his bare feet turned upward, a heavy blanket wrapped around his shoulders. His hair was damp, and there was a small bandage on his chin. Dark circles sank into the skin beneath his eyes. He didn't smile as his gaze flicked toward the new arrivals.

Cora rushed to his side and spoke in a low voice. "We should get you a lawyer. These people are making terrible accusations. They don't understand that you were dreaming. You've had bad dreams all week. And—"

"Ms. Wise," Paul gestured at the couch. "I invited you here as a courtesy. Please, have a seat."

"But—"

Chryss squeezed his eyes shut as if his head still pained him. "Cora, please. Listen to him. I can't abide any more violence. No violent words. No violent thoughts. Center yourself." He inhaled deeply. He held his breath. Then he exhaled slowly. Afterward, he looked at Paul and nodded. "You have questions?"

"Sir. I understand that last night you admitted to killing Teddy McIntyre in front of a crowd of people. Is that true?"

"Yes."

"But he didn't," Cora said.

"You don't need to protect me, Cor." He shot her a small, sad, smile. "You can't. I'm solely responsible for what happens when I'm channeling a spirit. And I will not lie. Neither should you."

"What happened last night?" Paul asked.

"I was preparing for my evening meditation. I showered, and I shaved, and I changed into my pajamas. While I was completing the light body exercise, I felt something hot and wet. I opened my eyes, and there was blood on my hands. I was covered in it. That's when I remembered everything." He took a shaky breath. "I was in an unfamiliar room. It was as if the world was tilted, somehow. I felt angrier than I've ever felt before. Rage consumed me like a firestorm. I saw a man standing across from me, holding up his hands. He said something, but I couldn't hear him. I laughed!" Chryss squeezed his eyes shut. "He ran outside. We struggled. I pushed him, and he fell. He fell so slowly! I saw his blue eyes. His soul looked into my soul. We both knew then that he would die. His face became my father's face. Teddy's work would remain unfinished. He knew it had all been for nothing. He disappeared beneath the waves, and I held up my hands. They were still covered in blood." He shuddered. "I remembered what I had done, and so I went to find Cora."

"Why Cora?' Ellie asked.

"I needed to confess," Chryss said. "I remember people yelling. They were disgusted by what I'd done." He touched the back of his head gingerly. "And I must have passed out. That's the last thing I remember."

"Mr. Tiano. When did you kill Teddy McIntyre?" Paul's voice was soft.

"I don't know."

"Why did you kill him?"

"I didn't want to. I didn't know him."

Tears squeezed out of the sides of his eyes.

Cora blurted, "Chryss, it was just *a vision*. You had a bad dream is all."

He shook his head. "No. It was real." He looked at Paul and frowned. "Given what I did, and the way I suppressed the memory of it, there's only one conclusion: I was possessed that night. A vengeful spirit entered my body, and it used me to murder that man."

"Sir," Paul's expression was dark.

"This isn't some crackpot legal defense, Officer Gumbs. It's merely what happened. I should have left this ship the moment I came aboard. I had a bad feeling in my bones. This vessel is cursed. Now, a man is dead by my hands, and I'll need to accept responsibility for that." He frowned to himself, then looked at Cora. "Perhaps I'm laboring under a karmic debt? There must be a reason why I was chosen."

"Mr. Tiano. Do you take any medications? Prescribed drugs? Recreational substances?"

"I never take drugs. Well, herbs. Rosemary for clarity. Ginkgo biloba for power. Sometimes, valerian to help me sleep. "

"Is it a pill? A powder?"

"A tisane." He took in Paul's confused expression and smiled. "It's like an herbal tea."

"And where do you get that tea?"

Chryss's forehead furrowed. "I get it over the internet from an herbalist friend in Los Angeles."

"You order it personally? And you handle the tea yourself?"

"No. Cora orders my supplies. Why?"

Cora shot Paul a fierce look. "You're so determined to solve your case that you're willing to pin the crime on anyone. Obviously, one of the dead man's friends killed him. We didn't even know him!"

Chryss unfolded his legs.

"Sir," Paul said quietly. "When the doctor examined you last night, his assessment was that you were under the influence of a powerful hallucinogen."

"But I don't take drugs. Ever." Chryss was adamant.

Paul took out his small notebook. "Pupils dilated. Patient describes vivid hallucinations. Do you remember what you said last night?"

"No. I remember pushing a man over the side of the ship and waking up this morning on an exam table."

"Our doctor's assessment, to skip the medical jargon, is that you were having a bad trip. After apologizing profusely for pushing Teddy McIntyre overboard, you claimed that the doctor's stethoscope was a cobra." Paul flipped to a second page in his notebook. "You told his assistant Trina that she was the most beautiful woman you'd ever seen. And then you muttered something about a koala? From that point, it was all gibberish."

Chryss Tiano seemed to be remembering something. "I do remember a blond woman. She had a halo of light around her head. Like an angel."

"That was the light above the exam table," Ellie said. "Chryss, did you drink your tisane last night?"

"I did. I was having a hard time sleeping, so I made a big cup of the valerian mixture."

Cora's cheeks were dark red. She was looking at Chryss, and her mouth formed a thin line. "You were having a night terror. There's no reason to assume you hurt *anyone*. Why would you ruin your life over one little mistake?"

"And what mistake was that?" Ellie asked.

Cora glared at her.

Paul put his notebook away. "Mr. Tiano?"

He nodded. "I need to apologize to the man's wife. She needs to know it wasn't anyone's fault but mine."

Cora was crying now. "You drank the wrong tea. You drank it, and you had a vision. It is not your fault." She wiped her eyes with her shirt sleeve.

"You've been helping Chryss have his visions." Paul's voice held a hint of frost.

She looked down at her hands. "Chryss has always used tea to prepare for his séances. And the last few events bombed. I thought maybe he needed a new formulation. Something to help him better access the spirit realm. It was a tiny, tiny change. And it helped! His Las Vegas show was incredible."

"You drugged me," Chryss's voice held a note of wonder. "I trusted you. And you lied to me?"

"You already use herbs, Chryss. You just needed a boost. That's all. Didn't we agree that you wanted to go deeper into your practice? I told you to use the blue tin. *Not* the red one. Don't you remember? I color coded them for you, and we went over it twice. I reorganized your whole system..." She dropped her gaze and whispered, "I'm sorry."

"You drugged me, and I *hurt* someone." Chryss's blue eyes brimmed with tears. "Don't you realize what you've done? You've taken on a karmic debt that will take *life-times* to repay!" He wiped his eyes and turned away. "And if you truly believed in me, like you said you did, you wouldn't have had to resort to dark magic." He shot her an anguished look. "You're fired."

Cora flinched. "Officer Gumbs, I screwed up. But you need to let Chryss off the hook. This was my mistake, not his."

"Do you have anything else to add to Mr. Tiano's statement before I take him into custody?"

"He didn't do it!"

"Can you verify Mr. Tiano's whereabouts between eleven p.m. Sunday and nine a.m. Monday morning?"

"No. He was asleep. So was I. So were most people! Are you going to question everyone aboard this ship?"

"Ms. Wise. Are you aware that people under the influence of hallucinogenic substances can become dangerous? Especially if they've been dosed without their consent and they haven't taken proper precautions? I recommend you contact the lawyer that you mentioned earlier. I expect you'll be investigated as an accessory to Mr. McIntyre's' death."

"You're a fool," Cora said.

Paul keyed his radio. "Officer Achebe, please send a security detail to *The Suites*."

"I *hate* you," Cora said. "This is wrong. And you know it." She stormed off, slamming the door behind her.

Paul lifted his radio again. "Officer Achebe, we have a runner. Please have Ms. Wise confined to her stateroom after you've secured it. Gumbs out."

"Understood." Kameron's Nigerian accent gave the word a musical lilt. Paul's radio crackled once more, then fell silent.

Paul stood. "Sir, I'm taking you into custody pending an investigation of your claims. We've already searched your room, and since we found nothing dangerous here, you'll be confined to your stateroom until we return to San Diego. At that time, you can make a statement to the authorities."

Chryss Tiano crossed his legs. He rested his hands lightly on his knees, palms up, and exhaled. He closed his eyes, and a tear escaped, running down his cheek. "I understand. And if there's nothing else, I'd like to try and recenter myself. This has been a most distressing morning."

Paul's voice was soft. "If you need anything, Sir, knock on your door. One of my crew will be outside to assist you."

Chryss opened his eyes. "Thank you. You've both been very kind, and I won't forget it."

As soon as they closed the door, they heard Chryss Tiano sobbing like his heart had been broken. Ellie turned, putting her hand on the door handle. Paul held the door firm. "Give him some space," he said.

Ellie stepped away from the door. "Paul, if Cora drugged him, he wasn't exactly himself. And there may still be another explanation."

"We have a full confession, in front of a hundred people. Chryss Tiano has no alibi for the time Teddy McIntyre disappeared. And his room was right down the hall."

"But he didn't mention the beef blood," Ellie said, waving a finger in the air.

"Why do you think I invited Cora along this morning? After Strunk told me Chryss was rolling dirty, I searched his room. But I couldn't search hers until she left it. That's where Kameron's been. Cora will probably run right into her."

"Do you really think—"

A radio crackled again. "ET? This is Tiffany from the guest services desk. There's an Ariana McIntyre here looking for you? She says she has some questions about last night."

She isn't the only one, Ellie thought. She keyed her radio. "I'll be right there." Turning to Paul, she said, "What do you want me to say?"

Chapter Twenty-Four

BEN LEANED FORWARD AND PICKED up the white teapot to refill Ellie's cup. The remains of a room service lunch were spread out over the clear acrylic surface. The base of the table was a scuffed wooden chest. "How did Ariana take the news?" Ben asked. His eyebrows had about hit the ceiling when she'd told him about Chryss Tiano's confession.

"Like you'd expect," Ellie said. "I told her Paul had arrested a suspect in her husband's murder, and she burst into tears. Greg was with her, and he basically bundled her up and took her away toward her stateroom. I mean, they all saw Chryss lurch into the lounge in his bloody pajamas, and they heard what he said, so it couldn't have been that much of a surprise. Still, I imagine they're as confused as we are."

"Well, I don't think anyone had drug-induced homicidal rage on their bingo card," Ben said. "That poor woman! She just wanted to bake some delicious food, and maybe win a prize. But she's lost her husband, and now she'll be dragged into a messy homicide trial."

"Manslaughter is more like it," Ellie said, picking up her teacup. "I honestly don't believe Chryss intended any harm. He reminds me of one of those people who doesn't eat eggs because it's cruel to the chickens. You know who I mean. They're sweet people, very compassionate, but kind of preachy about it."

"Vegans," Ben said knowingly.

"Exactly. He's like a vegan."

He scooted closer to her on the small sofa and put one arm around her shoulders. "I'm surprised you're not off with Gumbs, chasing down more leads. Isn't that what you two do all day while I'm on the bridge?"

Ellie chuckled. "Oh, I'm giving Paul a bit more space. He and Kameron have a little thing going on, but they don't want to admit it. They should work together more often."

"So, you're working an angle?"

She leaned her head on his shoulder. He smelled like spicy cologne, and she closed her eyes for a moment, resting happily in what felt like the safest place on Earth. "Nothing too crazy. Violet tells me that a direct approach backfired. But think about it! Long nights spent poring through the evidence. Steamy interrogation rooms. They won't be able to help themselves."

"We don't have any steamy interrogation rooms."

"It's an emotional steam."

"Have I been missing out?"

She looked up at him. "Nonsense. Besides, getting Paul and Kameron working together will give me more time for the important things. Like spending time with you. Crime schmime! Who needs it?"

"You're done sleuthing? Why do I find that hard to believe?"

"No! I'm just going to back off a little. I'll push Paul and Kameron in a room together. Wait for them to..."

"To do it like bunnies?"

Ellie laughed. "Yes. And thanks for the visual." She sipped her tea and set it down. "I do hope that Paul hasn't made up his mind yet. Maybe I'm getting soft in my old age, but I just hate to think of Chryss Tiano going to prison. When he found out what Cora had done, he seemed afraid for her. Karmic debt, he called it. But he wasn't even angry. Just hurt."

"You'd be surprised how much anger a person can conceal," Ben said. "When I was in the Navy, I knew a few men like that. Very soft-spoken. Eminently respectable. But sometimes there's darkness beneath the surface. And by the time you figure that out, you're on the wrong side of it."

"You don't talk much about your Navy days. Why is that?"

"Oh, it was a long time ago. But lately, those days have been on my mind," he said. "Do you know Captain West?"

"The Captain of the *Adventurous Soul*? Roberta has mentioned him a time or two."

"He got me my first job with Adventurous Cruises. Kevin and I go way back. He was my CO back when we were stationed on the USS Gunther. An aircraft carrier."

"I had no idea."

"Well, Kevin's planning his retirement. He plans to break the news to Roberta soon. We spoke on the phone and he told me he's going to move to a small island in the Caribbean and open a bait shop. He'll work only when he feels like it." Ben smiled. "I have to admit, it sounded kind of nice."

"Speaking of nice, tell me about this vacation you're planning?"

His eyebrows lowered. "Am I going on vacation? Because no one has told me."

"Violet said you were talking about taking some time off."

"Oh! That? Well, I may be considering a romantic trip for two."

"And were you planning on telling me about this?"

"At some point. Soon. But not yet."

"Intriguing."

Ben looked at her for a long moment. Then he gently pushed her off him and stood up. "While you were away, I went to see Madame Tiffany on St. John. And she gave me something."

He went into the bedroom. A drawer opened and closed. He came back holding out a rusty iron key. It was four inches long, with an ornate design of a schooner stamped into the side.

"What's it for?" She took it from him, turning it over. It looked ancient, but only the surface was tarnished.

"It opens a secret compartment in that chest." He tapped the massive wooden box beneath his table. "She gave me this, years ago. And she recently found the key. It opens a small compartment inside."

"And what's inside?"

He smiled at her. "Wouldn't you like to know."

"Oh. You're a man of mystery now!"

He took the key back and sat back on the couch. His arm went over her shoulders, and he pulled her close to whisper in her ear. "Here's the thing. The next time I give you this key, there will be a gift for you in that secret compartment. And maybe we'll take a vacation together, afterward. If you like the gift, that is."

He picked up her left hand and squeezed it, and just like that, Ellie's heart danced in her chest! She hugged him tighter.

"And you're telling me this today? During lunch?"

He stroked her hair. "You're the one asking me questions about my secret plans. And I know better than to think I could *ever* keep a secret from the one and only Ellie Tappet." When he spoke again, his words came out in a tumble. "Is it okay if I buy you a gift? If I wanted to? It's not too soon? You're—"

She put her hands on both sides of his face. She kissed the end of his nose. "No. It's not too soon."

He let out a shaky breath. "Good." He leaned forward and put his forehead against hers, closing his eyes. "You realize I have no idea what I'm doing, right?"

"You're doing just fine." She kissed him tenderly, and —

Her radio bleeped. Loudly! They both jumped.

"Ellie. This is Roberta. Get your butt to my suite, pronto. We have a problem."

Ben chuckled. "I swear. There are times I wish I'd never given that woman a radio."

Chapter Twenty-Five

STUART DIDN'T ANNOUNCE ELLIE'S NAME when he let her inside the owner's suite. Usually, that meant that Roberta was alone, so Ellie stopped in her tracks when she saw four pairs of eyes staring at her.

Ariana sat in the center of the sofa, her knees pressed tightly together beneath her pale pink dress. Her hair was tied back with a shiny ribbon. She was flanked by Mindie, who had one leg crossed carelessly over the other, and by Harvey, who had abandoned his heavy cardigan in his lap. His belly hung over his dark blue slacks, and his shirt buttons were tight enough to pop. Greg sat alone in an armchair, his mouth pinched tight like he was afraid of what might come flying out of it.

They all stared at her.

"Um. Hi, guys." Ellie stepped forward and looked to the right toward the kitchen. "Is Roberta here?"

Roberta walked in from the left wing of the suite. She was wearing a black pantsuit and her soft white hair was loose and fluffy. Her mouth was a diagonal line, and her eyes flashed with something stronger than her habitual annoyance. "She's here now," Roberta said to Greg. "*Now* will you please explain why you came bursting into my suite? I was on a video call with a friend in Beijing, and those calls aren't easy to arrange." Roberta sank into an unoccupied chair. "Ellie. Please sit. Greg says he has something important to discuss, but he wouldn't tell me what it was until you arrived."

"Is this about Teddy?" Ellie asked, sitting near Roberta. The empty chair was antique, possibly Victorian. The wooden legs were thin, and she sat down gingerly. It was stronger than it looked.

"Not at all." Greg's easy smile warred with the hesitation in his eyes. "I just wanted us to have a little chat. In fact, I was hoping to get your input on an idea for a new show. And I invited some of our bakers to weigh in as well."

"A new show, eh?" Roberta's irritation fell away, and she leaned forward. She shot Ellie a brief, eager glance. "Well, go ahead. And please tell me this show involves a cruise ship. But none of that *Love Boat* nonsense. Fixing marriages and solving crimes! Pure poppycock. I prefer a show with a bit more grit."

Greg glanced at the bakers. Ariana pressed her hands against her knees, and Mindie played with the ends of her auburn hair. Harvey's hands were folded in his lap. Greg hadn't invited Kitty along.

"I'm thinking about a new television show for The Sugar Network," Greg said. "And it's something unlike anything we've done before. A fantasy tale. I'm talking castles. Kings and queens. Maybe even a dragon or two! MTV had a highly successful run with *The Sword of Shannara*. We could do something similar."

"Seems like an odd choice for a baking channel," Roberta said. "Will there be food involved?"

Greg shrugged. "Sure. Even in olden times, people had to eat! The first time we met, ladies, right here in this room, I told you that I'm a storyteller. Stories are the most potent tool we have in this world. In fact, you've been hosting ghost stories all week. Today, I'd like your input on a story I'm working on. It begins with a very troubled young man from a faraway land. A prince. Let's call him..." Greg made a circular motion with one hand. "Benny."

"You want to tell us a story about a prince named Benny." Roberta glanced at Ellie with an incredulous look. But she'd missed the tremor of fear that had run through the bakers when Greg had started talking. Ariana had gone even paler than usual. And Harvey looked like he might be sick! A thin strand of worry threaded Ellie's gut and pulled taut.

Greg swallowed. "Benny was a very troubled young man. He was brilliant, in his own way. He had a lot of good ideas. But the prince struggled with his demons. He drank. He got into fights. And when he was at his very worst, he turned his rage on those who loved him most. Especially his wife, Tabitha. The princess."

Ariana was watching Greg, listening intently.

"The princess had many friends. But they didn't know how bad things had gotten between her and the prince."

"They should have," Harvey's voice was rough with emotion. "They should have seen the signs. Like the way she wore too much makeup to hide her bruises. Or how she tried to get the prince back to his room when he'd had too much to drink."

Ellie shot Roberta a questioning look, but Roberta wasn't paying her any attention. She was focused on Greg and his story.

"Then, one night, a knight stopped by Tabitha's room to offer her some pie."

"A knight?" Ellie couldn't help but smile at the sudden pivot.

Greg smiled. "Absolutely. A real one! And when he walked in the princess's room, he saw something that terrified him. The princess was *afraid* of the prince. They were arguing, you see. The argument had stopped when the knight walked in, but the princess was in trouble. But when the knight confronted the prince, the prince just laughed." Greg's face fell and he clasped his hands together in his lap. "To make his position clear to the knight, Prince Benny backhanded the princess across the room."

Mindie's hand squeezed Ariana's. Ariana swallowed and looked at the bookcase behind Greg, refusing to meet anyone's eyes.

Greg continued. "And while the knight was — um — retired from combat, his heart remained true. He rushed forward, heedless of his own safety, and he threw himself between the princess and the prince. The prince pushed him. The knight ended up outside. On the parapet." His voice wavered. "Above the moat."

Harvey looked distraught. Ariana said, "The knight saved the princess's life that day. He won't admit it. But it's true."

Greg cleared his throat. "A great battle ensued. The knight was — erm — he hadn't seen battle in many years, but he was stronger than he looked. When Prince Benny came at him, his eyes wild with the sickness that had taken him, the knight dodged, and he pushed the prince away. Just trying to deflect him, you understand. But Prince Benny had been running full force toward the edge of the parapet."

Harvey's voice was a hoarse whisper. "It all happened *so* fast."

Ariana reached up and covered Harvey's mouth with her small hand. She pulled her hand away, and he nodded.

"Prince Benny flew over the wall," Greg said. "And in an instant, he was *gone*."

"The knight wanted to turn himself in to the sheriff," Ariana said, wiping her eyes. "But the princess refused. She knew the knight had his own lady in waiting, in a distant land. And the knight would be punished terribly for saving the princess's life." She took a breath, steadying herself. She looked at Roberta, then at Ellie. "And the princess came up with a plan."

"The beef blood," Ellie said.

"I don't know anything about that!" Greg said, holding up both hands like she'd trained a gun on him. "I'm just telling you a *story*. But the princess's — um—"

"Advisor," Mindie interjected.

"Yes. Her advisor offered to help. When she rode off on her horse the next morning, she propped open the castle doors with a stone. Her advisor went inside the royal bedchamber and made the prince's treachery seem like a tragedy."

Score one point for Violet's doorstop theory, Ellie thought. "And why did the advisor do that? Forgive me for saying so, but it seems out of character."

Greg sat up straighter. "Because the princess asked him to. And because the knight was indeed a very good man. Too good to spend his golden years rotting in some dungeon. All for his decision to save the princess."

"The princess had a lot of help," Ellie said, looking at Mindie.

Ariana wiped her eyes. "The princess was grateful. But she still mourned her prince. Because before... before the madness took him, he was the love of her life."

"And the knight had many good friends too," Harvey said quietly. He looked at Mindie. "They spoke for him. They made sure no one would put him in a dungeon."

"So where does Chryss Tiano fit in?" Roberta demanded. She scowled at the looks she received. "What? I'm not making up names. You're all being ridiculous."

Greg looked at Harvey. "Well, when the princess heard that the sheriff had arrested a visiting wizard for the crime, she was shocked. But that person was not known to the princess and her friends. He was not involved. And if he were to go to the dungeon, it would be a great injustice." He looked Ellie in the eye. "It wouldn't be right."

Ellie's heart sank. *What a mess this is.* She looked at Harvey. "What do you expect us to do?"

Harvey stood. The others did the same. "The sheriff is a good man," Harvey said. "If he knocks on the knight's door before the week is out, the knight will surrender. Better that, than to see the wrong man punished."

Ariana walked over and stood in front of Harvey. She faced Roberta and Ellie. "But maybe, what you heard today is just a story. Maybe, if the princess's prayers are heeded, the storybook can close, and the knight can go home to his lady. I swear to you, that is her *only* wish."

A bead of sweat rolled down Greg's damp temple. "Anyway, the narrative concept for the show is still rather loose. Before I go further with putting resources toward the new production—"

Roberta's glare must have shut him up because his jaw snapped shut like it was on a hinge, and he pivoted toward the door. He held the door open while the rest of them filed out of the room. The front door shut with a thump.

Roberta swore, twice. "I *told you* that man would be trouble."

For a long moment, they didn't speak. Ellie broke the silence. "What do you want to do?"

Roberta stalked into her kitchen and opened her freezer. A moment later she came back with two shot glasses and a bottle of vodka. She filled both shot glasses to the brim and picked one up.

Ellie hesitated. "I don't think I should—"

Roberta downed the shots of vodka, one after the other. "I'm getting too old for this gig," she said to no one in particular. Then shot Ellie a stern look. "Why do I need to make all the decisions around here? Maybe *you* should weigh in." She flung herself back down on the chair with a heavy sigh and closed her eyes.

Ellie carried the cold bottle into Roberta's kitchen and put it back in her freezer next to the pints of ice cream. She filled the white metal teapot with water from the sink and heated it on the stove. Stuart came in and offered to help, and she asked him where the tea was. He pointed to a cabinet over the toaster. "I'll take care of it," she said.

She carried two hot cups of tea out into the parlor, and drank hers slowly, looking out Roberta's big windows. The sandy coast of Mazatlán stretched out behind the ship in a smooth arc. The day looked hot and bright outside.

They drank their tea in silence. Ellie stirred an extra lump of sugar into hers, and the tiny spoon clinked against the side of the glass. At last, she said, "We need to tell Paul."

Roberta regarded her warily. "Are you positive?"

"I am."

Roberta let out a weary sigh. "You're right. I don't like where this is headed, but here we are." She reached for her radio and turned the knob until the small orange screen flared to life.

⚓⚓⚓

"HE CONFESSED," PAUL STOOD BEFORE them, his expression incredulous. "You're telling me that old-man Harvey killed Teddy McIntyre. The scone man. The chubby Brit who spends his days mowing down the dessert station. *He* confessed to the crime. Seriously?"

"It was self-defense," Ellie said. "An accident."

"Then why didn't he come to us? My God. Why didn't he call for help so we could search the water?"

"Would it have made a difference?" Ellie asked.

"It doesn't matter!" Paul thundered. "When a man goes overboard, you call for help! That is the *only* decent thing to do. Period! Why on Earth did he think a clumsy coverup was the way to go? The nerve of these people!"

"Harvey wanted to turn himself in," Ellie said. "Ariana wouldn't let him. And before you get *too* mad, keep in mind that it was the rest of the bakers who did the cover up. Do you want to throw them all in prison? Would that be the right thing to do?"

He shook his head. "No. Don't lay that at my doorstep. I don't send people to prison. I complete my investigations thoroughly and honestly. You know that. Besides, everything they told you could have been a lie. By their own accounts, they've been lying this whole time."

"Then why confess to save the medium's skin?" Roberta asked. "They have nothing in common with him."

"They made a mistake," Ellie said. "We can all agree with that. All that's left is to figure out what we're going to do."

"You can't seriously be thinking about letting them off the hook?"

"What hook?" Roberta asked. "What proof do we have?"

"They confessed."

Roberta rotated her shoulders back. "They didn't. Give Greg Norris his due. If this ever went to trial, he and his companions will deny everything. They told us a fairy tale. Who on earth would confess like that? A jury wouldn't buy it, even assuming I cared enough to testify, which I would not."

"And neither would I," Ellie said. Her stomach tightened. "I'm sorry, Paul. I know this puts you in a tough position."

Paul sat down on Roberta's sofa with a soft thump. "You know I won't falsify my reports. That's out the question. What did you expect would happen when you brought this to me, eh?" He blew out his breath.

Roberta inclined her head. "If you're asking for advice, I suggest you fill out your report using verifiable facts only. No fairy tales. Send it off through the usual channels, and let the authorities deal with it as they may. If we're asked questions, we'll answer them honestly. We'll meet our obligations, and nothing more. Beyond that, it's not our business."

"The truth is *entirely* our business," Paul said. "And if anyone asks me, I'll need to tell them that Chryss Tiano confessed. Because that's what he did!"

"What did you find in Cora's room?" Ellie asked.

"LSD. And there are probably trace amounts in the tea we confiscated from Chryss Tiano's suite. She confessed to doping Chryss before his séances. Apparently, she whispered suggestions in his ear while he was in a hypnotic state. She'd heard about Teddy's suicide from one of the housekeepers, and she planted some of the details in his mind that night. She thought it would be good for business. A real live ghost. But apparently Chryss went off script that night. The bits about the wife being in trouble, and Teddy being pushed overboard, his poor addled mind just made those parts up."

Roberta crossed her ankles. She was still wearing her nice black pantsuit, but while Ellie had been in the kitchen, she'd traded her leather shoes for oversized pink bunny slippers. "The CIA tried the same thing with their MK Ultra program. They dosed people and tried to make them sleeper agents. Mostly it just made their subjects crazy. They did successfully train dogs with LSD, but I could do the same thing with a pocketful of bacon and a clicker. Paul, after the Picklewick affair, I promised I'd never interfere in your department again. And I meant it. You know where Ellie and I stand. Whatever you decide to do, let us know. We'll back you."

"I stand for the truth," Paul shot back. "The same as I always have. And so should the both of you."

Chapter Twenty-Six

LATER THAT DAY, ELLIE HEADED upstairs to the lido deck. She had a stomachache, one that had nothing to do with what she'd eaten for lunch. A brief nap had done nothing to alleviate her discomfort. She felt guilty for upsetting Paul, but she didn't regret what she'd said to him. Her late husband had been a cop, and she liked to believe that the justice system was, well, just! But she couldn't blame Ariana for swooping in to protect Harvey from prosecution. And the fact that she'd done so after facing such a devastating loss was commendable. Ellie's steps felt heavy and slow. How horrible it must be to be attacked by the man you loved? The mere thought of it made her heart ache for Ariana.

Your stomach hurts because it's wrong to cover up a crime, her mind retorted. *And an accidental death is still a crime! Who made you the arbiter of justice? What makes you and Roberta so high and mighty that you get to decide what truths are brought to light, and which ones can be hidden?*

She stepped out on the deck and looked around. Over the rail, the port town of Mazatlán waited. A sandy beach arced around the aquamarine water, edged with a tumble of buildings scattered across the coast like a child's wooden blocks. Here and there, white buildings stood taller than the rest.

Paul had wanted to be a police officer before he took a job with the cruise line, and he still viewed the world as a good police officer should. He didn't believe in treating people differently because they were rich, or famous, or a friend of his. He believed in the system, and the importance of finding the truth. More than anything, he viewed it as his job to be fair.

I believe as Paul does, Ellie thought. He's in the right! *So why can't I stomach the idea of turning Harvey in to the authorities?* The question made her stomach ache harder, so she headed for her destination, the Seashell Bar.

Manny had a line of guests waiting for drinks. Ellie stood in the back and waited her turn. When she got to the front, she shot Manny a wry smile. "Do you have any chocolate?"

He tilted his head inquisitively. "I have a chocolate martini, a mochatini, and a peppermint patty. And two packets of dark cocoa mix, which I'm guessing is what you'd prefer, despite this heat?" He wiped his damp forehead with a bar towel and tossed it in a bin beneath the counter.

"Please," she said, gripping the bar and hoisting herself onto the bar stool. "I'm suffering from an acute case of feeling guilty, and I could use a pick-me-up."

"I'm surprised you're not at port blowing through your social security check," he said, holding a mug beneath his hot water dispenser.

"Very funny" she said, smiling a little. "Anyway, I don't deserve to go shopping. Paul is mad at me, probably, and I feel like a heel."

"You could apologize." Manny had his back turned. He stirred her drink and topped it with something from a tall glass bottle.

"I should apologize for disagreeing with him?"

"I see. You're not feeling bad because Paul's mad. You're annoyed at him for not agreeing with you."

"No, I think he's right. I'm the one who is wrong."

"So, what's the problem?"

"I'm not prepared to change my mind."

He raised an eyebrow, then slid the cocoa over. "This may be above my pay grade. Drink that. I put some mint in."

She tried the cocoa. It was good! The mint gave it a refreshing lift, but it wasn't too sweet. "What's it like to be a bartender, Manny? Is it simple? I could use a bit more simplicity in my life."

His mouth quirked up on one side. "Life is full of conundrums. And bartending is like any other job. Most people want something, and they leave when you give it to them. But wherever you find happy people in this world, you'll find lonely ones too. They look at the crowd having a good time, but they don't feel like they're a part of it. Inevitably, those people spend time at my bar. We talk. And I like hearing their stories.

"Last night, I met a nice couple from Argentina. The wife, she had a sweet voice, and she was quite beautiful. Her husband is a successful businessman. They wore expensive clothing. And the wife's diamond bracelet was probably worth more than everything I own! From the outside, you'd assume the world was their oyster."

"But?"

"I found out why they took this cruise. They're grieving two miscarriages, and they're trying to find the strength to try again. They both feel alone in their grief. And they're trying to reconnect, to be a family, even if they don't know how big that family will be yet. Everyone on board this ship has a story, Ellie. And here, behind my bar, I'm allowed to listen." He smiled at her. "It has a way of putting my own small problems in perspective."

"I take it you heard about our incident last night at karaoke?"

"It's all over the ship. Did Paul arrest the guy?"

"Yes, but it's gotten complicated." She glanced up from her drink. "Have you been around the Sweetie Pie baking contestants? Did you form any impressions of them?"

"Harvey has been in here a few times. He's a sweet man. Extremely homesick, although he likes to joke away his problems. He brought the Australian woman with him a few times. She's lonely too, it's just that she makes less of a show of it. But you can see it in her eyes. She's always looking around, like she's looking for someone she knows. But whoever they are, they aren't here."

"She was friends with the man who died."

He nodded. "That might explain it."

"Do you think Harvey is a good person?"

"I just served him beer."

"Yeah." She sipped her hot chocolate.

Manny looked at her closely. "Something's changed. Hasn't it?"

"Paul is still investigating."

"No, not with the case. With you. You look different."

She thought back to her conversation with Ben, and she smiled. "All is well! I have something to look forward to; that's all." Manny's eyes were alight with curiosity, so she quickly changed the subject. "Although I think Roberta's disappointed that we won't end up on television after all. She thought it would help us expand. But between you and me, I like things as they are."

Manny looked over her shoulder. "It looks like you've got company."

HARVEY HELD HIS WOOL CAP in his hands. "Hi, Ellie. Can I join you?"

"Please do. But this chair is doing a number on my back. I'll get us a table." She shot Manny a grateful look and headed over toward the railing where she and Harvey could have some privacy. He came over a few minutes later, holding an amber-colored ale with a thin layer of foam.

"How are you holding up?" she asked.

He shot her a rueful look. "I'll be okay. But I wanted to apologize to you, personally. I'm an old man, Ellie, and I don't like to admit it, but I was too afraid to come forward. That night, when we fought, I believed Teddy was going to kill me. And when... when it happened, I was..." he took a shaky breath. "I think I've been afraid ever since." He looked down at his hands, holding the palms up, bending his fingers as if he were testing the joints. "I was a railroad man. I took the big engines apart. Put them together. Everything we did was about safety. These hands raised my babies. They comforted my wife. They make scones. Biscuits. Cakes. These hands have done a lot of good. But now?" His expression softened. "I look at them and all I can think about is what they've done. Taking a life. I'm..." He blinked rapidly. "Greg wouldn't want me talking to you, but I just... I needed to say that I'm sorry."

"Did you tell Samantha what happened."

"I did, over the phone. She's scared. We both are."

"I don't know what Paul has decided," Ellie said gently. "I wish I could put you at ease, but I can't. And honestly, I'm not even sure what's right here. But if it were up to me..."

Harvey quickly nodded. "There's no need to explain. As for Officer Gumbs, I know he had a long talk with Ari. Greg just about had a litter of pups when he found out. That man is determined to protect all of us, even if it destroys his career in the process. He's an uncommonly good person. And I think he's half in love with Ariana, to tell you the truth." He sipped his beer. "But I guess we're all in it now. We'll sink or swim together."

"Well, the princess, her knight and the royal advisor will."

He snorted. "If you and Officer Gumbs weren't so persistent, we wouldn't find ourselves in this mess. Not that I blame you, to be clear. My mother always told me that what goes around comes around. You shouldn't expect to cheat and win. God sees all. That's what she used to tell me when she caught me and my brother scrapping." He chuckled.

Ellie leaned back in her chair. Hot sunlight fell over her face and body, and she relished the heat. "Well, no matter what happens, you have one more night aboard the *Spirit* before we head back to California. Is there anything you wanted to do?"

Harvey considered the question. "I'll write to Samantha, as usual. Ariana said she'd teach me her pie crust recipe, and I promised to show her my special tricks for making scones. The test kitchen is still set up for us, and Mindie even promised to make her famous French rolls. One last bake, for old times' sake."

"And Kitty?"

Harvey chuckled. "Oh, we'll invite her. But I doubt she'll come. That kid exists in her own world. Do you know she once asked me if British people really talk this way? She seemed to be under the impression our accents are an attempt to be funny." He smiled at the memory. "That's us, the proud British, and entire nation of linguistic comedians, in on the same joke." He took a long drink from his beer and sat it down on the table. "It's just a pity that we can't have the baking competition after all." He sighed. "I wish you could have seen us in action. We were really something."

Ellie thought for a moment. "Maybe we could have the competition after all?"

"Darlin, that's sweet of you, but I'm not sure I'm in the competing mood. I know I said—"

"Okay, maybe not a competition. But like you said, you've got those ingredients ready to go. Would you be willing to bake for an audience?"

He looked skeptical. "You'd let us do that? After everything?"

"Secrets of the Dead is canceled. We have a whole ship full of people eager for entertainment. And we've already advertised the venue to everyone. Violet can host Cupcake Karaoke, and afterward, you could— Wait. Why are you laughing?"

Harvey was bent forward at the waist, laughing into his hands. When he sat upright, he wiped his eyes. "Oh! I was just thinking about poor Linda's face. The crew spent all night taking the kitchens down. When you ask them to put them back, her head is going to pop right off her shoulders!"

Poor Harvey was exhausted, frightened, and suffering from a case of the giggles. But his laughter was infectious, and she found herself smiling. "How's this? You talk to Linda and the bakers, and I'll talk to Violet. If everyone's on board, we'll give it a go."

Chapter Twenty-Seven

LATER THAT NIGHT, ELLIE SAT at the back row of the theater and marveled and how quickly the plan had come together. No one had objected to an impromptu baking show, not even Paul, who had asked her to save him a seat. Violet was on stage, taking her third bow, the shimmering pearl-colored dress she wore making her look like a bombshell out of the nineteen fifties. She'd had the entire theater crowd singing along with ABBA's *Honey Honey*, and the energy in the room was high.

She reached into her purse and checked her phone. The ringer was off, and there were no messages from Paul Gumbs. Aside from their brief conversation on the phone about the evening's festivities, she'd seen neither hide nor hair of the man since he'd stormed out of Roberta's suite. Why had he asked her to save a seat if he wasn't going to show up? Ellie set her purse on the empty seat to hold it. She'd chosen a row in the back, beneath the balcony level and near the right-side entrance to the theater. Every seat was full!

Raquel and Vick came out on stage. Violet tried to introduce them, but the cheering in the crowd overwhelmed the speaker system! Raquel's short strides were as prim and proper as her rose-colored suit, and Vick's big sunny smile beamed out at the audience like a beacon.

"Thank you, everyone!" Raquel's voice settled over the audience like a command, and the clapping and murmuring stopped. "Thank you for joining us for this special event. After the tragic loss of Teddy McIntyre, our contestants came to us and said they wanted to give something back. Each of our four contestants has chosen a charity for the evening. And the cash prize for the Golden Cupcake will be divided into five even *slices*. Vick, did you bring your cake knife?"

"A dessert joke? Now?" Vick groaned, and the audience laughed.

Raquel came over and pantomimed kicking him in the shin before turning to the audience. "The charity associated with tonight's winning recipe will be awarded *two* slices of the money pie. The other charities will each get a piece. But here's the twist!" She held up a finger.

Vick looked at the audience, "A twist! Like the twist of lime I put in my evening gimlet."

"Yes, dear Vick. Now shut up and stop stealing my light. Tonight, our recipes will *not* be baked by our esteemed contestants. Instead, they'll be baked by you! We're choosing four members of the audience to come up and bake with us. Each of you is carrying a ticket given to you by the usher. Turn your ticket over and look for the number. When I call yours, if you'd like to bake, you can come up on stage and choose your baker."

Excited murmurs ran through the crowd, followed by the shuffling of several hundred people hunting in purses and pockets for their tickets. Ellie smiled. It had been Ariana's idea to involve the audience.

"Now, I'm pleased to introduce our baking coaches! First up, please welcome Mindie Burton of Queensland!"

Mindie walked onstage, waving at the crowd. Her knee-length green dress swished around her knees as she walked, and she wore a white Adventurous Cruises apron on top. Ellie smiled at the sight of the purple mermaid logo. Perhaps it had been a tad impolite to stuff the official Sugar Network aprons in with the dirty laundry, but after all the trouble they'd had on this sailing, the cruise line deserved a little bit of attention! Ellie felt a smug sense of satisfaction as the camera panned over the apron and Mindie's smiling face.

That's a little something for you, Roberta.

Raquel held out her microphone. "Mindie? What charity will you be baking for tonight?"

"I'm baking for the Royal Flying Doctor Service of Australia."

Vick put his hand over his heart. "Oh my. Doctors *fly* in Australia?"

"Australia's a big country," Mindie replied. "So big, that sometimes when you need a doctor, a plane is the best way to go. Especially for rural areas." She pointed at the audience. "Come bake with me!"

"Our next baker is Kitty Gilbert of Malibu California. Kitty, who will you be baking for?"

Kitty snatched the microphone out of Raquel's hand and pivoted to face the audience. She paused, one hand on her hip, her body-skimming pink dress covered by an apron that looked far too big for her. "I'll be baking for The Sunlight Foundation. Because they make sure the government isn't doing rude things behind our back. Also, I *love* the sun. And I look really cute in sunglasses!" She giggled and handed the microphone back to Raquel.

Ellie felt a tap on her shoulder. Paul stood in the aisle, waiting. She smiled up at him and scooted over one seat. "What did I miss?" he whispered.

"Karaoke was great. Now they're preparing for the bake-off." She shot him a sidelong look. Paul looked far less stressed than he had the last time she'd seen him. Her heart sank a little. He'd made his decision, then. She looked up on stage, where Harvey was talking about his preferred charity, a Manchester-based organization for getting incarcerated youth into job programs.

When Ariana walked out, a hush came over the crowd. Raquel hugged her. Vick came over and hugged them both.

The crowd said "Awwwwwww!"

"That man is a horrible human being," Paul whispered. "Be glad you never had to meet him in person."

Raquel pushed Vick off, and he tumbled back like he was about to fall. The audience laughed, but she didn't. "Ariana, what charity will you be baking for?"

"I'm baking for the Catholic Charities of Chicago," she said. "They have an important program for people overcoming substance abuse." She blew a kiss at the audience. "Come bake with me!"

"Is everything okay?" Ellie whispered to Paul.

He nodded.

Raquel read out ticket numbers, and one at a time, the four volunteer bakers ran up to the stage. Ellie pointed at the last one. "Oh! Look! That's Rebecca Triumph! I know her."

Paul looked amused. "You've spent all week with our VIPs, and you're excited about knowing one of our *guests*?"

Rebecca climbed the steps, walked directly up to Vick, and hugged him hard around the middle! She whispered something in his ear, and his face turned a rather bright shade of pink. Rebecca waved up at the balcony level, grinning. She was waving at her sister, no doubt.

When the four volunteers were settled inside their tiny kitchens, the four Sweetie Pie contestants took off their aprons and settled them over the heads of their volunteers. Raquel said, "You know what comes next, my friends." She pointed her microphone at the audience.

"Ready! Set! Bake!" The audience shouted as one.

A huge clock appeared on the displays to the left and right of the stage. Linda came out, carrying her camera on her shoulder, going from kitchen to kitchen, projecting bits of the conversation onto the big screen.

Ariana was paired with a teenage girl. She watched as the girl mixed ingredients together into a big bowl. Ariana slammed a block of something covered in silver paper onto the counter. "We'll be using half butter, half butter-flavored Crisco."

Harvey looked aghast. He called over to her. "You use *shortening*? That's your magic pie crust ingredient?"

She grinned. "Yes! Shoot me. I use half shortening, half butter in my pie crust. It's how my mom made it! Don't give me that look. You're just a butter snob."

Harvey shook his head as if this revelation pained him.

In Kitty's kitchen, there was an argument in process. "No," Rebecca said. "You can't use chocolate chips in the brownies like that. You need either dark chocolate chunks, or peanut butter chips. Chocolate chips are boring!"

Kitty's smile was brittle. "Fine! Why don't you just ignore my recipe and make your own? Since you're such an expert."

Rebecca nodded and pushed the bag of chocolate chips onto the floor. "That sounds like a plan! Will you go find me some better ingredients?" She peered into the bowl, and Kitty stepped back, a hurt look on her face. The camera panned in to capture every moment, and Ellie could have sworn she saw a gleam of satisfaction in Kitty's eyes, half-hidden beneath her pout. Kitty Gilbert knew what she was doing.

Paul leaned over and whispered. "I see why people watch this show. It's not about the baking at all, is it? It's about the drama."

Harvey delivered his baking advice directly into the camera. "A good scone is all about texture. The flour should feel like damp beach sand. Feel it and imagine you're in the Mexican Riviera. Squish it between your toes if you like. Just don't tell the family!"

The crowd laughed, and Harvey's volunteer baker nodded and began squishing the flour mixture between his fingers. The man had a purple mohawk, and he was wearing a Secrets of the Dead t-shirt. "I see what you mean!"

With fifteen minutes left on the clock, the big screens on the sides of the stage turned into countdown timers. Harvey's baking partner playfully shooed Harvey's hand away as he reached for a scone.

"You *have* to test them," Harvey explained.

Rebecca was fanning her brownies with a piece of paper while Kitty stood nearby, looking wistfully at the camera. Linda aimed her camera at Mindie, who was crouched down with her volunteer baker, scrutinizing French rolls through the oven window. "They'll continue to cook for a moment when you take them out," she explained. "That's why we'll pull them out when they're *almost* done."

Ariana walked over to Harvey and tried to hand him a bar of shortening. He pretended to refuse, and she shoved it into his shirt pocket.

Ellie leaned over to whisper. "Harvey told me they had great chemistry together. I'm glad I finally got a chance to see it."

"You should know," he whispered back, "I've decided to do what Roberta suggested. You can give Greg the good news if you'd like."

Ellie kept her voice low. "Are you sure? I don't want you to feel pressured."

His glance was salty! "Well, I *do* feel pressured. You both saw to that, didn't you? But it doesn't matter. You know I make up my own mind. I talked it over with Kameron, and she agrees with the two of you. Teddy has no living family aside from Ariana. There's no life insurance claim. And they'll all need to live with what happened. If we get a call, later on, we'll cooperate, like Roberta said." Paul frowned. "I may *want* to be a police officer, but I'm not one. I work for the cruise line, a private business. And I've done my duty. Do I like this situation? No. Can I live with it? I hope so."

"And the beef blood?"

"The doc told us that he was guessing. And I don't have to put guesses in my incident reports."

"And what about Cora Wise?" Ellie whispered.

"I offered to write a report for Chryss, to give to the police, but he told me that my 'violent paperwork' was no path to universal peace. He put his hands together and bowed. Then he blinked at me like an owl, for like an hour."

"He's back to his old self, then."

Paul's voice was too casual as he dropped his next bomb. "Kameron and I are having lunch tomorrow. Her idea, not mine. She wants to discuss security procedures."

Ellie's heart double-thumped in her chest. "Is that so?"

"Calm down. It's just lunch." A smile played at the corner of Paul's lips. He pointed up toward the stage. "Look, they're taking Ariana's apple pie out of the oven."

The camera zoomed in on the pie. The sugary brown filling bubbled beneath a golden lattice crust. Up on the massive display screens at the front of the theater, the apple pie was approximately fifteen feet tall.

Ellie's stomach growled loudly. "I'm feeling extremely hungry all of a sudden."

"Me too," Paul said mournfully. "I was too busy to eat lunch."

"Investigations, huh? They *do* work up an appetite."

Next to them, a woman shot them a fierce look. Despite their whispering, they were distracting her from the show.

Paul lifted his hips and reached deep into his pocket. He pulled out a large set of keys and dangled them. "I know where Devon keeps the pies," he said, leaning close to her ear. "Should we get out of here?" Without waiting for an answer, he stood and stepped out into the aisle, heading for the back door.

She followed him. As soon as the theater doors closed, she put her hands on her hips. "You can't just go stealing Devon's pies! Back in my day, Officer Gumbs, we had this little thing called inventory control."

"Victor does it better," he said, jingling his keys. "Let's make a pact. If we're heisting pies, let's agree that this is a *one-time* crime. Because after we return to San Diego, I plan to pretend that this sailing never happened. We'll drop the baking contestants off at port, and then we'll begin our *very first* Mexican itinerary. Deal?"

She shrugged with supreme indifference. "Mexico? I've never been! At best, I've been Mexico-adjacent." She looked him up and down as they walked toward the center of the ship. "You should wear something nice for lunch with Kameron. That dark blue button-up really brings out your eyes. But would it be too formal for a daytime meal? Hmm. You need to show Kameron you've made an effort. Get your hair trimmed and switch out that plastic watch for something shiny. Wear one of your nice polo shirts."

"Did I ask you for dating advice?"

"Don't talk about anything too heavy. Stick to business since that's what she invited you out for. And if the past comes up, just say you wish you'd handled it better."

He scoffed. "But she was the one who dumped *me*."

"It doesn't matter, sweetie. Always apologize. It puts your adversaries at a disadvantage."

He shot her an amused look. "Kameron is my adversary now? When did that happen?"

Ellie looped her arm through his. "She is! Because you're going to steal her heart, Paul. And she'll hand it over, but not without a fight. Luckily, you've got me on your side."

He squinted down at her, skeptical. Was that a glimmer of hope in his eyes? "You seem rather certain about all this."

"Oh, I had a vision," she said sagely.

"Are you sure it wasn't LSD?"

"Yes. And I know *exactly* what's going to happen next. But only if you get your act together, Gumbs. This is your last shot."

"Now, you're being silly. You don't even believe in visions!"

She rested her head against his arm for a moment. They passed a window. Outside, white capped waves slid by, almost too fast to see. The sky was a dark, inky blue. She looked up at Paul and beamed out her sunniest smile, the one that said she loved him like a son. Did he know? She hoped so.

"There *may* be things in this world that defy our understanding," she said slowly. "Phenomena that we can't control or explain. Strange experiences that defy all logic! And falling in love? Well, that happens to be one of them."

What's Next for Ellie Tappet?

Thanks for joining me for another Ellie Tappet mystery. I hope you had fun!

Ellie's headed into rough waters in The Case of the Fond Farewell. When Captain Kevin West comes aboard the Adventurous Spirit for his retirement party Ellie can't wait to meet him. Before long, the death of a senior officer raises uncomfortable questions about someone very dear to her.

Let's Stay in Touch!

Sign up for my list to receive fun and nerdy notes, travelogues, and a free starter library. Visit **cheribaker.com/News** to get started.

More from this Series

For a complete list of books in this series and for the latest Ellie Tappet news, visit **cheribaker.com/Ellie**

Find Your Next Series

Want more cozy mysteries that celebrate friendship and fun? Check out the **Butterfly Island Mysteries**.

Do you love snarky sleuths, office mysteries, and workplace drama? You'll enjoy the **Kat Voyzey Mysteries**.

How about a world of corporate espionage and betrayal? Meet Jessica Warne in the **Emerald City Spies Trilogy**.

Excited for more Ellie Tappet? See what's available and what's coming next at **CheriBaker.com/Ellie**

More from Cheri Baker

The Kat Voyzey Mysteries

Involuntary Turnover
Orientation to Murder
Death by Team Building
Cutting the Track

The Ellie Tappet Cruise Ship Mysteries

The Case of the Missing Finger
The Case of the Karaoke Killer
The Case of the Floating Funeral
The Case of the Lady in the Luggage
The Case of the Red Phantom
The Case of the Fond Farewell

Emerald City Spies

The Assistant
Power Play
Hostile Takeover

The Butterfly Island Mysteries

A View to Die For
Death at Dagger Cove
Shadow of a Doubt

About The Author

Hey there. My name is Cheri, and I'm a writer from Seattle, Washington.

I've been a book lover my entire life, and for many years writing was my hobby, something I did on the weekends or in the early morning before work. My first novel, *Involuntary Turnover*, was loosely based on my experiences working in human resources. Not the murder part; just the setting! It took me ten years to write my first two novels, working around the demands of a busy job, but eventually I traded my business suits for jeans and began writing full time. Now, I'm lucky enough to have wonderful readers all around the globe.

When I'm not writing I spend my time reading, hanging out with my husband, watching terrible monster movies, drinking coffee, having movie nights with friends, playing Dungeons and Dragons, walking through the city, and thinking up twisty murder plots. Rainy weather makes me happy, and so does the fact that you read one of my books! Thanks so much for supporting my work.

www.ingramcontent.com/pod-product-compliance
Ingram Content Group UK Ltd.
Pitfield, Milton Keynes, MK11 3LW, UK
UKHW020224250726
13967UKWH00001B/174